I0632367

William Senior

Waterside Sketches

William Senior

Waterside Sketches

ISBN/EAN: 9783337144098

Printed in Europe, USA, Canada, Australia, Japan

Cover: Foto ©Andreas Hilbeck / pixelio.de

More available books at **www.hansebooks.com**

Waterside Sketches.

(*CHEAP EDITION.*)

BY

W. SENIOR ("RED SPINNER"),

Angling Editor of " The Field."

*Author of " Travel and Trout in the Antipodes;" " By
Stream and Sea;" " Notable Shipwrecks;" Fisheries
Exhibition Handbook, " Angling in Great
Britain;" " Anderton's Angling,"
&c., &c.*

LONDON :

SAMPSON LOW, MARSTON, SEARLE, & RIVINGTON

CROWN BUILDINGS, 188, FLEET STREET.

1885.

PREFACE.

THE reader will probably observe from the cover that this is the first of a projected series of shilling books, directly or indirectly refering to Angling. The number and character of the series will be regulated by the support given to the venture by the purchasing public. I have almost pledged my word to our worthy publishers that the angling body of Great Britain will appreciate the opportunity now given them for the first time, of obtaining cheap and handy editions that may be clapped into the pocket to fill up odd half hours, either by the fireside or on fishing excursions ; and that a very large section of readers who are not anglers will also encourage the scheme, which for many years I have had at heart. It is entirely at the publishers' request that " Waterside Sketches " has been placed first on the list, but I humbly hope the series will not suffer on that account.

The original edition of " Waterside Sketches " was published ten years ago. Before it ran its natural course a fire destroyed the copies in stock. The book was also so kindly received and reviewed in the press that I confess to requiring but little pressure to republish it in its present form. Some alterations have necessarily been made. They have been chiefly in the direction of curtailment, demanded by the march of events in the angling world. Even in ten years that march has been rapid and far. Anglers have multiplied exceedingly. Numerous additions have been made to angling literature, as a perusal of the Rev. J. J. Manley's Fisheries Handbook, and the invaluable " Bibliotheca Piscatoria," of Westwood and Satchell, both published during 1883, will show. In 1877 the " Fishing Gazette" gave the anglers of Great Britain, for the first time, a journal exclusively devoted to their interests. A decade is not much after all in an ordinary way, but it is enough to make one fear, when revising work done before its commencement, that it may be considered old-fashioned. Be it so. There are worse faults in the world than that.   W. S.

CONTENTS.

WATERSIDE SKETCHES.

CHAPTER I.

OUR OPENING DAY.

"Away to the streamlet, away, away !
The Sun is up in his realms of light.
But it is not alone from his captured prey
That the fisherman wins his keen delight.
Ah no ! 'tis the breath of the infant day,
'Tis the air so fresh and the sky so bright—
In these is the fisherman's best delight."

THAT is all very true and pretty, but I am still inclined to agree with Charles Kingsley—one of the best anglers in the lowland country where he lived, died, and was buried, loved and lamented by rich and poor—that it is best to say little about the poetry of sport.

Truly, the worthy Hampshire rector delivered this sentiment in the red deer country, and rather

B

in reference to the huntsman and marksman than the less active angler, but never was truer sentence spoken than that concluding remark of his that we English owe too much to our field sports to talk nonsense about them.

Yet if any sportsman has the right to foster sentimentality it is the fisherman. We anglers of this and every other period have been charged with being coxcombs, fools, and what not ; and such we may or may not be. I do not mind crying " Peccavi," however, to one accusation made times out of number against us : we are no doubt a gossiping race, and all we can plead in mitigation of sentence is that our garrulity is at least harmless ; which is more than some gossipers dare aver.

Come with me for an hour or so to a haunt sacred to fishermen's gossip, and judge for yourself. Following the example of the immortal Izaak, I will trouble you, as we walk, with some preliminary prosing. You will find, then, that angling is not the thing it was when Piscator overtook Venator and Auceps on the road to Ware ; Auceps on his way to look at a hawk at Theobald's, Venator to join in an otter hunt at Amwell, and Piscator, the avowed brother of the angle, to pursue his gentle art, sitting and singing under the high honeysuckle hedge, while the showers fell gently upon the teeming earth, and gave a sweeter smell to the lovely flowers adorning the verdant meadow. Hawking no longer takes place at Theobald's ; there is no necessity for rising before the sun to meet the otter pack on Amwell Hill ; and the times are gone when the Hertfordshire milk-woman would offer the passing angler a syllabub of new verjuice, a draught of the red cow's milk, and her honest Maudlin's sweetly sung song.

The modern Waltonian, nevertheless, has, on the whole, little cause to grumble at the change which has come about. There still remain pleasant haunts and moderate chances of sport, and if he be unable to kill roach at London Bridge and fill his basket within an hour's walk of town, increased facilities by rail and steamboat bring new opportunities within his reach. In the great law of compensation upon which the world is said to move the modern Waltonian shares. The mines, manufactories, and mills do their best to pollute the good fish-breeding rivers that are left to us ; but there is a keen spirit of preservation abroad, and all over the country influential associations are continually imitating the noble example set them by the Thames Angling Preservation Society.

Taking us the country through we are a very numerous body. Year by year additional recruits avow their conversion to the "Contemplative Man's Recreation." Angling fraternities with various names and mottoes flourish in many a town ; aye, in the most dismal and poorest quarters of London's City. For angling literature there is a healthy and perpetual demand.

The town fishing club somehow is treated with a derision it hardly deserves by the fortunate gentleman who is able to kill salmon in Norway or Ireland, deer in Scotland, and trout in Wales. This is neither fair nor considerate. The city-pent Cockney, poor fellow, must do what he can, and the shabby apprentice who walks from Shoreditch to Tottenham, bait-can in hand, every Sunday morning, and is content with such results as his humble rod and line may bring, may be at heart— why not ?—as true a sportsman as the happy individual who goes forth with a couple of keepers at his heels, and the costliest tackle and the finest streams at his command.

But a truce to prosing, at least for the present, for here is the Waltonian's home. You may see that we are a very united family, and not ashamed to avow ourselves followers of quaint, pure-hearted Izaak Walton. We aim, in our several ways, to emulate his spirit, which was eminently unselfish. We are unknown to the world, but we know each other, and hold as a primary article of faith that the man who possesses a good fishing-rod, a stout walking-stick, and the opportunities and means of using both in moderation, ought to be happy and healthy. This brotherhood of men who love the gentle art with unswerving fidelity includes persons who can afford to frequent costly salmon rivers, but some of these days you shall see them enjoying with the keenest relish an afternoon's roach or gudgeon fishing by the banks of a prosaic stream. We earn our right to recreation by work of divers kinds—on Exchanges, in Government offices, in establishments where printing-presses groan and struggle, in Westminster Hall, in chambers; we buy and sell, we toil by brain and hand, we are rich and poor, we are old and young, but we are not ashamed a second time to avow ourselves followers of quaint, pure-hearted Izaak Walton, whose nature was eminently unselfish.

By listening quietly awhile you will discover how true it is that we are a gossiping race. But note that our talk is all of one warp and woof. This is the hour when the smoking-rooms of clubs where politicians and the great ones of the earth do congregate are handling freely public and private scandals, questions of national pith and moment, controversies weighty and bitter. Here we are in the town, but not of it. We are bodily present, but in spirit far away. Possessing in common a devotion to angling, there are all kinds of branch fondnesses by which certain men are known, each warranting, however, Washington Irving's observation, "There is certainly something in angling that tends to produce a gentleness of spirit and a pure serenity of mind."

There is not a man present to whose love of angling there is not grafted some other pleasant pursuit or liking. Here is a fern lover who has actually been known to miss the striking of a fish on suddenly espying a novel specimen of his favourite plant. To another the pocket sketch-book is the most necessary item of his fishing kit; his friend is full of learning as to forest trees and wild flowers; ornithology is a common acquirement with the majority. I could point you to one who captures more butterflies than fish; to a second whose weakness lies in tadpoles, newts, and snakes. Out of the fulness of the heart the mouths speak, producing a medley of conversation truly, and an exchange of miscellaneous experiences, but no ill-humour, no treason, no railing.

It is the last night in March, and we muster in force amongst our old acquaintances, the trophies encased around the walls. How we fight our piscatorial battles over again! That monster pike glares as if he were cognisant of the story re-told of his folly and fall—how, greedily grabbing at the gudgeon that was intended for a passing perch, he, twenty-eight pounder though he was, was struck, played, exhausted, and landed with a single hook, which you may observe coiled up in the corner of the case, to his everlasting disgrace.

The eyes of our old friend whose prowess

amongst the salmon and white trout is a proverb at
Glendalough and Ballina, and has been known
there these twenty years, will glisten again as he
describes the history of the three large trout overhead, caught in three casts within a space of thirty
minutes.   And soon a patriarch takes up the
parable.   He is as enthusiastic at three score and
ten as he was when, a truant, he slew small perch
near Sadler's Wells Theatre, and he will set us in
a roar by his comic recital of a day's bream fishing
on one of the Norfolk Broads, and the cowardly
behaviour of the flat bellows-shaped brute in the
compartment next but one to the sixty-three-ounce
perch.

And so we pass the time, silently overlooked by
specimen trout, tench, carp, barbel, dace, roach,
perch, and pike, which strangers come from afar to
admire, and which recall many a pleasant memory
to be fondly lingered over and cherished ; and
smiled upon benignantly by the ancient picture of
a wholesome-looking old man, with long white
hair, smooth face, steeple-crowned hat, and broad
white collar—the man who was father of us all.

To-morrow a small party are bound on an expedition to the waterside according to annual custom.
We begin our campaign on the 1st of April. News
of fish feeding and moving has arrived by express
to gladden our hearts.   Some of us have already
opened our fly-books by the early streams else-
where, and are hoping to do gallant deeds with a
particularly neat March brown that is never out of
season.   Others have been busy during the day
removing rods and tackle from their winter resting-
places, and in lovingly preparing them for active
service.

Do you smile at the high character given to so

simple an occupation ? Then you know not how fertile are the sources whence spring the angler's joys. When the north winds blow, and the east winds bite, and the yellow floods overflow the spongy banks, and the fisher is a prisoner at home, he forgets, in overhauling his stock, both his ill-luck and the unfriendly elements. He sits at the blurred window with his scissors, waxed thread, varnish, feathers, fur, and wool spread out before him ; he tests his lines and casts, oils his winches, and resolves himself into a committee of inquiry respecting the joints and tops of his rods, which he regards as companions to be communed with, praised for merits, and remonstrated with for faults. Rest satisfied, therefore, that our friends who to-day have brought their implements into the light for the first time since autumn have set about their task in the spirit of no common or vulgar ransackers.

To morrow arrives : All Fools' Day, as we pleasantly remind each other. Happily March had come in like a lion, or rather like a bellowing bull, and had, true to tradition, departed like a lamb, leaving immediately behind it the loveliest of spring mornings. Two hours before, we had the smoke and noise of London ; now we are surrounded by sights and sounds that make us glad at the mere thought of life. Our veteran, whose rod the keeper is carrying, drinks in the balmy air in great gulps, and if the grass were a trifle less wet, would frisk it merrily amongst the lambkins in the mead. The birds, still in their honeymoon, make unceasing melody in the hedges, and you can hear a grand responsive chorus away in the dark wood, from whose trees the grip of winter has just been relaxed. The impudent water rats evidently hold us in supreme contempt, scarcely deeming it necessary to plunge from their holes and perform that light-hearted somersault which so often startles the unsuspecting rambler. There is life and the promise of life everywhere, and we revel in it, and feel kindly towards all mankind.

Rods are put together, and it will go hard with not a few innocent fish if the eager looks of certain of our band carry out all they express. April clouds are scudding softly over an April sky, and there is a friendly breeze from the west ready to aid the angler. The river runs smooth and deep here, but a little space ahead it tumbles into a noisy weirpool, boiling and fretting, and ejecting from its troubled depths an occasional weed or stick. At the rear of the osier bed a placid back-water winds, and here one, two, three, and four of our brotherhood are settling down to a few hours' special correspondence with the tench, just now in their prime, and, with this wind and water, almost certain to be off their guard.

We will stroll round that way by-and-by. But *en passant* I would advise you never to hurry by this corner with your eyes shut, for as the April days multiply there will appear in all their vernal glory a host of marsh flowers and pants. The village children, romping and hallooing in the distance, are bound for the copse to search out wood anemones, the woodruff, the wild hyacinth, lords and ladies, strawberry blossoms, primroses, violets, crane-bills, and (as they will call them) daffydowndillies ; but our ruddy-faced little friends are too early in the season, and will meet with but a portion of the treasures they seek.

Now let us pause at the weir, and watch our gay young comrade do his will with the phantom

minnow. If he handle his papers at the Circum-
locution Office as deftly as his spinning-rod he
ought speedily to reach a distinguished position in
the Civil Service. But he does not find a fish
instanter, nor will he succeed until the cast places
his bait in command of the furthest eddy and scour.
This our gay young comrade in due time neatly
accomplishes, and his reward is a vicious snap, a
taut line, and a thrilling rod.

It is a heavy trout, as you may see by his pull ;
a lively trout, from the speed with which he darts
round and across the pool ; an artful trout, by his
rush for the woodwork ; a beautiful trout, self-pro-
claimed in a succession of leaps into the air, during
which the sun lights up his ruby spots and bur-
nished vesture ; a princely trout, as you must
admit, for the keeper, who knows that the first
fish of the season is always an extra coin in his
pocket, stands by with the weighing machine, and
announces him a few ounces short of five pounds.
He is a goodly fish, yet personally I hold him in
light respect, being convinced that nothing would
ever induce him to rise at a fly. We have been
long familiar with these lusty trout, with their
haunts, their vices, their virtues, their dispositions.
Sometimes they take a clumsy dead gorge bait,
sometimes a live roach, or gudgeon, sometimes
minnow or worm, but seldom a fly, artificial or
real.

This straight level run is a roach swim, famous
amongst us. By these fast-springing flags three
years ago a young gentleman who had never seen
the water before, and was apparently a novice in
the craft, in one afternoon caught a great weight of
roach, four individuals of which turned the scale
at eight pounds, several of which were over a

pound, and none of which were less than six
ounces. Presently we reach another weir, and
soon a third, and in each our gay young friend
will before night seek a companion for the beauty
we assisted, a few minutes since, to smother in
newly cut rushes of last year's growth.

We are now, let me whisper, making our way to
a tributary streamlet, upon whose rippling surface
the flies dangling over my shoulder will receive
their first baptism. The brotherhood have various tastes, and agree to differ with perfect good
humour. Our friends at the backwater are not
unfriendly to me, personally, but they pity my
weakness for fly-fishing. I dote on our victorious
young comrade of the weir, but nothing could
induce me to toil throughout the live-long day
spinning for a brace of heavy trout, if the chance
remained for me of a dozen of smaller size fairly
killed with the artificial fly. Each man to his
liking, and good luck to us all : that is our motto.

When we turn out of the next meadow, in whose
trenches a few weeks hence will blow—

"The faint sweet cuckoo flowers,"

and where—

" The wild marsh marigold shines like fire in swamps and
      hollows grey,"

look straight at the rustic bridge spanning the ford,
and you will see a couple of fellows lounging upon
the hand-rail. They are poaching rascals on the
watch for the trout that prowl up from the wider
water below to chase the small fry on the shallows,
and when the sun comes that way it would be
worth while spiking your rod into the coltsfoot-

covered bank, lighting another cigar, creeping
stealthily behind the willow bushes, and watching
the actions and habits of the fish. Such time is
never thrown away, and you will soon discover
that the fish are not unworthy of your inquiring
study. As to the hulking scoundrels beyond, after
nightfall there will be a splash and a struggle, and
an hour later the poachers will probably be offering
a brace of handsome trout for sale at some village
pothouse.

Across a bit of young wheat, down a lane where
we could find a posy of white violets if we had the
leisure to pluck them out of their modest retirement, and we reach the narrow winding streamlet
where, fortune favouring us, I may ply the fly to
some purpose. But what with poaching, the increase of anglers, and vile pollution everywhere,
trout, alas! except in very remote parts, are becoming scarcer and scarcer every year, and it
requires the utmost skill to bring the fish to basket.
Unfortunately this streamlet is poorly stocked, and
there is not a solitary tree or bush to cover its
banks. On the other hand, the water is neither
too high nor too low—an inch makes a vast difference here—and the factory above has been good
enough not to pour out its discolouring refuse to-
day. But I must creep to the water and move
stealthily.

As it is a small stream, of course, on that strange
law of contraries which guides the angler in these
matters, full sized flies must be employed—the
invaluable March brown as stretcher, the cowdung
(considering the warm wind) for dropper number
two, and the blue dun number three. You cannot
detect the ghost of a rise anywhere, and cast after
cast ends in the same monotonous disappointment.

Try every art within your knowledge, still no success.

At last I have carefully covered every yard of the short length of streamlet at our disposal, fishing according to orthodox rules, and—pardon the egotism—fishing it thoroughly. I am too much accustomed to the certain uncertainties of angling to be disheartened, although it must be confessed I am anxious not to return to the brotherhood empty-handed. Now let me be unorthodox. One of the lessons I was taught in the early days was not to use a red spinner till May. The red palmer is permissible in both February and March, and often very killing; and in April your book is not complete without both brown and grey spinner; but the red spinner by very many worthy folks is not regarded as appropriate till later. In that case I mean to anticipate the season by a month, and substitute my favourite red spinner for the fly which has been unsuccessful. The cowdung-fly must remain, for that insect is unmistakably abroad, circling in the wind with its usual activity. The March brown has been so firm a friend that I seldom discard it, early or late, and it shall not be discarded now. Still something must be done.

One method is left untried. I plump down upon my bended knee, well away from the brink, winch up the line to a few yards, and cast close under the opposite bank, upon it if possible, and rather below than above. This, too, some dogmatists would condemn as unorthodox : but is not the proof of the pudding in the eating ? The flies, sinking somewhat, are borne with the stream, and I am keeping my eye closely upon the red spinner, which the wind dances naturally upon the surface, and which it is my intention to work slowly, dib-

bing fashion, across to my own bank. In a few
minutes I feel a trout, and I want no information
as to his quality ; he has shot athwart stream with
a deep strong pull, and bent my light rod like a
whip. He was lying almost close to the bank on
my side of the water, and never broke the surface
in seizing the fly : he waited until the red spinner
dipped, and then in a business-like way closed
upon him once for all.

Twice afterwards my attendant has the pleasure
of using the landing net, but only with the normal
half-pounders of the stream. Yet we are quite
content and happy, and stroll lazily back to the
brotherhood with clear consciences.

The gay young comrade it seems at mid-day has
found a fitting mate for his captive from the weir,
and is, as we pass, engaged with his friends and
the keeper in a vain endeavour to rescue his spinning
flight from a submerged tree trunk. We comfort
him with the assurance that the chances are twenty
to one in favour of the willow-wood holding its
own. Our brethren at the backwater, comfortable
on their campstools, with two or three empty bottles
upon the trodden grass, and the *débris* of a heavy
luncheon at their feet, have had the premier sport
of the day—measuring sport by numbers. The
tench have behaved themselves in a freehearted
and appreciative manner, and, save that they
manifested an unaccountable dislike to one
gentleman, showed no preference for particular
anglers.

Four rods have been constantly at work, and
three have been constantly taking fish. The fourth
is in the hands of the undoubtedly best angler of
the party, and he uses the finest gut and hooks,
but, to his chagrin and surprise, while his friends

have caught fish whether careful or careless, he has
not perceived so much as an accidental nibble.
Finding him accordingly in a despondent frame of
mind, we cheer him with such cheap comfort as we
can find at a moment's notice.   Even as we speak
his delicate float trembles, and then rises slowly
and mysteriously until it lies flat upon the sluggish
water.   Every angler knows the meaning of that
welcome token.   There is much jubilation over
such a beginning, and we feel it right, in duty
bound, to drink each other's health in a flask of
brown sherry, which one of the brotherhood—a
City man of course—produces with a flourish.

What follows aptly illustrates the unexplainable
fancies of the fish world.   For an hour the previously unsuccessful fisherman hauls out as fast as
he can bait his hook, and his three friends, who had
been pitying him for hours, are now recipients of
our compassionate regrets.   There is no rhyme or
reason for this sudden whim of the tench, and at
the termination of the hour, the biting ceases as
suddenly as it began, and not another fish is brought
to land.

The tench had taken well-scoured marsh worms,
absolutely refusing to touch either striped brandlings, tempting lobs, or able-bodied gentles, and
it was noticed as a curious circumstance that while
at one spot the bites were sharp and vigorous, the
float disappearing without much hesitation, a few
yards off the fish dawdled over the bait, as tench
frequently do, leaving the angler in doubt whether
the movement of the float was not a mere accident.
As the bottom was muddy rather than gravelly,
the anglers had fished a couple of inches from it,
and, all told, were, on quitting the field, able to
show a total of over twenty pounds, which, for

so capricious a fish as the tench, may be considered, for that water, great sport.

Our Opening Day we deem on the whole all that could be wished. We can say with the philosopher "Our riches consist in the fewness of our wants." If we can boast of no sensational creels, we are all satisfied and at peace with each other. Hungry as hunters, we gather in the eventide round the table of our pleasant room, beneath whose balcony a bye-stream hurries, mad with the impetus received from a weir at the bottom of the garden, and foaming with anger as it shoots under the roadway. Incidents of the day, trifling in themselves perhaps, and bits of observation and experience, not startling or profound it may be, are exchanged, while the click of the knife and fork beats time to the soothing plash and flow outside the window.

And so our Opening Day, like all other days, runs to its close, and to-morrow we shall be at our posts in the busy spheres of the big city, better surely rather than worse for those pleasant hours by the waterside?

CHAPTER II.

THE MAYFLY.

" Fly disporting in the shade,
Wert thou for the angler made?
To grace his hook—is this thy fate?
And be some greedy fish's bait?
　　　Fly aloft on gladsome wing!
See one comes with eager spring,
He'll dip thee far beneath the wave:
And doom thee to a watery grave."

MAY has nearly run its course. We have an ancient promise that the seasons shall never fail, and though sometimes our variable climate makes it difficult to draw a hard-and-fast line between summer and winter, in the long run you may be sure seed-time and harvest come round in very much the same fashion as they appeared to our forefathers. I pack my portmanteau as I make these sage reflections, and am grateful that the spring has been one of the time-honoured sort. March winds prevailed at the proper time, the April showers fell soft, and the May flowers bloomed without delay. And there has arrived a letter announcing the advent of the green drake.

Mayfly fishing is not, to my mind, altogether a

satisfactory style of angling, yet I grieve me much if
the Mayfly season pass without taking advantage
of it. The fish are so terribly on the "rampage"
at this time that it seems like catching them at a
mean disadvantage. The silly trout evidently take
leave of their senses for a fortnight or so, at the
beginning of June, and, of all ranks and sizes, lay
themselves out for unlimited gorge. The angler,
however, places himself more on an equality with
his game if he forswears the live fly. If I were
asked for my advice I should say :—Seldom use
any but the artificial Mayfly, if you would live
with a clear conscience ; then you will have the
additional gratification of knowing that the special
difficulty experienced in producing a really good
imitation is a slight set-off against the greediness
of the trout at the Mayfly period.

Cotton speaks of Mayflies as the "matadores
for trout and grayling," and he adds that they kill
more fish than all the rest, past and to come, in the
whole year besides. It should be remembered that
Cotton was then writing of the picturesque Dove,
not so stocked with trout and grayling now as it
was in his days, but still as limpid and romantic as
when Piscator welcomed his disciple to the Vale of
Ashbourne with—"What ho! bring us a flagon of
your best ale"—the good Derbyshire ale which
Viator had the sense to prefer, scouting the idea
that a man should come from London to drink
wine at the Peak.

As a rule—and there are not many exceptions to
it—the flies that suit one river do not suit another ;
but the Mayfly is the touch of nature which makes
most rivers kin. With some allowance for difference
of size, your Mayfly will answer on any stream, or
on lake and stream, during the few days in which

the green and grey drakes make the most of their chequered existence. What Cotton wrote of the Dove will therefore apply to streams that in no other respect could be compared with it.

It is not the Dove to which I am bound. My stream is not half so well known either to anglers or to the non-angling world. It has a name nevertheless, and appears accurately marked upon the Ordnance Map. Let us for convenience sake call it the Brawl. In most instances you will not err greatly in disliking the fisherman who refuses to tell his brother where to find sport. It is true, necessity has no law, and the necessity is often laid upon one, sadly against his will, of withholding information which might be of service to a brother angler. He may be the best and most generous hearted fellow in the world, but he may lack that essential backbone of wisdom, discretion.

Therefore the stream now in question shall be named the Brawl, and I give fair warning that the rest of my nomenclature in this chapter is also drawn from the source whence a member of Parliament was accused of drawing his facts— namely, the imagination. There is no objection to your knowing that the spot is not far from the cradle of the queenly Thames; so near, in fact, that you may almost hear the first babblings of the infant river. Green hills stand in rich undulations of pasture high above the surrounding country, giving to the sheep grazing on the luscious downs a name that is distinctive and far known. The Brawl does not rise, as many streams do, through the silver-sanded floor of a bubbling spring sequestered in the dell, but it spurts sharply out of a hill-side, and commences its course, as it were, with a grand flourish of trumpets and waving of flags.

Tennyson might have had the Brawl (but of course had not) in his mind's eye when he wrote "The Brook." The forget-me-nots are there, and the cresses, and the shallows, and the windings, and all the melody which tinkles in the Poet-Laureate's exquisite song.

When a man travels the best part of a hundred miles for one day's amusement he is generally prepared to crowd as much work into that day as human possibilities allow. How fresh the country looks in its May garment of many colours, and how majestically the sun sinks behind the great hills towards which I am rattling in the ravenous express! As if the landscape is not already gay enough with its foliage and flowers, the sun clasps it in a parting embrace, and at the touch it becomes radiant and rosy and soft.

The village is hushed in repose by the time I am left, the only passenger, on the rude platform, and the ancient churchyard is wrapped in shadow that becomes weird and black in the avenue of cypress and yew. The bats wheel hither and thither over the housetops, and beetles drone as they fly. The last roysterer—it is but ten o'clock— is leaving the Hare and Hounds at the moment I lift the latch to enter. The landlord eyes my rod and basket, and glances sidelong at me during supper time.

At length, he informs me that he himself is an angler and proprietor of a willow bed through which runs about two hundred yards of the Brawl, and that if I would like to try my casts upon it in the morning before starting up the country I am welcome so to do. He does not give this privilege to every one, he says, and could not if he would, since he has let the right of fishing to an old gentleman living on the spot, reserving to himself the power which he now offers to exercise in my favour. The programme for to-morrow includes a small lake across country, and then a drive of six miles into the uplands to where the newly-born Brawl turns its first mill-wheel. Still, no reasonable offer or likely chance should be refused, and the landlord's kindness is accepted with thanks.

Before the lark is fairly astir next morning, I am being brushed by the dew-charged branches of the trees in the landlord's willow bed. The tenant, the old gentleman previously spoken of, is known to the world as "the General." He was a sergeant of dragoons in his younger days, and now in the evening of life lives in a honey-suckled cottage overlooking the bit of animated stream in which he finds so much amusement. Perhaps if I had known this earlier I should not now be trespassing upon his preserves. Quite Arcadian the place must be ; his rods, used beyond doubt last evening, he has left by the river, and they lie without attempt at concealment on the wet grass.

It is a very likely locality for a good trout, and circumscribed as the bounds are, there are deeps, eddies, and scours in excellent condition. More by way of wetting the line than anything else, I cast up towards a sweeping shallow, around whose edge the pure silver-streaked water swirls sharply, and at the second throw rise, and, I am free to confess, to my surprise hook a fish. The accident being attributed by the landlord to masterly skill, he stands by admiringly and excitedly with the net. The trout, however, is in no hurry, and runs straight into a forest of weeds, from which it seems impossible to extricate him without loss of tackle and time. The landlord rushing to the cottage

for a pole brings with him "the General," half
dressed, and in a pitiable state of alarm and anxiety.
Almost with tears and in broken accents he says :
    " I've been working three days for that fish, sir,
early and late ; he rose once yesterday, and twice
the day before."
    Poor old General! I feel sorry indeed, but
sorrow cannot undo the unconscious wrong I have
perpetrated! After tremendous exertions with a
pole and hay-rake we loosen the tangled weeds,
and the trout comes in on his side, not the patriarch we had supposed, but a burly little fellow
not much larger than a Yarmouth bloater. Then
"the General" rejoices, and I too rejoice on hearing that "that fish" which has been tantalizing
him all the year is still left to tantalize him again.
    "The General" begs me to remain for five
minutes, and disappears. In his absence I notice
that he has been using the live drake, the dead fly,
a humble bee, and a worm. Those baits remain
transfixed as he left them last evening, and admirably do they conceal the hooks. Now he reap-
pears with a ruddy-faced girl, his daughter, who
having, by my gracious leave, studied the artificial
fly which has proved so effectual, thanks me with
a smile which breaks upon her countenance like the
rise of a tranquil trout, and hurries back into the
cottage to manufacture an article exactly like mine.
    Sir Melton Mowbray did not hesitate to grant
me a day's fishing in his park when I met him in
the lobby a month previously. I had rescued him
from a deputation of farmers and churchwardens
who were worrying him about some highway business, and I am sure he was grateful to me for the
service. I, on my part, was equally grateful to
him when he added that I might with surety antici-

pate some sort of sport, inasmuch as his lake had not been fished (to his knowledge) for three years.

It being now the Whitsun recess Sir Melton is at home, and receives me in a charming country house in the midst of an old-fashioned park laid out in some parts to resemble the best features of a natural woodland. Not fifty yards from the lawn I notice a hawk on the wing, and the rookery overhead is a Babel. The aged trees have been respected, and their picturesqueness, as I make bold to tell the baronet, is worth more to him than the felled timber. Wild flowers bloom upon the banks, and bramble and fern and bracken have not been removed if their presence suits the surroundings. The consequence of this is that Mowbray Park furnishes a perfect example of what Nature, assisted but not stamped out by Art, can do.

The lake is not large, but it is deep, and graced by numerous trees down to the water-edge along seven-eighths of its margin. Sir Melton Mowbray, introducing me to the water, wishes me luck, places a gardener's boy at my disposal, and goes back to his Blue-books. The only way of fishing the lake is from a boat, and boat there is none. There is instead an overgrown square washing-tub, used by the boy for fetching duck's eggs from a little island in the centre. You do not dare to stand upright in this remarkable specimen of naval architecture, but you may sit on a rail nailed across, and must balance yourself to a hair if you would avoid a capsize. Having procured a pole, I punt to the end from which the wind comes, and it is fortunate that it blows steadily, and not too strongly. Then I deliver myself and fortunes to the will of the breezes.

Though I have been apprised that the Mayfly

is out in unheard-of quantities, I can see none.
Smaller insects are on the wing, but in spite of
the rushes around the edges, and a thickly wooded
ravine through which a tributary brook runs into
the lake, there is no rise of drakes. It is a game
of patience, then, in which I have to engage. I
am aware that the Mayfly is quite as capricious as
the rest of the insect creation, and disappears
suddenly and mysteriously, without any apparent
cause. In angling, too, it is safe never to take
anything for granted. At the same time it is with
just a modicum of faith that I tie on a most
elegantly made fly of medium size. The fish, I
find, as I drift and whip, are very lively, and I get
excellent sport for the space of an hour ; and the
trout are all within an ounce of the same size, each
being about a pound and a quarter in weight.

This is a trifle strange, but so it is. A dozen
and one of them lie in my creel, thickset fish ;
much darker in colour, however, than I care to
see, and as like as peas. It does not require very
careful fishing to get them, for the wind assists
you in the casts, and the trout take the Mayfly
boldly the moment it touches the rippled surface,
or not at all. The wind drops, and the sun, letting
a searching daylight into the bottom of the lake,
reveals all its pretty traceried labyrinth of aquatic
vegetation. Deep down, cosy amongst the weeds,
I descry shoals of perch, and now I am no longer
puzzled. In the mud no doubt there are eels also,
and perch and eels, it is well known, give the
spawn and fry of trout little chance. There being,
as I conclude, few small trout in the lake, the
heaviest fish have very likely fallen to my share.
On the whole I have done passing well for so brief
a time, but sport wholly ceases when the calm

comes. The fish, however, are leaping on every hand, whereas before, when the remunerative fun was fast and furious, not a rise was to be seen. But every trout angler is aware that those frivolous splashes which make most noise and commotion are ominous signs—another illustration, in a word, of the adage, "Great cry and little wool."

Until now I have frequently heard of perch taking the fly. Without going so far as to say I was incredulous on the point, I may here confess that I would not believe it except from authentic information. But there is no length of impudence to which a hungry perch will not go; and a humorous angler in the far west of Ireland once told me that the perch of Lough Corrib were, the moment your back was turned, in the habit of climbing up the banks, stealing a worm from the bag, and slinking again into the water to devour it at leisure. That may not have been true, but it was his story, and in return for it I gave him an appreciative laugh, and a pipe of tobacco.

These urchin perch to-day, however, rise madly at my Mayfly. I am whipping carelessly right and left as the wind wafts me towards the shore, and from a shallow part where the weeds are not two inches under water I decoy something which comes with a bang, and that something to my amazement is a perch. For the fun of the thing, and to thin out the undesirable companions of the trout, I lessen the number by a couple of dozen. The body of the fly looks like a fat caddis worm, and I put the folly of the perch down to that score, but adding a large red spinner to test the matter, they still come and pursue both lures close to the punt. The teeth of the game little zebras of the water do not improve my Mayfly. The imposing

feathers become ragged, then as perch after perch
is caught the gauzy wings and long tail vanish, and
finally there is nothing left but the half yellow half
buff body, wrapped round with brown silk ribbing
frayed and torn.   This is a serious loss when, as I
have discovered too late, there are but three Mayflies left in the book.

Sir Melton Mowbray at lunch promises to take
my advice, buy a net, and remove the perch ; and,
beholding my good fortune, he betrays a sudden
interest in the sport of angling, and carefully copies
the address of the best tackle shop I can recommend.   But the hon. baronet must build a proper
boat before he begins, for the rickety washing tub
was never intended to carry fifteen stone, and he
himself confesses—and his park-hack would not
contradict him—to that modest weight.   I bid
him good morning, and terminate my flying—might
I not say Mayflying ?—visit to Mowbray Park, not
directly coveting my neighbour's goods, but perhaps
resolving to think once, twice, aye, and even thrice,
before refusing, should Sir Melton ever take it into
his head to offer the place to me as a gift.

The sun smites fiercely upon us on our way to
Brawl Mill.   The road lies over a stiff hill country,
and the valley of the Brawl is far beneath us, a
lovely panorama of English scenery.   The stream
meanders through its course, a mere thread of
silver from this distance.   Two gentlemen, with
a keeper in the rear, are whipping away, now and
then resting to mop the perspiration from their fore-
heads, and appearing to us from our elevation no
bigger than the Shem, Ham, and Japhet of a Lowther
Arcade Noah's Ark.   The driver knows them to
be both peers of the realm ; one of them owns the
estate, and is a man of note in the racing world.

Every year at the first appearance of the May-fly his lordship is telegraphed for wherever he may be, and the earliest train brings him and a companion or two to the nearest station. They take quarters at a roadside inn (where we halt to water our reeking horse) and remain there until the fly has gone, enjoying the sandy floor, the flitches of bacon on the rafters, the bunches of lavender in the drawers, and the fragrant snow-white bed linen. The only member of the party who seems put out by a temporary residence at this rural hostelry is the earl's *valet de chambre:* Mons. Adolphe has, I regret to state, taught the rustics the use of the word *sacré*, and saturates himself with *eau de Cologne* night and day, that he may not be polluted by the hinds and dairymaids about him.

Brawl Mill might be a bodily transfer from Switzerland, nestling there as it does in the silent hollow, with a slope of dark pines rising straight from its little garden on the hill-side, with its drowsy old water-wheel, with its farmyard poultry and pigeons, with its wide porch smothered in roses, with its wooden loft steps, grey granary, and primitive out-houses. It is shut out from the turmoil of the world ; not another human habitation is visible from the higher garden. It possesses two gardens—the first gained by ascending a flight of ashen steps above the mill ; the second reached by similar means to where, below the house, the stream, after being released from the mill, tumbles over a fall.

Farther down the Brawl deserves the name I have bestowed upon it : it ripples and complains, it frets and hurries away to find its level in a water-mead beyond. Above the mill the stream

is wide and placid, as if conscious of its usefulness
in feeding the hatches communicating with the
mill, and desirous of sticking to its post of duty to
the last. A bank of impenetrable weed, filling
half of the river-bed, affords hiding-place for the
trout, albeit it compels you to bring all your
strength and ability into play to send your fly
freely and gently across the stream ; and a morass
of rushes adds to the difficulty. The water is too
clear, the sun is too bright; the fishable spaces do
not give sign of a rise, and the flies alight and
float down unnoticed. A stranger would not
hesitate to pronounce the river untenanted as an
empty house.

Ladies greet us here. I never yet knew the angler
who regretted their society by the riverside, and
there is one sauntering up the lane who has herself graduated with credit in bank-fishing. They
have been rambling, and the children gleefully
display the flowers they have gathered. Little
Rosebud asks me to accompany her a field or
two down the stream to pluck the forget-me-nots
her small arm cannot reach. These sunburnt
folks are spending their holiday at the old mill-
house, and have much to tell me of bird, and
beast, and fish.

Little Rosebud, let me inform you, has often
aforetime been my companion at the waterside.
She can distinguish a roach from a perch, and a
trout from a pike, should the pike happen to be
large enough, and she will trot along proud as a
queen if allowed to carry the landing net. So,
yielding to the fair-haired tempter, I lay aside my
rod, and stroll lazily along on the banks of the
Brawl, inwardly making observations to guide me
in the evening's fishing. Little Rosebud, it seems,

has seen a kingfisher, and last night she heard an owl hooting in the pine-wood.   A prostrate trunk invites us to spend an idle half-hour in a sweet natural bower, from which we can command a capital view of one of the best bends of the stream.   Little Rosebud, flushed in the hedge-row out of the heat, sits crowned with flowers, clapping her hands at the large sportive Mayflies on the water.   She thus receives her first lesson in entomology, and hears the story of the nautilus which the insects are imitating.   They fall on the water light as snowflakes, spread out their wings like sails, and run free before the wind or grace-fully tack, as it may please them.   Little Rose-bud claps her hands at the furious leaps of the trout, and shouts for very joy when the fly, after skimming daintily along the surface, and dallying with doom, takes wing once more and escapes scot-free.

But let us pass on.   We will dwell no longer on this remembrance of a happy day ; but should I live to the extremest span of human years, when-ever the Mayfly appears in its season, the picture of little Rosebud in the shade, following the airy flights of the heedless insects, now up, now down, with her dancing eyes, will be ever before me, for little Rosebud, alas, alas, needs no more to sit in the hedgerow out of the heat.

The evening fishing repays me for the idle hour, and, to be honest, I meet with far more good fortune than I deserve.   Above the mill, by the hatches, the placid current, when the day declines, is troubled with the movements of many trout. They appear to make no distinction between the insects that touch it.   Drake or moth shares the same fate.   My artificial Mayfly is quite as good as the plumpest reality. The ladies hover round, observing that fly-fishing is a most gentlemanly pastime, and that a trout is entitled to special consideration as one of the upper ten of the finny tribes. I strike an attitude and resolve to treat my audience to something artistic. I dry the fly : one, two, three, and then for a cast that shall win a compliment and a fish. The great wings float trembling down to the verge of an eddy, and lo ! a plunge and——Alack, the cast rebounds with no fly at its extremity. I have by sheer stupidity lost both my compliment and my fish ; it is the usual result of trying for too much, and the pinch of the mishap is that it has reduced my stock of Mayflies to a solitary specimen, with yet another hour of daylight.

That unfortunate trout will be telegraphing danger to all his relatives and acquaintances, unless he has darted into a quiet corner to persevere if haply he may rub the hook out of his jaws; in which operation I wish him speedy success.

It is better after this blunder to shift quarters for a few minutes, and take care that the fault does not recur. But how true it is that misfortunes do not come singly ! Not five minutes elapse before a wild attempt at an impossible cast deprives me of my last Mayfly. I have left it driven hard into the overhanging bough of an alder, that any tyro should have avoided. With varying success I now move up stream, picking out a trout here and a troutlet there with an orange palmer and a medium blue dun. The still summer night steals on apace, and the half-hour remaining must be devoted to the broader part where the ladies witnessed my discomfiture.

In point of numbers that half-hour turns out to be the most remunerative of the whole day; the trout rise freely at the soldier palmer, and are partial to a small coachman. Twice I have a brace of young fish on the line at once.

The lower part of the stream I am compelled to spare, and even then it is dark before I have arranged my spoil on a broad kitchen platter, artistically disposing the finest fish to catch the eye of the ladies chatting in the homely parlour of Brawl Mill. Supper being eaten, I plod up the creaking stairs, pondering that to tire the arms, stiffen the back, punish the right hand, develop the power of the lower limbs, and sharpen your appetite, you could pitch upon nothing better than a long day by the waterside in the Mayfly season.

CHAPTER III.

THE THAMES.

"From his oozy bed
Old Father Thames advanced his rev'rend head,
His tresses drooped with dews, and o'er the stream
His shining horns diffused a golden gleam.
Graved on his urn appeared the moon, that guides
His swelling waters and alternate tides :
The figured streams in waves of silver roll'd,
And on his banks Augusta, robed in gold ;
Around his throne the sea-born brothers stood,
Who swell with tributary urns his flood :
First, the famed authors of his ancient name,
The winding Isis and the fruitful Thame."

T is a little singular to read in an angler's
book published forty years ago that
while pike and perch fishing seemed to
be followed only occasionally, "as it
is very uncertain sport in the Thames," trout were
fairly numerous.   Then, as now, the proper thing
for the angler was to perch upon the top of a
pile with the uproar and gallop of the weir flood
beneath him, and spin patiently for the expected
monster ; but there were spinners and trollers
also in those days, piscatorial sons of Anak whose
deeds were, and here and there are still to be

seen, commemorated in the rudely outlined fish drawn on the walls of the comfortable hostelries on Thames-side.   In 1835 Jesse speaks of a large trout that took its daily airing opposite the water-gallery of Hampton Court, but had defied every endeavour to capture it.   The wish expressed by Jesse that "something will be done for the protection of the fish during the earlier stages of their existence" has been fulfilled, and we can still say, with that rare old contributor to *Frazer's Magazine,* that "persons of every class seem to participate in the amusement of Thames angling, from the Duke of Sussex to the little fat cobbler of Hampton."   Jesse lived at Hampton, and naturally gave a preference to that portion of the river, and many modern anglers agree with him in that preference.

It was the Thames that inspired Jesse to recommend to his brethren of the Walton and Cotton Fishing Club the old song :—

"Come, lay by all cares, and hang up all sorrow,
Let's angle to-day and ne'er think of to-morrow :
And by the brook-side as we angle along,
We'll cheer up ourselves with our sport and a song.

"There, void of all care, we're more happy than they
That sit upon thrones, and kingdoms do sway :
For sceptres and crowns disquiet still bring :
But the man that's content is more blest than a king."

Not so much as a trout river, however, as the cosmopolitan resort of miscellaneous anglers, let us bestow a few thoughts upon the Thames.   I will openly confess myself a very indifferent Thames fisherman.   Imprisonment in a punt has no delights for me.   To me one of the chief charms of the angler's pursuit is the infinite

variety of scenery into which it leads him. Give
me a supple fly-rod; equip me in all respects in
light marching order; introduce me to a few miles
of stream that meanders through flowery mead and
leafy dell—that now rolls dark and deep, and anon
splashes and foams over stones and shallows; that
at every bend opens up a new prospect; that
brings me here to a rustic weather-browned foot-
bridge, and there to a ford through which the
ploughman or harvestman takes his team; or to a
simple hamlet, perfumed with wood-fire, thatch,
and homeliness, where morning newspapers are
unknown; thence into the sheltered glade, and,
by smiling homestead, away from the haunts of
man; give me all this on a day when the larks
sing loud and untiringly, and the insects rehearse
in happy chorus; when "waves of shadow" pass
over the glad fields and woods, and all God's
beautiful earth seems to murmur in grateful soft
ness of spirit—give me this, and you present to
me one of the masterful attractions of what has
been so appropriately termed the "contemplative
man's recreation." I shall like it all the better, to
be sure, if my fly be not cast upon the water in
vain; but in no case shall I bewail the day as a
positive blank.

This is a type of happiness which often falls to
the rambling Waltonian's share, but seldom to the
share of the Thames angler. Yet what exquisite
scenes are commanded by the Thames! Verily it
were a work of supererogation to recount them,
since they have been the subject of poet's song and
artist's pencil from time immemorial. Thus :—

> "But health and labour's willing train
> Crowns all thy banks with waving grain;

D

With beauty decks thy sylvan shades,
With livelier green invests thy glades ;
And grace, and bloom, and plenty pours
O'er thy sweet meads and willowy shores.
The fields where herds unnumbered rove,
The laurell'd path, the beechen grove,
The oak, in lonely grandeur free,
Lord of the forest and the sea ;
The spreading plain, the cultured hill,
The tranquil cot, the restless mill,
The lonely hamlet, calm and still ;
The village spire, the busy town,
The shelving bank, the rising down ;
The fisher's punt, the peasant's home,
The woodland seat, the regal dome,
In quick succession rise to charm
The mind with virtuous feelings warm ;
Till where thy widening current glides,
To mingle with the turbid tides,
Thy spacious breast displays unfurled
The ensigns of th' assembled world."

There are, I know, many anglers who prefer
streams on a smaller scale, and the liberty of the
solitary roamer ; but for the life of me I cannot
understand why Thames punt-fishing should be
sneered at and abused by those who have no personal liking for it.   If to yield the greatest happiness to the greatest number is to benefit mankind,
in the matter of angling the Thames punt must
be held in supreme veneration as a benefactor.
Thousands of citizens, for the major part of the
year immersed in the grinding mill-round of business and business cares, thanks to the square-
cornered squat Thames punt, find innocent amusement and healthful draughts of fresh air.

Yet how easy it is to laugh at the spectacle, say,
of those three stout gentlemen in their shirt-sleeves,
sitting cosily in Windsor chairs, engaged throughout the livelong day in jerking back to their feet
the gaily-coloured float which perpetually races

away from them, as if anxious to escape the everlasting check put upon its motions ! These gentlemen are Smith, Jones, and Johnson, and it is
both probable and possible that they will be punted
to the snug waterside hostelry at night with no
more fish than they could hide in a quart pot.
They are men in flourishing lines of business when
at home, but to-day, happy as the kings of proverb, they sit there under the broiling sun, hoping
a good deal, dreaming a little, eating, drinking,
and smoking somewhat, and caring for nobody in
the wide universe. Money may be tight in the
City, markets bad, things on the Exchange
gloomy ; but for the time a lusty barbel or a
wriggling roach would concern them more than
all your dividends, discounts, or exchanges.

And there is no part of the Thames—certainly
no portion of its fishable parts—where there is not
shorewards something worth looking upon. No
doubt your superfine critic would consider punt-
fishing at Richmond, or anywhere between Richmond and Teddington, to be Cockneyism of the
most pronounced type ; but if only for the sake of
the manifold playings of light and shade upon the
trees, the glints of golden sunlight falling each
hour differently as the eventide draws on upon the
river, and the ever-changing, ever-interesting
traffic of the tideway which you get on a summer
afternoon, stationed within sight of bonny Richmond Hill, or further up by the pretty lawns and
villas of Twickenham, you would do well not to
think too lightly of a few hours in a Thames punt,
even so close to the Rialto as are those near-at-
hand " pitches."

It does your heart good to ramble along the
banks and see how much happiness the bounteous

river gives to old and young. Cockneyism? Sit down upon this bit of soft turf, your feet dallying with the meadow-sweet on the brink, and watch the inhabitants of the nearest punt. There is the fisherman in his usual commanding position—ground-bait, gentles, landing net, customer's lines, and (may I without offence add?) commissariat department, all within reach of his hand. You see this is a family party. Paterfamilias in the straw hat will be at the receipt of custom to-morrow morning, and would politely but firmly request you to endorse your cheque if you had omitted that necessary formality. He watches the fisherman (who is generally Bob or Bill Somebody) dispense ground-bait much as yesterday he would watch the junior at the bank shovelling sovereigns into the bags; only he is free from anxiety, and the master eye of a superior is not upon him.

The two boys are absorbed in their sport, striking vigorously at the end of every swim, and clamouring for more ground-bait. Their mother, working quietly in the background, has to duck her head and lower her parasol when Master Henry perceives a bite, for Master Henry's idea of sport is swishing the fish high in the air over his shoulder. The little girl, lounging in the bottom of the punt, laughs musically at these performances; and the merry voices of all are never wholly still. Quite content are these anglers with the six-inch victims transferred, as fortune varies, into the well.

What a hubbub there is in the punt when Paterfamilias after a dexterous "strike" finds his float doggedly held beneath the surface! The fisherman warns and directs after the manner of fishermen, doing, of course, his best to increase the

nervousness of an inexperienced angler. Even
mamma gets excited over this crisis. To right of
them, to left of them, the taut line is borne. The
angler is commanded to "let him go," to lower
the point of his rod, and to take it easy. Miss
Mary's oval face peers over the side of the punt,
and her brown eyes try to pierce the two fathoms
of water. Master Henry shouts aloud his conjec-
tures. Master Robert saw the monster turn over
on his side.

"It's as long as your arm, papa," he cries.

The float is gradually being coaxed above water
at last, but it still makes sharp, slanting stabs,
pointing to the depths where the prey, whatever it
may be, is making angry efforts to free itself. It
is a little disappointing, no doubt, when, after all
this fuss, the monster is netted in the shape of a
bronze, wiry barbel, of not much over a pound and
a half ; but the consoling reflection remains that if
it had been a salmon itself it could not have fought
more pluckily. Our last glimpse at this scene of
"Cockneyism" reveals the proud citizen surrounded by his family, to whom he is confiden-
tially explaining that to slay such a fish with a foot-
line of fine gut is a particularly clever and artistic
feat—a proposition no one gainsays. Made-
moiselle is much interested in the demonstrations
of the barbel now sulking in the well, and the
boys are busy separating their lines, which in the
agitation of the last quarter of an hour were allowed
to become entangled.

Young Browne Browne, Esq., pulling up stream
with two brass-buttoned ladies in the stern-sheets,
rests on his sculls to make game of Smith, Jones,
and Johnson, in their shirt-sleeves. He wonders
how "these fellaws" can sit in the punt after that

fashion, pities the weak intellect which angling denotes, and mightily amuses his pretty, gaily-dressed companions by his wit.   It is strange that S., J., and J. are on their part at the same time laughing at Browne Browne's amazing nautical costume.

Browne Browne sometimes trusts himself on board a small toy steamer, and then he is apt to become a serious nuisance.   The little spit-fire craft ruthlessly invades many a "swim," and pursues its reckless way in triumph.   And it would be all the better if Browne Browne would forswear that unmanly trailing propensity of his, and leave the small jack to reach years of something like maturity.

The extension of railways has brought the Thames within easy reach of the angling classes. The river may now be "tapped" at all points, beginning with a Great Western station not far from the source.   The number of anglers in the Thames multiplies with every season, and the pastime itself is more generally followed, if not in its higher, in its lower branches.   The angling clubs in the metropolis probably have a good deal to do with this addition to the rank and file of anglers.

The most courteous and genuine-hearted Waltonian I ever met by the waterside was a Bloomsbury locksmith's apprentice.   I was stopping at Henley, and although I never actually indulge in my favourite amusement on Sundays, conscientious scruples do not prevent my watching with the keenest interest any sort of rod-work that comes under my notice on the day of rest.   The first train on Sunday morning would bring down scores of rods, and most amusing it was to watch the anglers disperse along the riverside.

In the course of a few Sundays' quiet observation of these men, I could detect signs of un-Waltonian selfishness, for which I suspect the club prize system—its abuse, not its use—is to a great extent answerable. Some " brother of the angle," as you might soon perceive, was stimulated by the hope of a prize to excel honestly in the craft ; it sharpened his wits, and put him upon his mettle. In others, on the contrary, very undesirable qualities were developed. They forgot that though everything might be fair in love and war, in angling there are certain rules not to be transgressed. Their one desire was to bag fish—honestly if possible, but at all costs to bag fish.

The sportsman thus became, in the worst sense of the term, a pot hunter. He leaped from the railway carriage before the train stopped, panting to be first in the field. One morning I saw a dozen young fellows racing as if for dear life towards the meadows, foaming with rage at a dapper little French polisher who outstripped them all. Just as the peaceful church bells were calling the people to prayer, and the musical chime floated across the waters to die away in the magnificent woods rising grandly on the other side, a regular fight took place among the competitors. Throughout the day men tried to mislead and even to interfere with each other's fishing, a miserable contrast to the ancient angler who quaintly asked no higher bliss than to live harmlessly :—

"Where I may see my quill or cork down sink
With eager bite of perch, or bleak, or dace ;
And on the world and my Creator think
While some men strive ill-gotten goods t'embrace,
And others spend their time in base excess
Of wine, or worse, in war and wantonness."

My courteous locksmith's apprentice would hold no intercourse with these ne'er-do-wells. He had discovered a sweet nook at the junction of the main with a smaller stream, and there, hidden in over-hanging alder boughs, he perseveringly plied his lures. The lad was very poor, and, as he confessed to me, denied himself all superfluities, and some necessaries, to raise the four shillings which his fortnightly trip to Henley cost him. He had never missed his Sunday for two seasons. He was great in theories. He had a theory about everything— about tying a knot, about impaling gentles, about striking and landing. His greatest achievement was the killing of a Thames trout without running tackle and with an ordinary roach rod. Some club men refused to speak to him because he wore fustian; but, as he informed me with a comical smile, they could be very gracious to the youth if they ran short of baits or hooks. With all their wiles and questionable play, the locksmith could beat them hollow at fishing. When to most eyes there was no movement of his porcupine float he would be fast to a fish. The prettiest bit of angling I ever saw was his handling of a vigorous pound-and-half roach in a roughish stream. I have often wondered what luck has fallen to this casual waterside acquaintance in the every-day of life. He was very original, and, for one of his class, well-informed. A tattered ready-reckoner, he always carried with him, as a receptacle of rare entomological or floral specimens. A present of a "Walton's Complete Angler" brought tears of gratitude into his eyes. It was not necessary to warn him, at any rate, against a certain selfishness which I fear, though not peculiar to Thames-side, is much more prevalent there than it used to be amongst Waltonians. Because of this I do not say the prize system should be abolished, but it is an additional reason why every club should cultivate a spirit which is fatal alike to unbrotherly and un-sportsman-like behaviour. Surely, surely, anglers are so comparatively few and the world is so wide that there is room enough for all !

If the anglers who have not the opportunity of punting farther than Teddington or Hampton are to be congratulated upon the fair scenes surrounding them as they pursue their avocation, what shall be said of the more fortunate who pay leisurely visits to Windsor, Maidenhead, Cookham, Marlow, Sonning, Caversham, Pangbourne, Goring, Mouls-ford, and Wallingford? It is a very trite saying that we despise what is nearest home. One has no patience with travellers who persist in shutting their eyes to the beautiful scenery of the Upper Thames, or in placing her charms lower than those of other rivers, which they feel constrained to adore because they are more remote. The Thames, it is true, boasts of no bouldered bed, rocky banks, or turbulent currents that roar their troubled journey to the sea : but its landscapes in many respects have no equal. They tell in every feature of peace and plenty : of corn, and wine, and oil.

To the angler the Thames offers a wide choice. It contains fish for all fishers. Towards the close of last year's season I saw a dainty little lady, sitting in a punt near the bridge at Hampton, catch with most graceful skill a fine dish of gudgeon, who might truly have said :—

"And Beauty draws us with a single hair."

While the preservation of the Thames has been

worthy of all praise, there is something yet to be
done. Mede and Persian laws cannot be laid down
upon angling, and the experience of one year, without any apparent reason, often directly contradicts
the experience of another. But upon one point
there need be no hesitating utterance—fishing for
pike in June is opposed to both law and common
sense. Roach may have recovered from spawning
in that leafy month, though that is by no means
certain, even when the season has been a forward
one. In the last week of April I have caught
with a fly dace that were perfectly recovered, and
this in a stream where the previous year they
were rough and flabby so late as the middle of
May.

The professional Thames fisherman, though not
half so bad as he is painted, is all the better for
being looked after. Fishing from the punt necessarily involves an almost childlike trust in the
fisherman. If you succeed, you reward him ; if
you fail, you execrate him and all that is his.
Your prosperity you place to the credit of your own
skill ; your adversity you lay to his charge. In
both you may be right, but it is not hard to see
that between the two the fisherman runs a capital
chance of being spoiled. Much of the objection
which many entertain to Thames angling arises
from dislike of the fisherman. Still the fisherman's
position is a safe one, for to fish the Thames profit-
ably you must perforce use a punt or boat. The
fishermen are capable of some improvement, although in fairness to them let me say that, considering how they are pampered by one set of
anglers and bullied by another, the wonder is they
are not worse than they are.

You will forgive a man much if he is equal to his

business, and the Thames fishermen as a body do understand the river, and the habits and haunts of its fish. It does not of course follow that they will give every stranger the benefit of their knowledge. Why should you expect them to be above favouritism and scheming when Society, from its Alpine heights of fashion to its plebeian base, is full of it? The fisherman, naturally too, sometimes loses patience with the amateurs who frequently occupy his punt ; they are out for a day's jollity, and he fools them to the top of their bent. On the other hand, nothing can be more irritating than to be pestered by a talkative fisherman, or a man who will meddle and dictate.

Last year a friend persuaded me to join him in a day's punt-fishing at one of the higher stations. I was warned that I should find the fisherman a most disagreeable necessity, and the anticipation quite spoiled that pleasure of hope which every angler knows is not the least ingredient of a happy day. The man introduced himself to us at our hotel, and ordered breakfast at our expense—not at all bad as a beginning. Bottled ale was good enough for our hamper, but the fisherman, volunteering to pack the meats and drinks, coolly told us *he* could not drink beer, and must have whisky. A pint of Kinahan's was forthwith added for his special consumption ; he was, I remember, particular as to Kinahan.

He punted us down the river, and brought up at a notable "pitch." Till then we had rather enjoyed the young man's cool, and not in manner at all offensive, assumption, but when he proceeded to forbid my companion to bait his own hooks, plumb the depth, or touch a fish ; when a jack hooked himself upon my ledger line and I began to winch him in, and our friend peremptorily took the rod—my rod !—out of my hands, and by his clumsiness allowed the jack to escape, matters were brought to a crisis.

Some language ensued. The air, I rejoice to say, quickly cleared, and our friend was none the worse for the setting down he received, and for the remainder of the day a more docile, intelligent fisherman never wielded pole. He had after all acted according to habit ; upon discovering that we understood our part of the business he devoted himself to his own. He was not at all a bad fellow when we came to know each other, but he had been spoiled by foolish customers, and required to be kept in his place.

Fly-fishing in the Thames, though the pursuit of a few, is a fascinating and not unremunerative method of dealing with the river. Though the fly occasionally takes a *salmo fario,* especially in the early spring months, fly-fishing in the Thames for trout alone is scarcely worth the time and trouble it involves. Dace and chub rise freely, and in the very hot evenings of July and August roach may be included. The fly-fisher is independent of the punt and the fisherman. A hired boat with a friend to manage it answers every purpose. Or an evening's moderate sport may be enjoyed from the bank if you understand where to go.

A boatman's boy at Richmond with a peeled willow wand, a length of twine, and a small black gnat begged from some passing possessor of a fly-book, will, when the humour takes them, whip out dace with every cast. The Thames dace never runs large—six to a pound being perhaps under rather than above the average size. He is a game, handsome little fellow, and not to be despised as a table delicacy. Learn how to master the art of dace-fishing with your fly rod, and you have graduated to a fair trout degree. Indeed, a quicker eye and lighter wrist are necessary for dace. The thing must be done on the instant if at all. Should you, as I have had the felicity of doing in the Colne, find the fish feeding voraciously, and have a couple of bold half-pounders on your line at once, you may be ready to admit that, in the absence of trout, dace are not beneath an experienced man's notice.

Chub take a large fly well in the Thames, and the easiest road to their good graces is this : let your boat drift quietly with the stream—the slower the better—about a dozen or fifteen yards from the bushes under which the chub are known to congregate, and parallel with the bank. Use a large black or red palmer ; drop it upon the boughs, and thence seductively into the water ; and it will warm your heart to see how heartily the lumbering chevens rush to their destruction. Beware of the first bolt. Here, as everywhere else, it is the pace that kills. " Let him go "—that is always serviceable advice for an angler, although, in this instance, I must add a reservation. Let the chub *not* go into the bank or under the roots of a tree ; should he accomplish that, invariably his first impulse, the chances are fifty-two and a quarter to one in his favour. The chub, nevertheless, is a chicken-hearted fish. He soon gives up the fight, and comes in, log-like, without a grumble.

NOTE.—Since this chapter was written Mr. Spreckley and his colleagues of the Thames Angling Preservation Society Committee have turned large quantities of fish into the Thames. Great pains have been taken in stocking

with trout.   One result of the careful preservation is an undoubted increase of that noble fish.   Mr. W. H. Brougham
was able to report in 1883 that eighteen Thames trout from 2 lb.
to 14 lb. were taken between Kingston and Chertsey in one
week.   In the new Thames bye-laws, which came into
operation in 1883, the regulation sizes of fish were thus
specified :—Pike or jack, 18 in. ; perch, 8 in. ; chub, 10 in. ;
roach, 7 in. ; dace, 6 in. ; barbel, 13 in. ; trout, 16 in. ;
bream, 10 in. ; carp, 10 in. ; tench, 8 in. ; rudd, 6 in. ;
gudgeon, 4 in. The measurement the extreme length.—W.S.

CHAPTER IV.

A HOLIDAY IN DEVONSHIRE.

" Fair are the provinces that England boasts,
Lovely the verdure, exquisite the flowers
That bless her hills and dales,—her streamlets clear,
Her seas majestic, and her prospects all,
Of old, as now, the pride of British song.
　　　But England sees not on her charming map
A goodlier spot than our fine Devon ;—rich
Art thou in all that Nature's hand can give,
Land of the matchless view !"

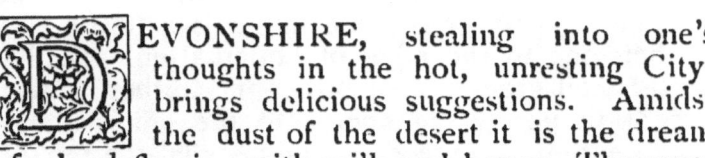EVONSHIRE, stealing into one's thoughts in the hot, unresting City, brings delicious suggestions. Amidst the dust of the desert it is the dream of a land flowing with milk and honey. The overworked man looks forward to its green lanes and luxuriant meads, to its cool darkened woods and refreshing streams, with a grateful sense of coming rest and freedom. Other counties have their special nooks and corners famed for picturesqueness and noted as the beaten track of tourists ; large though it be, there is no other county in England bearing in its entirety so excellent a general character as fruitful Devon.

Announce that you are going down into Devon-

shire, and you have said enough.   No one asks to
what particular district you are shaping your
course : so long as it is Devonshire you must
perforce enjoy yourself.   Does it not possess a soft,
warm coast of surpassing loveliness, where the
myrtle flourishes in mid-winter ? Has it not gentle
lowlands and bleak highlands ?   Does it not rise
into open-browed moors that catch the earliest
snows, and sink into valleys sequestered from the
storms and turmoils that roughen the rest of the
world ?

These thoughts were not unwelcome as I stood
apart from the shifting, bustling throng at
Paddington terminus, mounting guard over creel
and rods, until the express was ready to whisk me
through the night to Plymouth.   The confusion
and bustle of this station, immortalized in Frith's
picture, were positively soothing to the Devon-
shire-bound passenger, for the contrast between
the fleeting present and the immediate future was
a whetstone to the edge of anticipation.   So, let
porters and grooms rush hither and thither, ladies
appeal in perplexing chorus to the officials, and
testy gentlemen rage and scold—what mattered ?
To-morrow I should be knee-deep in west country
clover, my flies would be sailing down Devonshire-
streams, and for a whole week, behold, London
should know me no more. The greater the hubbub
around, the more placid I.

It was a long ride in prospect, for Reading,
Bath, Bristol, Taunton, Exeter, and Plymouth had
to pass in review ere I could exchange the iron
horse for that more primitive carrier through whose
good offices I hoped by to-morrow's noon to climb
up into the free air of Dartmoor.   It was the 1st
of June, a date of no significance to ordinary

mortals, though a red-letter day to the London
angler. Wherefore, though perchance I should
sleep by-and-by, it must not be until I had caught
such glimpses as time would permit of the stations
along the Thames.

In a brief space of time the train was at West
Drayton, where the mellow fading sunlight slanted
across the Thorney Broad water, and revealed on
the willow-lined banks rods flashing like bayonets.
In a few minutes we crossed the narrow Iver, with
just a glimpse, through the elms up the meadows,
of the bridge, by which doubtless lay trout, over
which since the first day of the season many a fly
had been thrown. At Slough there might be seen
upon the up platform a small contingent of returning anglers who had been honouring the 1st of
June on the Thames at Eton.[1] These were for the
most part gay young ladies and gentlemen who had
been combining a large measure of picnicing with a
soupçon of angling ; who had been, in short, using
the rod and line as a justification for and aid to flirta-
tion. It was at Maidenhead, Taplow, Reading, and
the higher stations that the real anglers were found ;
there they clustered, leaning tired on their rods,
recounting their day's experiences. And soon, the
last bit of gold having been extracted by greedy
nightfall from the sky, it was meet to settle cosily
into the corner to doze, and see visions of speckled
trout and silvery salmon.

The Dart, with whose upper waters I proposed
to make intimate acquaintance with all speed, is
crossed by the South Devon line at Totnes, and I
had an opportunity of reconnoitring it at unexpected
and unusual leisure. A deep sleep had sealed

---

[1] The Thames season now opens on the 16th June. —W. S.

our eyelids as we ran down close to the estuary of
the Exe and skirted the sea wall at Dawlish and
Teignmouth ; but we by-and-by became conscious
of something uncommon, and awoke to find the
train brought to a standstill in the midst of the
purest country surroundings.

An hour or two before a luggage train had
wrecked, and our passage was now stopped. In
the freshness of the balmy morning we had—
men, women and children—to tumble out of the
carriages, and struggle with bag and baggage
through a couple of fields, across a country lane,
and up a high bank of nettles and brambles, to a
train composed of odds and ends of rolling stock,
hastily constructed and despatched from Totnes.
The sun, newly risen, shone upon this singular
picture of wreck and confusion in a frame of rural
fertility, and the sleek Devon herds and a few
open-mouthed rustics looked on in astonishment
at the novel occurrence which had taken place
amongst their promising orchards and richly-
cropped fields.

The Dart at Totnes is a very sober-minded river.
That morning not a breath of wind ruffled its
greenish waters, and a couple of troutlets a
hundred yards up stream, gently rising at a frisky
midge, covered the whole surface with concentric
circles. The trees and bushes in full leaf were
repeated in the glassy water. North and south
alike, the scenery is of the most fascinating description even here, where the Dart, having pursued
its devious way from distant uplands, seems to
pause for a brief interval of repose and thought
before entering upon that magnificent, sweeping,
more dignified course through the South Hams to
the sea at Dartmouth. The Devonshire people

are proud to hear the Dart designated "The
Rhine of the West," and no unprejudiced voyager
who has taken steamer from the ancient town of
Totnes to the almost equally old seaport of Dartmouth will deny that the name is deservedly
applied.

It is doubtless a very ill wind that blows good
to nobody, and our delay had given me, at least,
the opportunity of taking a leisurely look at the
landscape. The railway guards and porters did
their best to remedy the mishap ; and in a surpris-
ingly short space of time we were once more
en route through the finest part of pastoral Devon.
Every new prospect proves that it would be
almost impossible to praise it too highly. The
great officers of State take the Viceroys, Sultans,
Shahs, and Czars of the earth to see our soldiers
and guns, our forts and ships, our densely populated
centres ; but who ever heard of their being brought
down into this Eden ? Surely here was an aspect
of the nation's life in which some, and not a little,
of its strength was indicated !

But who cared for emperors and kings ? Here
came South Brent, and running through it, with a
bridge across, another Dartmoor-born stream, the
Avon. Now I might form a pretty correct opinion
upon the state of the rivers I had travelled so far
to fish. For six weeks there had been no rain,
and very ill reports of the rivers of the three
kingdoms had been troubling the Waltonian world.
The Avon was not encouraging ; it was so reduced
in volume that it was difficult to see where there
was room for a trout, and throwing a fly into
those mere saucers which now represented the best
pools was out of the question. It was, one had to
confess with sorrowful misgiving, a hopeless

prospect, unless the banks of clouds brooding over
the moors would come to the rescue and unlock
their long-sealed fountains. Anxiously I waited
till a few miles further we crossed the Erme at Ivy
Bridge. The Erme confirmed the dismal story told
by the Avon. The stones in the rocky bed shone
with the unwetted smoothness of a long drought.
Although it might be better nearer the source, I
began to wish that the creel, capable of stowing
away 18lb. of fish, had been left at home. Nasmyth
hammers were not made to crack eggs.

But the woods were leafy, the air was charged
with the scent of hawthorn blossom, the landscapes were magnificent, and if the worst must
be endured, there would in all this be a certain
compensation for an empty basket.

> " Nature never did betray
> The heart that loved her ; 'tis her privilege
> Through all the years of this our life, to lead
> From joy to joy."

Still, remembering how the Erme and Avon in
their average condition tumbled and swirled and
gambolled from rock to rock, and beholding their
present melancholy dead level, it was but too true
that just a trifle of sunshine seemed to have
departed. Would the Yealm, yet another of the
Dartmoor brood, dispel the cloud ? Two or three
miles further, and lo, the Yealm coincided with its
sister streams. My only consolation was that in
the same carriage journeyed to South Brent a
young gentleman who was in worse plight than
myself : three salmon rods, a huge wooden-framed
landing net, fit receptacle for a shark ; wading
apparatus, gaffs, and an outfit generally that would
stock a tackle-maker's shop, he had brought with

him from town ; and certainly he looked the picture of misery when I showed him the sort of brook upon which his costly machinery was to be exercised.

The valley traversed by the Tavistock Railway, to which at Plymouth we were transferred, is not to be surpassed in Southern England for sustained sylvan beauty. Lord Morley's property at Saltram is the beginning of a stretch of woody hillside that continues with unbroken picturesqueness for miles. Such beeches, elms, ashes, sycamores, aspens, firs, maples, and oaks seldom indeed are to be looked upon from the windows of a railway carriage.

A few local anglers, who, it cheered the despondent stranger to think, would not have ventured forth unless there had been *some* chance of sport, got out at Bickleigh, and descended through the foliage towards the Plym, there almost hidden by over-spreading branches and bushy under-growth. Higher up, losing themselves in the Plym, are the Meavy and the Cad—the Cad of which Carrington, the poet of the Devonshire waters, wrote :—

> " Yet when, sweet Spring,
> Thy influence again shall make the bud
> Leap into leaf, and gentlest airs shall soothe
> The storm-swept bosom of the moor, thy feet
> Shall tread the banks of Cad."

Both Meavy and Cad are good trout-yielding streams when the conditions are anything like favourable, but at this time they suffered more perhaps than any from lack of water. Onward and upward still, through new phases of scenery, the train proceeded to Horrabridge, where we crossed the Walkham, now no longer the popular trout stream it used to be ; for here, unfortunately, as in other parts of Devon and Cornwall, the mines had been doing serious damage.

Tavistock, compact and thriving, lies in a natural basin, surrounded by a belt of hills. Where Dartmoor ends the Cornish hills continue the duty of encircling the small town, dooming it to more than a full share of wet weather. The Tavy runs through it ; and later in the year, when the salmon peel are in their prime, there is no river in the county that yields better morning and evening sport. A well-organized fishing association preserves the stream, its tributaries and sub-tributaries ; and under one of its wise regulations the angler below Denham Bridge is restricted to the use of the artificial fly. It is in these associations the hope of preserving our English fisheries chiefly rests ; wherefore, let every angler, whenever he has the opportunity of acting as an amateur waterbailiff, do his best to enforce their laws.

Eminently clean and respectable is Tavistock, on the border-land of the two great western counties. Nay, it is quite ecclesiastical in its staid appearance. There is an air of repose within its borders of which you become immediately sensible. A rollicking blade the visitor may be in London, but at Tavistock it will be useless to struggle against the subduing influences around him. On entering the hotel I was on the point of doffing my hat, fancying I was on the threshold of a church. The markets had all the quietness of the cloister ; the public buildings struck me as decidedly smacking of the cathedral style ; and the police went their rounds with a verger-like tread. The town, celebrated in the fifteenth century for its mitred abbey, would seem to have cherished to the present day

its ecclesiastical associations. Some remnants of
the time-worn stone-work of the abbey are there,
in keeping with the spirit of serenity which still
lingers in the highways and byeways.

It is seven miles into the heart of Dartmoor,
and, as you will speedily discover, seven miles pat
against the collar. He who is able to ride and
drive safely and boldly over Dartmoor is fit to take
a horse anywhere. It is a typical drive from
Tavistock to Princetown, for it affords fair examples of many peculiarities of the moor. Steadily
ascending from the lowlands, the atmosphere, like
the scenery, gradually changes. For the first mile
or so out of Tavistock I noticed the foxgloves, in
regular red-coated battalions, standing at ease in
the hedgerows, while all descriptions of flowers
were blooming in the profuse natural ferneries so
common to Devonshire banks and woodlands. As
the milestones were left in the rear, the foxglove
bells became less open, until on Dartmoor they
had not begun to expand into blossom. Up
amongst the billowy downs, blocks of granite,
wild ravines, shaggy sheep, and brawling brooks,
we followed the road, now this, now that Tor
challenging attention. Why this was ever called
the Royal Forest of Dartmoor it is hard to say,
although the bogs suggest forests primeval, and
some years since no inconsiderable traces of tropical
trees and plants were discovered in one part of the
moors. It is the general absence of wood that is
the primary characteristic of Dartmoor.

But then the place is a puzzle from first to last.
The masses of granite, cast, apparently, in Titanic
volleys out of the bowels of the earth, and the Tors
crowning the summits of the downs, as if systemati-
cally placed there for specific purposes, may well

account for the theories and superstitions and
dogmatisms associated from time immemorial with
them. From the top of the first hill, looking behind,
Tavistock appeared in its hollow like a snug bird's-
nest. Cornwall, its hills crowned with mine shafts
instead of granitic masses, confronted us. Far
away over the end of a long, wooded valley, and
sparkling like silver beyond the radiant woods, was
Plymouth Sound. Ahead and around were the
endless risings and fallings of the moor, now fresh
and green ; and the sun, fierce overhead, was printing cloud-pictures upon their broad bosoms.

At Merivale Bridge, spanning one of those
romantic rocky glens which intersect Dartmoor at
every point, the Walkham, not yet polluted by the
mines, passes downwards. It is a good sample of
a Dartmoor stream, plashing from point to point
in a quiet musical fashion, the banks open and
bare, and the water clear as crystal. It was, indeed,
so clear that I on the spot abandoned my original
intention of half an hour's fishing.

Besides there was other game on foot. A number
of prison warders were abroad stalking convicts.
Three of the wretches had escaped in a sudden fog
that, enveloping the moor as with a blanket two
hours before, had disappeared as suddenly as it came.
The convicts had got away ; two of them had been
shot when the fog lifted, and the warders were
searching for the third, examining every boulder,
every peat stack, every bit of ditch and bog.
Nearer Princetown we saw the warders bearing
the prostrate runaway, number three, to the convict
establishment, winged with a bullet from a carbine.
Princetown is most desirable head-quarters for the
angler, since it immediately commands several of
the moorland streams ; and there is admirable

hotel accommodation for man and beast in the place.

To fish Dartmoor properly a horse is necessary for a man of only moderate walking powers, and if he be fortunate enough to engage for the term of his stay a moorland pony it will be a decided advantage. The man who can trudge fifteen miles a day may, however, consider himself independent of anything but a sensible pair of boots, and it should never be forgotten that there, more than 1,500 feet above the level of the sea, fatigue is seldom felt as in the lower country. There is a comfortable little inn at Two Bridges, about two miles from Princetown, in a fine situation, and close to the West Dart and its tributary the Cowsick.

These Dartmoor streamlets, it may be convenient here to explain, have many, indeed most, things in common. Besides the larger streams there are, I believe, fifty brooks abounding in trout, but of them all these conclusions may be taken for granted :—the trout are remarkably small, delicious eating, and so plentiful that one is almost afraid to mention the undoubted "takes" that, with suitable water and wind, may be expected. As I had feared when once I had surveyed the chances from the railway carriage, my visit to Dartmoor, as a mere matter of fins and tails, was not profitable. The water had not been so low in the memory of our dear useful friend the oldest inhabitant ; it was offensively pellucid ; and, to make bad worse, the wind blew either north-east or not at all. Slimy weeds had accumulated in the pools, and nothing but a tremendous freshet would clear them.

Still with these overwhelming disadvantages, to which a bright sun may be added, and fishing, as

on the last day (of course) I found, with not the
most appropriate flies, it was easy to take an
average of two dozen each day, and 1 might have
basketed double that quantity on the first day had
I known how small it was the custom to take them.
The fish were verily Liliputian, even smaller than
Welsh trout.   One fellow weighed close upon half
a pound, but that seemed of mammoth proportions
amongst its brethren, and a three or four ounce
trout was considered by the Devonians a really
large moorland fish.

The bulk of the trout were about the dimension
of sprats, and these on the first day I in my ignorance returned to the water.   Three or four, however, injured beyond redemption by the steel, went
to the cook with what I deemed to be the sizeable
fish, and at dinner I made a discovery.   The Dartmoor troutlets are the best flavoured and sweetest
eating fish it was ever my good fortune to taste.
You devour, or rather scrunch, them, body and
bones.   A Plymouth friend afterwards told me
that parties of epicures frequently made expeditions to Princetown for the sake of a dish of *petite
truite.*

Four, five, and six dozen of trout are no uncommon result of a day's persevering and intelligent
angling on the moors.   An old man, whom I had
no reason whatever to doubt—for similar state-
ments were made to me by others—assured me
that he once caught fifteen dozen in eight hours.
This assertion will probably take away the breath
of the incredulous heretic who shrugs his shoulders
and drops the corners of his mouth at any record
of rod and line work ; but with very exceptional
luck, or perhaps it should be said through a combi-
nation of fortunate circumstances, such an enviable

capture is at least possible on the Dartmoor streams. Of course it will not often occur, and three or four dozen is the total which under ordinary conditions should give complete satisfaction, and send the angler home in good humour with himself, his tackle, the water, the weather—and, in short, the world at large.

The Dartmoor streams should always be fished upwards. Their direction being, roughly speaking, from north to south, this course is the easiest as well as the best to pursue when the wind sits in the right quarter for piscatorial pursuits. It will save time and trouble to lay in a stock of flies at Plymouth or Tavistock. If one could make sure of finding that infallible native who generally lurks somewhere near the waterside, and who manufactures flies more killing and more natural than the living insect, he is the man to buy from ; but it may happen that the worthy is not to be found, and life is too short to waste a day in unearthing him while the fish are eagerly rising. The flies at both Tavistock and Plymouth are good, and the shopkeepers thoroughly understand Dartmoor, and will give the customer honest advice as to the streams.

The knowing ones in Devonshire never use winged flies, and many of the most successful fishermen go through the season with, at the outside, not more than half a dozen different hackles. Of these, the essentials are a blue upright, a red or red-and-black palmer, a fern web, and a black fly, which for convenience sake we may also call a palmer. The coch-a-bondhu is not amiss, and there is a gaudy little fly called the Meavy Red, which kills well on the Meavy.

The upper streams being very small and broken,

the artificial flies used are, as is not uncommon in mountain streams, much larger than could be ventured upon in broader and deeper rivers whose flow is more placid. It is only once now and then that the Dartmoor angler encumbers himself with wading materials or landing net.

Beginning at Two Bridges, fish the West Dart to the spot where the East Dart, amidst beautiful wooded scenery, joins. In the higher land, far above the meeting of the waters (Dartmeet), the two Darts run through unadulterated moorlands. No bushes take a mean advantage of your carelessness ; no trees are near. The outlook, if it were not so .picturesque in its wild ruggedness, would be inexpressibly dreary ; and to many visitors very likely Dartmoor is a howling wilderness, fit only for convicts, anglers, lunatics and—artists. It is a merciful dispensation of Providence that all men do not see with the same eyes. When, years gone by, we had prisoners of war who were confined at Dartmoor (the convict establishment was built for that purpose), a French writer described it as a terrible Siberia, covered with unmelting snow.

"When the snows go away," he added, "the mists appear."

In the desolation of winter Dartmoor is naturally not so pleasant as Torquay or Brighton. In summer, spite of the frequent mist, the Frenchman's description must not be entertained, for then the heather is everywhere abloom ; the graceful ferns fondly sweep the edges of the old grey rocks ; the foot sinks into an elastic velvet pile of moss, herbage, and alpine plants ; the distant coppices catch and hold the shadows of the clouds in the trembling tree-tops ; the colours of earth and sky imperceptibly change and blend morn, noon, and night ; the cuckoo tells and re-tells

"His name to all the hills ; "

the peewit, concealed among the rushy hollows, utters its shrill cry at your approach, and tries, with instinctive cunning, to entice you away from its nest ; and there is music in the rarified air, performed by such united choirs as are made by myriads of merry-lived insects, the tinkling of streams, and the half-mournful cadence of many zephyrs journeying over the moors.

In sceptical mood I have sometimes doubted whether Mrs. Hemans, though she won the prize offered by the Royal Society of Literature for the best poem on Dartmoor, had herself looked much upon the place ; but these lines are most appropriate :—

"Wild Dartmoor ! thou that, midst thy mountains rude,
Hast robed thyself with haughty solitude,
As a dark cloud on summer's clear blue sky,
A mourner circled with festivity !
For all beyond is life !—the rolling sea,
The rush, the swell, whose echoes reach not thee."

Near Dartmeet, woods begin to diversify the landscape. They cover the steep declivities that rise precipitately from one or both banks. Below the bridge there are numbers of the most tempting pools ; but the local fishermen, admitting the superior scenery, give the sportsman's palm to the West Dart, which for a mile or two above the bridge is the beau-ideal of a lovely highland stream. Its bed is strewn with boulders that in drought, as in flood, irritate the impetuous current into ebullitions of boil, bubble, foam, and headlong plunges very beautiful to watch, and

presently, when the torrent moderates into a less
violent flow, most serviceable to the dexterous
handler of the fly-rod. The Dart, on its down-
ward course to Buckfastleigh, more especially in
its windings through Holne Chase, is the paradise
of painters.

Time and space would fail me to recount the
legends to which Dartmoor Forest has given rise.
It was my privilege on one of my rambles to fall
in with a gentleman renewing an old acquaintance
with the moors. For years he had been doomed
to frizzle in the West Indies, and returning to the
mother country for a year's holiday, repaired at
once to Dartmoor to fish familiar streams and be
braced by the invigorating atmosphere. Of course
he was a sportsman, and accustomed to both rod
and gun. We had whipped the West Dart,
growing narrower and shallower every day, and
then by common consent, meeting no reward, one
day spiked our rods, lay down on the grass, and
in the heart of Dartmoor smoked our pipes of
peace like a couple of lotos-eaters to whom there
was no future.

He knew the moors as the Londoner knows
Fleet Street. He had shot blackcock in certain
bits of scrub where a few regularly breed ; he had
tramped in the September days over the Tor far
away to the north-east, returning at night with
six or seven brace of snipe picked up in the bogs,
and an odd woodcock or two recruiting on Dartmoor before starting for their inland haunts. He
had ridden to hounds when the fox made straight
over the open, up and down hills steep as the roof
of a house.

Finally, after a true Devonshire luncheon of
"bread and cheese and cider," he took me to

Wistman's Wood. From the valley I had previously noticed what appeared to be a rather extensive shrubbery to the north-west of Crockern Tor. In the great heat it was a stiff climb up the slope, over which immovable blocks of granite lay thickly peppered. The shrubbery turned out to be a wonderful plantation of dwarfed, gnarled, uncanny-looking oak trees, reputed to have been a veritable Druidical grove. The trees, though not more than seven feet high, put on all the airs of hoary forest patriarchs. In age they must have been the Methuselahs of their tribe; in shape they were the counterparts of the finest and most venerable oaks of Windsor Forest. Their branches were wrinkled to such a painful extent that various plants and shrubs that usually prefer the ground seemed to have entered into a league to hide the marks of extreme antiquity from the light of day. Brambles, ferns, ivy, lichens, and other growths had taken root in the branches and covered them with tangle. The roots of the oaks, after centuries of fight with the granite soil, were doing their best either a few inches below, or on the exposed surface. Leaving this extraordinary spectacle we leaped the West Dart where it was a yard wide, and climbed the steep to the Cowsick River, gaining the high road through a wooded glen of the most exquisite loveliness, and passing a rude bridge of slabs said to have been put together by the Ancient Britons.

The Tamar, I had been informed, is generally fishable when other Devonshire rivers are dry, and to the Tamar I accordingly determined to go. This involved a sunset—and what a sunset!—journey back to Tavistock, a night's sleep in that quiet stannary borough, and an early drive to

Horsebridge, six miles in the direction of the Cornish hills surmounted with tall chimneys. The experienced superintendent of the Tamar and Plym district had kindly "coached" me, but my ill-luck doggedly pursued me to the Tamar; the water was in good order, but the north wind blew dead down stream, rendering the likeliest scours and eddies almost unfishable from below. Wading and landing net were here indispensable.

The Tamar is a good river, with steep wooded slopes on either side, slaty bed with occasional boulders, of fair width, and it is one of the troutiest-looking streams imaginable. But my meagre basket would have satisfied even Major-General Incredulity. In two days only nine brace gladdened my eyes, but the trout were excellent representatives of the river—handsome, plump, fish of two and a half to the pound, and game as trout of double and treble their size from some other counties I know of. The Dartmoor trout, like the denizens of all peat-bound streams, were dark; the Tamar fish were perfectly coloured, spotted, and shaped.

The Inny is a tributary of the Tamar, and full of trout. Wading in the main stream should be done with care, for there are shelves which, without warning, will drop the heedless sportsman from five inches to five feet of water. The scenery at Endsleigh I shall not attempt to describe—it is lovely. The Duke of Bedford's lodge is perched up on the side of a finely wooded declivity, on which whole shrubberies of rhododendrons gleamed purple and scarlet. The famous trees of Fountains Abbey are not more towering or wide-spreading than those in the Duke of Bedford's woods at Endsleigh. A little cottage maiden

brought me a plate of brown bread and fresh
butter and a mug of new milk at midday; and
this meal, after laboriously whipping three miles
of river in the teeth of the wind and against strong
currents, was, I fancy, better appreciated than
frequently happens with my Lord Mayor's turtle
and champagne at Egyptian Hall feasts.

Then was the time to use Golden Returns in a
meerschaum service for dessert, and to take note
of details. A hawk swooped at a ringdove within
pelting distance. Kingfishers flew by like flashes
of sapphire and emerald; rabbits openly continued
their nibbling in the next clearing; and the vermin
—adders, my little handmaid said, were much too
numerous—rustled in the intervening thickets.
When a dragon-fly pitched upon my ebony winch
and crawled a few inches on a tour of inspection
up my line, there was no more to be said. It was
wonderland pure and simple.

But musing is one thing and trout-fishing
another. Standing out in the Tamar, a bit of
shoal water landwards revealed to me some of its
treasures, and I recalled the minute description of
Keats :—

> " Where swarms of minnows show their little heads,
> Staying their wavy bodies 'gainst the streams,
> To taste the luxury of summer beams
> Tempered with coolness. How they ever wrestle
> With their own fresh delight and ever nestle
> Their silver bellies on the pebbly sand !
> If you but scantily hold out the hand
> That very instant will not one remain,
> But turn your eye, and there they are again."

From the minnows, to be frank, I *had* turned
my eye upon a radiant kingfisher, which flut-
tered through the brambles and ferns, and poised

F

himself on a bough overhanging the water, at which he looked intently while I looked at him. Meanwhile, a trout took advantage of my fly floating at will with the current, and rudely recalled me from my bird-study by hooking himself, leaping out of the water, and escaping with a shillingsworth of tackle. The kingfisher darted up stream, but came back again in a few minutes, hovering restlessly about, waiting, no doubt, until the neighbourhood was clear of his human rival. It looked as if he was at the same time quietly amusing himself over the penalty I had to pay for inattention to rod and line.

CHAPTER V

IN THE MIDLANDS.

" The stately homes of England !
 How beautiful they stand,
Amidst their tall ancestral trees,
 O'er all the pleasant land !
The deer across the greensward bound,
 Through shade and sunny gleam ;
And the swan glides past them with the sound
 Of some rejoicing stream."

HEMANS.

COWPER must indeed have been a poet to find so much in the River Ouse worthy of his attention. True, his was a humble soul, and very little gave him content. Musing and wandering he saw more sermons in stones, books in the running brooks, and good in everything than most men. The Ouse is an interesting river, but it is not romantic. It is prosaic and business-like from beginning to end, fulfilling its course through the fat pastoral counties of Northampton, Oxford, Buckingham, Bedford, Huntingdon, Cambridge, and Norfolk, like a respectable commercial traveller who has to "work" a certain district, and is prepared to do it conscientiously to the last.

Cowper had a favourite expression for the Ouse. He called it "slow-winding." The poet was accurate : the river is slow, and I believe it pursues the most serpentine journey of all our rivers, through the flattest part of the great grazing shires. Thus it fully justifies Cowper's repeated use of the expression referred to. He says :—

> "Shut out from more important views
> Fast by the banks of the slow-winding Ouse :
> Content if thus sequestered I may raise
> A monitor's, though not a poet's praise."

In such words terminates the not half appreciated poem of "Retirement." Yet again the poet returns to his idea. He has not written many pages of his "Sofa" before he draws a picture of the river he knew so well and loved so much, which, like all his pictures of the country about Olney, is Wilkie-like in its fidelity to details :—

> "Here Ouse, slow-winding through a level plain
> Of spacious meads with cattle sprinkled o'er,
> Conducts the eye along the sinuous course
> Delighted.   There fast rooted in their bank
> Stand, never overlooked, our favourite elms
> That screen the herdsman's solitary hut ;
> While far beyond, and overthwart the stream,
> That *as with molten glass inlays the vale*,
> The sloping land recedes into the clouds,
> Displaying on its varied side the grace
> Of hedge-row beauties numberless, square tower,
> Tall spire from which the sound of cheerful bells
> Just undulates upon the listening ear ;
> Groves, heaths, and smoking villages remote."

This sketch is as faithful now as ever it was, and it is a description that may be said to apply not only to the particular district in which the poet lived and suffered, but to the general character of the river. Here and there the Ouse is not without picturesqueness, but there is always that fine suggestion of molten glass inlaying the vale. By no chance will the Ouse ever be taken into custody for brawling or riotous behaviour. When the rains descend and the floods come the Ouse swells, muddens, and overspreads the meadows in a methodical manner, doing its overflowing with dismal thoroughness, but conducting itself with persistent respectability, under circumstances which would warrant any other river in roaring and trampling over all that lay in its way.

In summer and in winter, going to Ouse-side with a pocket edition of Cowper in my pocket, I have, when sport failed, beguiled the time by following his minute observations of the scenery. I could give you the address of that boy of freedom of whom it is written :—

> "To snare the mole, or with ill-fashioned hook
> To draw the incautious minnow from the brook,
> Are life's prime pleasures in his simple view,
> His flock the chief concern he ever knew."

The young rascal will get you a can of gudgeons for a consideration, and forsake his flock to accompany you on your piscatorial wanderings in the fields. And as you wander you shall be ever and anon reminded of the river's poet. By Sandy I have met that "reeking, roaring hero of the chase" who hunts that part of the world to this day. The little inn where you stay has its "creaking country sign," and "ducks paddle in the pond before the door." On every side "laughs the land with various plenty crowned." Many is the time when, smoking "the pipe with solemn interposing puff," I have stood "ankle

deep in moss and flowery thyme," or taken shelter
from showers under "rough elm, or smooth-
grained ash or glossy beech," and in the absence
of luck have returned "at noon to billiards or to
books." Whether poor Cowper added fishing to
his simple amusements has not to my knowledge
been recorded, but you may remember how sagely
he observes :—

> "So when the cold damp shades of night prevail
> Worms may be caught by either head or tail."

—an unvarnished statement of fact which leads me
to suspect that the poet had at some period of his
life been interested in that familiar operation to the
angler of stalking "lobs" in the garden with a
lantern and flower pot, having an eye to the bream
to whom such dainties are an irresistible bait.

The Ouse roughly speaking runs in a north-
easterly direction. Rising in Northamptonshire,
it for a while divides the counties of Northampton
and Buckinghamshire, touching and indeed almost
encircling the town of Buckingham, and afterwards, beyond Stony Stratford, receiving the
Tove, which passes near the rare old town of
Towcester, and takes in the drainage of Whittle-
bury Forest. At Newport Pagnell the Ouse is
increased by the little Ousel ; it then flows to
wooded Weston, where stands the park placed at
Cowper's disposal by his faithful friends, and to
Olney, where he lived in neighbourship with John
Newton, of Olney hymn fame. By-and-by it
comes to Bedford. At Tempsford it is joined by
the Ivel ; it becomes a broad deep river in Huntingdonshire, takes in numerous minor streams in
its course through the Fen Level, and after 156
miles of persevering twisting and turning delivers

up its tribute in goodly volume at the estuary of the Wash.

The Ouse is an excellent pike river, and remarkable for the size and quantity of its bream. For the greater portion of its length until recently it was under no law but that most wholesome law of trespass, which, judiciously enforced, is so potent a preserver of wood and water when other provisions fail. And there is probably no stream in England which has been more poached than the Ouse.

But that spirit of preservation which in a former chapter I mentioned as so beneficial to the Thames is not confined to metropolitan head-quarters. In all parts of the country, rivers, to foul and poach which the public from time immemorial fancied they had a prescriptive right, are being protected by local societies.

Two autumns ago I myself had the pleasure of finding a "hot corner" amongst the Ouse jack. If I had a Cowper in my pocket, there was despair in my heart. Two days had I been sojourning at a pleasant waterside inn at Barford Bridge, a melancholy example of the strange reverses to which the angler is subjected. The "tip direct" had been sent me that the pike were feeding, and off I went straightway to Sandy by train, and to Barford per dogcart, with a companion who meditated valiant deeds with his bait can. Even while alighting from the two-wheeler—as a matter of fact my companion, encumbered with three rods and little short of half a hundredweight of miscellaneous baggage, tumbled out head foremost, and smashed the baiting needle he had ostentatiously stuck in his hat—we saw an urchin, wielding a clothes prop and line to match, swish out a pikelet close to the bridge : and rubbed our hands at the prospect.

But the entire day was a blank. Somehow the fish "went off," and fed not. Perhaps the wind had chopped round to the east ; perhaps the fish knew, as they are said to do, that atmospheric changes were pending ; perhaps they had retired into the magnificent thickets of tufted reeds which rose like a wall out of the other side of the river ; perhaps the sportsmen were not sufficiently skilful with their lures. Anglers are often laughed at for that ready excuse they have under any circumstances and at all times to explain ill luck : the water is too low or too high, too bright or too coloured, or the weather is unfavourable, or has been, or threatens to be so. Nevertheless, laugh as you may, it is undoubted that fish do suddenly and without any apparent reason drop into listlessness and lie at the bottom like a stone, to be tempted by no bait whatsoever.

On this morning we tried every expedient ; roach, dace, and gudgeon were in turn placed upon the live bait tackle ; every spinning flight in the box was attempted ; artificial trout, phantoms, and red-tasselled spoon bait succeeded ; and finally we settled down to trolling. A dozen times during the day we distinctly saw pike lazily follow the spinner or dead roach to within a few inches of the surface, never intending—the cheats !—to touch the bait, but pursuing it out of mere shark-like instinct. We thus returned to our hostelry, muddy, silent, out of heart, and hungry ; and stamping our feet at the door confronted the country postman.

There he was to the life as drawn in "The Winter Evening." We had heard his horn twang-

ing o'er yonder bridge while we passed through
the third meadow with the rods slanting over our
shoulders. He was the poet's " post " with but a
few touches of difference. The boots were spat-
tered, and the waist strapped as of yore, but his
locks were not frozen for an obvious reason—it
was not frosty weather ; and

> " He whistles as he goes, light-hearted wretch."

We did not whistle as *we* went, and I have already
intimated that we were not exactly light-hearted.
Not at any rate until we had plodded upstairs into
our snug sitting-room.

Ah ! what a friendly friend a blazing wood fire
is ! How the flames seem to wink at you, and
how the crackling and sputtering suggest somebody laughing and nudging you under the fifth
rib ! Why, a ten pound note, or three fives at the
outside, would have purchased the entire furniture
of that cosy room, outside of whose window the
sign swung and creaked. But it was a palace to
us, though the branches scratched the window as
if they were angry fishwomen clawing at a husband's face. There was a storm brewing south-
eastward, and the rising wind made mad work
with such few leaves as were left upon the branches,
while the day faded out in the sullenest of moods.

What more suitable time for relishing the warm
chamber, loose slippers, cleanly spread tea-table,
and savoury ham and eggs ! We made love to the
Dresden shepherdess in china on the mantelpiece,
and admired the cheap hunting scenes on the walls ;
and as, tumbling out the winches to wind the sodden lines round the chair backs—never neglect that
precaution, Mr. Pikefisher—we tumbled also the
Cowperian pocket edition out of the wallet, what

more natural than that, thawing into good humour, we should hold forth in recitation ?

My companion, the "Gay Comrade" of our first chapter, rather prides himself upon his elocutionary gifts and graces. The shadows of the wood fire flickered about his curly head in the darkening room, as he extended his right arm and in commanding tones began—

"Now stir the fire, and—"

Margaret of the ruddy cheeks and white apron at that precise moment silently entered, bearing candles ; with a little shriek she observed :—

"Oh, no, sir, please don't ; them logs churkle dreadful, and the sparks 'll pop out and you'll burn the carpet if you poke the fire."

The G. C., somewhat abashed at being caught in a tragic attitude, at my laughter, and at being so ruthlessly brought down into the ham-and-eggs atmosphere of every-day life, pierced the poor woman straight in the eyes with a fearful glance of Othelloish, Macbethical, and Hamletian power. Then he resumed :—

"And close the shutters fast,
Let fall the curtains, wheel"—

"I'll try," quoth Margaret, "to fast up the shuts, but I know two of the hinges is broke, and the blind don't come only half ways down."

The reciter here found it convenient to gaze vacantly out into the gloom and hum something until the handmaid had descended into the lower regions, and then good humouredly, and with a fine sort of frenzy in his expression, he finished the broken measure :—

—"wheel the sofa round,
And while the bubbling and loud hissing urn

> Throws up a steamy column, and the cups
> That cheer but not inebriate, wait on each,
> So let us welcome peaceful evening in."

We forthwith welcomed according to our lights. The sofa, weak and ruptured in the hind off castor, refused to be wheeled ; the steaming column arose, not from the dear old urn now so seldom seen, but from the hot-water jug doing duty as a reserve force to the teapot ; and to be honest (poor *but* honest as the story books have it) the cups were not quite so innocent as those handed round in Mr. Newton's Buckinghamshire Vicarage or Mrs. Unwin's parlour, for, as a precaution against cold—and understand, once for all, from no less praiseworthy motive—our tea was flavoured with just a suspicion of cognac, which increased the cheering quality without producing actual inebriation.

It is Cowper's fault that by this time I have almost forgotten my " hot corner " experience on the Ouse. I apologize and pass on. The morning after we had welcomed our peaceful evening in it blew a gale, and we had not been out of doors five minutes before we were drenched. At length we got a mile or two down the stream, but the blank of the previous day was repeated. Like those very old fishermen we read of, we toiled long and caught nothing. The sun began to set in a copperclouded and wild sky about five o'clock, and in the midst of a discussion as to whether we had not better go back to welcome another, &c., the wind fell—soughed convulsively amongst the quivering forest of reeds, sighed, and went to sleep.

Now was the time. A lively gudgeon cast within a few inches of an island of rushes in the middle of the river did the trick ; in a twinkling the float darted away and the winch spun round merrily.

In all directions the small fry, leaping out of the
water and fluttering on the surface, betrayed the
whereabouts of the ravenous fish.   Released from
the mysterious spell laid upon them to our loss
during the two previous days, they now appeared
to throw caution to the winds.   As fast as I re-
baited, my float disappeared and a fish came to
bank.   Who shall account for the unaccountable?
The G. C. is in all points a better angler than myself: his tackle was finer and his style of fishing
more artistic.   Yet, when too dark to see the river
we reluctantly reeled up, his bait had not been
touched, though half a dozen pike taken in the
manner I have described by my rod were hopping
about in the grass.   It was all the more singular
because my friend had thrown his baits into places
where fish were visibly moving and where directly
he shifted his position I was instantly successful.

In July and August there are almost miraculous
draughts of fishes amongst the bream in the Ouse.
Not a hundred yards from Bedford Bridge there is
at least one bream hole out of which sixty pounds
of fish have been taken in a morning, and you
hear of bream of six pounds.   That, however, is a
very unusual weight, but a three-pound fish is not
at all uncommon in any part of the river.   I must
confess to no great respect for the *Cyprinus Brama.*
A fish that is shaped like a bellows, that is as thin
as a John Dory, that is as uneatable as the John
Dory is delicious, that is capricious in its habits,
and that rarely rises at a fly, cannot be termed
beautiful or useful to either cook or sportsman.

In the Ouse country, notwithstanding its bones
and general insipidity, the poorer people do eat the
bream and like it passing well.   At Huntingdon
on one of my outings by the Ouse the landlady of

a small inn served up a breakfast dish which I relished to the extent of absolute consumption. It was a thin fillet of white fish, from which the bones had been extracted, and which was served up yellowish brown with some description of savoury herb sauce. Having eaten every flake, upon inquiry I found it was the bream I had on the previous night so execrated. But frequent trials since have utterly failed to make the bream a decent edible. Yet I do not forget that the French proverb says, " He who hath bream in his pond may bid his friends welcome," and that Chaucer, who may be said to have known a thing or two, wrote :—

> " Full many a fair partrich hadde he in mewe,
> And many a breme, and many a luce in stewe."

A recital of a little personal experience of bream-fishing will give some insight into the habits of the bream. Having at odd visits to John Bunyan's pretty and interesting old country town seen Howard's workpeople returning home staggering beneath burdens of fish taken from the bank in the meadows near Cardington Mill, I resolved to lay myself out seriously for rivalry : but unfortunately it was October before I could carry out my intention. This I did not require to be told was fully a month or six weeks too late ; but a celebrated professional bream-catcher at Bedford, nevertheless, got his boat ready and took me a couple of miles down the river. We tied ourselves to the reeds with fourteen feet of sluggish water beneath us, and to our dismay found the surface smooth and clear as glass. The bream angler in July should be at his post on the river and quiet as a mouse by daybreak, for the chances are that he will have finished all his work by breakfast time.

But as later in the season it is necessary to let the
morning chills evaporate, seven o'clock had struck
before we began.

Balls of mingled slime and brewers' grains the
size of bombshells were first cast into the water
five yards from the boat, the boatman observing—

"You'll see a lark presently, guvnor." He then
began to make ready his tackle—long, heavy,
rudely made rods, coarse lines without winches,
clumsily leaded gut hooks, and seven or eight nasty
little worms affixed *en masse* to each hook, of which
there were two to each line.

"Why don't you throw out?" I said, all being
ready, and looking out upon the dreadfully unruffled
surface of the broad river.

"You hold hard, guvnor; there'll be a lark presently," he still replied, looking down the stream
with a patient, wistful gaze.

"There they are," he said, by-and-by; "don't
move, guvnor. I know the beggars, bless you—
I told you so. You keep still, guvnor."

He now made a monster cigarette from a leaf of
Bradshaw's Railway Guide (having forgotten to
bring out his pipe and tobacco), and watched what
he had termed a "lark" with a benign expression
of countenance. It was certainly amusing. Quite
fifty yards down the river large dark somethings
splashed, twisted, and plunged upon the surface of
the water in hundreds, all advancing slowly towards
the point where we were stationed. This the boatman said was a favourite winter-home of the bream,
and his theory was that they had scuttled away in
shoals at our approach, and were now slowly returning in good skirmishing order. Steadily the
host advanced, the splashes and backs of the fish
appearing at intervals of four or five yards. The

signs ceased when they should have appeared opposite our boat, and this led the bream master to remark—

"The darned skunks, they've winded us, guvnor."

Be that as it may, in a few moments the hubbub recommenced many yards above us, and then all was silent as before. After a decent pause, the bream having evidently retreated upon their former position below, the plunges began again, and another cautious upward movement commenced ; and to our delight this time there were no indications that the fish had passed us.

The boatman then deftly threw out his baits and fixed his rods under the thwarts, and I followed his example with my lighter implements. Five minutes elapsed, when down went both of his floats. They came up, went down, came up, and again went down, while the fisherman grimly sucked his Brobdingnagian cigarette. Soon a decisive slanting movement of the long float led him to strike sharply, and his great rod bent to the encounter. Two or three struggles appeared to exhaust the bream, and they were netted in succession without much finessing or trouble. My companion thus caught seven fish in the course of an hour. Then my turn arrived. To my chagrin I had been wholly unable to throw my delicate tackle out to the baited ground, but now the porcupine quill went clear away at a shoot ; to be brief, the drawn gut parted at the sullen resistance to the too eager strike, and the boatman, emitting a great oath, said we should get no more sport.

"If it had been summer," he said, "it would not have mattered so much ; we should have whacked 'em out like a shot ; but it's all up now."

And even so it proved.

The processes necessary to successful bream-fishing, like those insisted upon by barbel-fishers, are not nice. Ground baiting hours before you fish is a necessity. Great fat lobworms, or unsavoury brandlings, are the orthodox bait, and the fish himself is covered with slime that is not pleasant to handle. No angler would care to fish often for bream if there were other fish within his reach, but in Bedfordshire and Huntingdonshire men of the artisan type manifest a rooted affection for the sport ; and wherever bream exist, having found the same predilection, I always look upon the broad, forked-tailed, light brown bottom-grubber as a kind of working man's candidate.

Hard by a village I once visited in Yorkshire there ran a canal in which there were a good many bream. Amongst the men who at about six feet intervals lined the banks on a summer's evening was a quaint, shrewd Barnsley pitman, with whom I became very familiar. He would think nothing of a fourteen miles walk for the sake of three hours with his pet bream, than which, he firmly believed, no nobler game swam the water. He was a consummate coarse fish angler, and a hero amongst the Yorkshire Waltonians. Poor fellow ! Years passed, and I had forgotten him. Then I saw him, blackened and dead, one of a ghastly row of unfortunate colliers just brought up from a pit, laid out on benches, and ticketed, till the coroner should inquire into the miserable circumstances which without warning cut them off from the land of the living.

*   *   *   *   *   *

Without intending to be disrespectful or unfaithful to the queenly Thames, I must profess an undying adoration of the Trent, the many armed Trent that takes much of its inspiration, if not its source, from the breezy highlands of Derbyshire. It is a kingly river, and terminates its long stately journey by mingling with the waters of another river, many-armed and mountain-flavoured as itself —the Yorkshire Ouse. The only resemblance existing between the Ouse of the Midlands and the river which is supposed to be the north and south division line of the kingdom is that each has its poet. Cowper sang of the Ouse, Drayton and Kirke White of the Trent. Drayton, adopting a prevailing legend, has a somewhat off-hand way of accounting for the word "Trent" :—

"There should be found in her of fishes thirty kind ;
And thirty abbeys great, in places fat and rank,
Should in succeeding time be builded on her bank ;
And thirty several streams from many a sundry way
Unto her greatness should their wat'ry tribute pay."

Including the Derbyshire streams which are swallowed up in it, the Trent, no doubt, could yield specimens of every fish known in English rivers. The Ouse I have chosen to describe as sober-minded and substantial. The Trent, so far as I have seen it, is a sparkling genius that makes its presence known by infinite brightness, dash, and impulse. The Ouse is a solid line of infantry, the Trent a glittering squadron of light cavalry. Serving the busy Potteries in the outset of its course, the river soon becomes aristocratic, and runs through Trentham, whose trees it lovingly laves, flowing with moderated pace through the beautiful park, and lending new charms to its far-famed gardens, terraces, temples, fountains, and hanging plantations. In the valley which the Trent glad-

G

dens are other great family seats—Meaford, Sandon, Ingestre, Tixall, Hagley, and Donington, where cliffs enter into the composition of the landscape.

I have some angling acquaintance with the Trent, and unkind is the fate which prevents me at least once every summer from standing knee-deep for a day or two in the broad gravel bedded and rippling stream. It is Kirke White who applies to the river the term "rippling," and the term is photographic. The hapless lad loved to escape from the drudgery of the hosier's shop to the river's brink; and, if possible, afterwards, when more congenially engaged at Mr. Coldham's law office, where in busy times he attended from eight in the morning till eight in the evening, finding an hour still later for Latin study, thither tended his footsteps. In his seventeenth year—"scarcely the work of thirty minutes this morning" he told his brother Neville—he wrote seven four-line verses of elegy on the death of a gentleman, drowned in the Trent while bathing, and says :—

> "Of thee, as early I, with vagrant feet,
>   Hail the grey-sandal'd morn in Colwick's vale;
> Of thee my sylvan reed shall warble sweet,
>   And wild-wood echoes shall repeat the tale."

When the dark days of disease and anxiety called upon the poet to recruit his overworked frame he went across to the little village of Wilford, near the Clifton woods, and it was in its churchyard that he applied to the Trent the designation I have repeated :—

> "It is a lovely spot ! The sultry Sun,
> From his meridian height, endeavours vainly
> To pierce the shadowy foliage, while the zephyr
> Comes wafting gently o'er the rippling Trent,
> And plays about my wan cheek. 'Tis a nook most pleasant."

The Trent, notwithstanding the proverbial variety of its finny population, is chiefly interest- ing to the angler for its dace, barbel, and pike.[1] Sport with them may be reckoned upon at times and in places where nothing else could be pro- cured. Here and there—and it is yearly becoming still more "here and there"—you may pick up a grayling. The Trent was once a noted grayling stream, and Hofland, a pleasant writer, and a prince of fly-fishers and fly-makers, thought well thirty years ago of the river in that character. A few grayling are still caught every season.

As to barbel, take the following quotation from a published paragraph : " Mr. B. and a friend captured over 100 pounds in one day near Colingham, and Mr. C. and a friend sent over eighty pounds on Wednesday night, with instruc- tions to meet the trains every night, for they were hooking them every swim. Some were over nine pounds each."

I saw a pretty afternoon's sport one August day under the lee of a lonely wood below Lowdham. A groom and two friends in a boat, after a few swims finding no bites, went ashore for an hour and returned. The barbel at the previous trial were splashing like porpoises and turning over on the top of the water ; now they were still as mice, and the three men at their first swim were fast to a fish each. So they went on catching great ruddy brown lively fellows which gave capital sport, and required every one of them careful playing and a strong landing net. The bottom of their boat was covered with spoil when the game was thrown up.

---

[1] Of late years salmon may be included.—W. S.

Old Nottingham, or, as I believe it should be called, Trent Bridge, ancient as the times of Edward the Elder, was a many-arched and picturesque structure from which it was possible between the racing currents, to catch barbel. There was a noted angler in the town whom, for convenience, we will designate Bowles, and he was quite historical as to barbel—a Gamaliel at whose feet stocking-weaving Sauls sat to learn the wisdom pertaining to greaves, dew-worms, marsh-worms, brandlings, gilt-tails, red-worms, tegg-worms, peacock-reds, dock grubs, and so forth : in which your Trent anglers, let me say, are remarkably learned. Bowles was an institution on Nottingham Bridge. Tradesmen and work-folks, strolling that way in the cool of the evening naturally looked for Bowles, his spectacles, and his strong barbel rod. But he, I am informed, was never seen at his post after the following occurrence :—

The word was passed that Bowles had hooked a monster barbel. The news penetrated into the town, ascended to the workshops, ran along the meadows up and down, and caused great excite-ment. Looms, counters, tea-tables, business and pleasure were alike forsaken, and there was a regular stampede in the direction of Nottingham Bridge. Sure enough Bowles was engaged in a mighty struggle. The old man perspired, but never blenched.

The crowd became immense. Bowles would winch the monster in within a few yards of the shore, when, whew ! out it shot into the stream like an arrow from the bow. The superb skill and patience of Bowles were audibly commended ; he was too wily to check the monster in those

furious rushes, but waited till the line ceased
running to winch him cautiously and proudly in,
amidst such cries as "Bravo, Bowles," or "He
won't get over you, guv'nor," or "Give him time,
Georgy."

The noise of the crowd hushed at last, for
young Badger had, by direction, gone down to
the water's edge to use the landing net. Bowles
was bracing himself up for a final effort. Wind,
wind, wind went the winch; in, in, in came the
monster; "Be careful, Badger, be careful," said
the crowd; "Now, then, nip him, nip him,"
shouted Bowles. Ah, me! what a tremendous
roar there was when the monster was landed—a
drowned retriever, with whose blown-out carcase
the eddy had been playing unkind pranks!

Would you not consider sixteen dozen of dace,
the lawful capture of the artificial fly, a pretty
decent day's sport? I saw it with my own eyes
done by a Nottingham angler, on a July day. It
was at a part of the river where, broad though it
is, you may wade across : and wade you must to
do the best that can be done. This dace-angler
had occupied the same compartment of the train
as I had, and had courteously, considering my
strangerhood, offered to show me the best shallows and to place his fly-book at my disposal.
He laid stress upon the latter because a special
description of small hackle is required. His
fishing boots, however, gave him an unapproach-
able advantage. Sixteen dozen dace, and three
or four pound roach lay in his rush basket when
we met at night, all taken by a thinly-made red
palmer with gold twist. Even I, the stranger,
whipping from the bank, could show over four
dozen silvery fish, running about three to the

pound, exquisitely shaped. Anglers, perhaps I need not labour to show, do not always return from the Trent with sixteen dozen dace, but they would be downcast indeed if they did not surpass my four dozen, of which, nevertheless, I was very proud.

Of the higher waters of the Trent—and it may be assumed as a safe rule with all rivers which minister to large towns and ultimately become navigable, that they improve for the angler as you ascend them—Armstrong writes :—

" If the breathless chase, o'er hill and dale,
Exceed your strength, a sport of less fatigue,
Not less delightful, the prolific stream
Affords. The crystal rivulet, that o'er
A stormy channel rolls its rapid maze,
Swarms with the silver fry. Such, through the bounds
Of pastoral Stafford, runs the brawling Trent."

A chapter upon Midland Streams would be incomplete without a word upon those classic tributaries of the Trent, the Dove and the Derwent, and the sub-tributary the Wye. And a word only may suffice for rivers immortalized by Walton and Cotton, and by the numerous disciples who have spoken or sung their beauties until this day. Time has, unfortunately, considerably reduced the trout and grayling as to numbers, but the angler may still reap honour in the well-known dales of Derbyshire. The straits of Dovedale, romantic Ashbourn, Cotton's fishing house, and the steeple shaped rock in Pike Pool— could we not sketch each from memory, so familiar are we with the written and pictorial descriptions of them, even if we had not rambled and angled there? Of the modern angling I will say no further than that the bungler will not deprive

Dove, Derwent, or Wye, of its wary denizens. It is difficult to rise them at any time, and, that accomplished, the battle has to be won with the tiniest hook and finest of gut lines.

Once these waters were free, but there is little left now unpreserved. Some portions, however, may be reached through the consent of local fishing clubs, and at Rowsley and Bakewell, where both Derwent and Wye are within short distances, the hotel landlords are allowed by the Duke of Devonshire to grant tickets to customers. There are plenty of flymakers in all the Derbyshire fishing villages, and it is impossible to improve upon the neat little bumbles which they provide according to the sky, water, and season.[1]

[1] See "The Amateur Angler in Dovedale," published by Sampson Low & Co.—W. S.

CHAPTER VI.

WHARFEDALE.

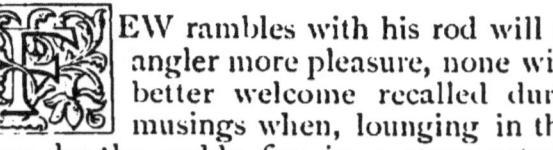

"A day without too bright a beam,
A warm, but not a scorching sun ;
A southern gale to curl the stream,
And, master, half our work is done."

FEW rambles with his rod will afford the angler more pleasure, none will be with better welcome recalled during those musings when, lounging in the winter-time by the ruddy fire in a stormy twilight, he turns over page after page of that wonderful and never-failing photographic album which is stored with the plates of memory, than his visit to Wharfedale. It is an autumn's amusement that will well bear the winter's reflection.

The Southrons of this kingdom are guilty of a heavy fault ; they do not know as much about Yorkshire as they ought to do. Most people I have noticed exercise the right of remaining remarkably ignorant of their own country : and it must be confessed with shamefacedness that we English are not a whit behind other nations in general ignorance of the beauties of our own fatherland. Yorkshire especially suffers from this singular neglect. You meet with men and women who are aware that the St. Leger is run at Doncaster, and maybe that Doncaster is in Yorkshire; that there are springs of nasty, though perhaps wholesome, mineral water at Harrogate; and that Scarborough is a fashionable and late watering-place. They may possibly, too, remember being taught at school that Yorkshire is the largest county in England; they may be in a position to assure you that it produces a popular pudding which mates worthily with the Roast Beef of Old England; they have vague ideas that it is famous for "tykes."

Yet Yorkshire has been gifted with great natural charms. I have set to myself in this chapter the task of gossiping chiefly about the grayling as you find him in the romantic Wharfe, else I could fill many a page with heartfelt glorifications of the sweet wooded dales, the lofty fells, the far-stretching wolds, the rolling moors, the rare historical associations, and the bounteous mineral and agricultural features of the rich county which covers 5,983 square miles of territory as important as any to the welfare of the State :—

> "The lofty woods; the forests wide and long,
>   Adorned with leaves and branches fresh and green,
> In whose cool bow'rs the birds with chanting song
>   Do welcome with their quire the summer's queen.
> The meadows fair, where Flora's gifts among
>   Are intermix'd, the verdant grass between ;
> The silver scaled fish that softly swim
>   Within the brooks and crystal wat'ry brim."

In justice to my readers I feel moved to admit the possibility of looking upon Wharfedale with eyes that refused to behold defects, of hurrying to its woods and streams in a frame of mind under which I should have magnified into picturesqueness the most ordinary landscape. In a word, I had been attending the annual meeting of the British Association. I had drenched myself with science : had perseveringly sat out the sectional gatherings ; had courageously endeavoured to follow dissertations on dirt, dust, and brickbats ; had pretended to be interested in discussions on shoddy, in the homologues of oxalic acid, thermal conductivity, protoplasm, the electrical phenomena which accompany the contraction of the cup of Venus's fly-trap, hyper-elliptic functions, and serpent worship in the pre-historic era.

These are serious subjects, and far be it from me to scoff at the learned papers read to explain them. On the contrary I owe them a special vote of thanks, which I hereby propose, second, and carry *nem. con.*, for the excellent preparation they proved for the moment of release. Bradford was eminently hospitable and pleasant during that British Association visit, but there was one member, I can honestly vouch, who joyfully rushed to the ticket office and booked "straight away," as the railway porters have it, to Otley, and who, putting away the spectacles and solemn demeanour that became a *savant* of the nineteenth century, lit his meerschaum and began to overhaul his fly-book the moment the train started.

The Wharfe illustrates the old saying, "Variety is charming," for it is a decided mixture of gentleness and anger. You would scarcely fancy, standing on the handsome bridge spanning it at Tadcaster, that the docile river which here begins to be navigable is so obstreperous in the upper part of the dale. The scenery of Lower Wharfedale is not so striking as that which delights you as you push upwards, but the grayling fishing is infinitely superior. Strolling down stream on the right bank at Boston Spa, for example, there is some open water that should be tried in passing.

It would be convenient perhaps to make known to all whom it may concern that some of the best portions of the Wharfe are strictly preserved, and that the angler generally should fish rather down than up the stream. Bearing this in mind, let us proceed towards Wetherby ; at a place called Flint Mills there is a splendid piece of grayling water, but it is difficult to obtain the requisite permission to bring it under contribution. Wetherby may be passed by lightly, but not Collingham. Even now the angling there is good, but it has, in common with that of every fishing station in the country, greatly deteriorated during the last few years. Above Harewood, if you are fortunate enough to possess the "Open Sesame" to the preserves at Arthington, you may capture plenty of grayling and a few trout. About twenty years ago an angling club at Harewood rented one side of the stream, and then the grayling fishing of the Wharfe was in its prime. I recently conversed with a middle-aged gentleman who was born in the district, and he assured me he once saw a basket of seventy-five grayling taken with the fly in one day by one rod between Collingham and Woodhall—a piece of luck, I need scarcely add, never to be approached in these later days.

At Otley, for some cause not very explainable, grayling are not so numerous as trout ; but whether your purpose in visiting Wharfedale be rambling or angling, or both (which is far better), Otley will be found a convenient starting-point, or even head centre. Here I had proposed making a somewhat protracted halt, knowing that sport would diminish in proportion as the scenery of Upper Wharfedale increased in variety and beauty. Besides, Otley is in itself a pretty place—a sweet refuge for the weary. If it be any gratification to know that long before the Conquest the manor hereabouts was given to the Archbishops of York, open that red-covered book on the coffee-room table, and you will see the details in black and white.

I remember reading somewhere in a treatise on grayling that the fish was introduced into the country by monks when England was undis-guisedly—to coin a word, and of course without offence to any creature—a monkery, and that the good St. Ambrose was particularly fond of the grayling. The saint in that case knew what was good for himself. This thought occurred to me on glancing at the guide-book literature of the coffee-room, and I then further remembered how the saints and abbots and holy friars invariably pitched their abodes near a river of great fish-producing capabilities, and how they often supplemented the stream with ponds and stews for the more ready and certain supply of their larders. It is generally conceded that the grayling, not being indigenous to English streams, must have been imported from the Continent, probably from Germany, and the monks might as reasonably be credited with the importation as any other class of men.

I should have remained longer at Otley had I not on the very first day encountered a hair of the dog that had bitten me at Bradford. A learned Dryasdust, full of archæology, having remembered my face at the sections, fancied my pleasure would be consulted by giving me relief " in kind," where-

fore the worthy gentleman forthwith pursued me
relentlessly with his facts and fancies, which were,
truth to tell, a pretty equally mixed assortment.
He told me that Athelstan had had dealings with
Otley, and I asked him if he knew whether that
eminent Saxon king tied his own flies. The philosopher at first, I fear, suspected me of trying to
get a rise out of him, but after a pause meekly informed me that he had perused most of the ancient
documents concerning that part of the Riding, but
had observed nothing that would throw a light
upon that subject. I am not sure to this moment
whether the patient antiquarian said this in humble
innocence or as a covert rebuke.

A short distance out of the town stands a cliff
called the Chevin, and this, as readers of old-
fashioned angling books know, with a trifling
difference in the spelling, is also the name of a
certain fish.

"The Chevin," said the rev. gentleman, "used
to present "——

"Ah! talking of chub," I remarked, "do you
ever find any in the Wharfe?"

Then the archæologist—who, by the way, was
not the genial informant whom we are always glad
to meet and grateful to hear, but somewhat of a
bore, given to conceit—gave up the angler as a bad
investment, and shuffled behind him. It did so
unfortunately happen that just then the latter was
on the point of casting his flies upon the stream,
and somehow or other the archæologist managed
to receive the dropper in the rim of his wide-
awake; indeed, it might as well be confessed that
another inch and the evening's sport would have
included an archæologist's ear. The worthy man,
however, insisted upon accompanying me, saw me

to my chamber door at night, and was waiting at
the bottom of the stairs on my appearance in the
morning. The grayling of Otley were perhaps
gainers by this intrusive companionship, inasmuch
as the persecuted angler who was in search of—

"Respite—respite, and nepenthe"

from the parliament of science, lost no time in
reckoning with his host and departing from the
"field of Otho."

The railway has accomplished many wonders
and overcome many difficulties. Steadily and
surely it has intruded into the realms of romance
and reduced them to its own utilitarian level.
But Upper Wharfedale hitherto has defied it. Nor
is it easy to perceive how it is possible to lay
down a permanent way over Barden and Conis-
tone Moors, or to convert Bolton Abbey into a
station and Great Whernside into a terminus. It
fills me, I confess, with glee to spread out the
map and behold how the iron horse has snorted
and screamed up to the very foot of the balmy
moorlands, and then stopped short, sullen and
defeated. Thrice did he start off to invade the
district of which Skipton may be taken as the
southern, Ripon the eastern, the Westmoreland
border the Western, and Barnard Castle the
northern limits. At Ilkley he was frightened by
Rombald's Moor and the uplands towards Bolton.
At Pateley Bridge, Dallowgill and Appletrewick
Moors blocked the way; and at Leyburn a
judicious halt was sounded, at least for the
present.

None but strong, enduring pedestrians can,
therefore, do Wharfedale full justice, and it may be
here said generally that every turn of the stream

from Otley to its source under the brow of Cam
Fell will repay the pedestrian, and reveal new
surprises in itself, in the vistas beyond, and in the
ever-varying quantities and qualities of its steep
wooded banks.

Ilkley and Ben Rhydding receive much of their
popularity from the scenery of the Wharfe, and
the former watering-place, so well known to
hydropathists, owes its repute as much to the
little impetuous stream galloping over the breezy
side of Rombalds, as to the bracing mountain air.
But we cannot afford to linger here, with Bolton
Abbey beckoning us onward. Bolton Bridge,
reached from Ilkley by a delightful five miles of
road, overlooking the Wharfe on the right and
skirting umbrageous woods on the left, will serve
admirably as the wanderer's temporary head-
quarters. The hamlet itself offers nothing extraordinary either in landscape, architecture, or com-
merce, but the view above and below from the
bridge charmingly combines the pastoral and
romantic in harmonious proportions.

Having procured his ticket, easily obtainable at
the inns, and turned into the meadow on the left
bank of the river, it would save time if the angler
did not put his rod together until he had arrived
at the plantation adjoining the grounds of Bolton
Abbey. Indeed he would be wise, if a stranger
to the far-famed ruins, to inspect them before
going down to the river, and possess himself of
the legends and architectural features of the
place. Both are fascinating. Let us sit down
upon this meadow grass and hear the legend-in-
chief.

First look abroad. For a little space in front
and across the stream you have a park-like

prospect, lawn and trees appearing at intervals. Towards the priory, however, the noble woods close in high and thick, making us curious to see how the Wharfe, "the swift Werfe" of the poet Spenser, threads its way through the devious, overhung course. In many places yonder the foliage touches the water. The earlier tints of autumn are already stealing over the leaves, for the sportsmen have for three weeks been amongst the stubble and turnips, and we can hear the frequent crack of their fowling-pieces away in the fields. When the autumn tints are at their prime, you shall not be able to deny that Wharfedale hereabouts is one of the most entrancing of sights for those who love the garment of many colours with which the declining year adorns itself: for this reason, and also perhaps because the grayling is in good condition in October, it is the resort of anglers when other places are deserted.

A fine herd of Herefords, most effective of all cattle as component parts of a landscape, contentedly muse under the trees or crop the succulent herbage. The smoke rises above yonder orchard blue and straight, sure sign that the harvest is passed and summer ended, and that the atmosphere is flavoured with frost. A healthy-faced Yorkshire boy swings on the gate, which his sisters—as little sisters, bless them! always cheerfully do—laughingly set in motion. The stream is here shallow and wide, but the bouldery bed has been, and anon will be again, washed by a furious torrent, the scouring of moor and fell for many a mile. It is a peculiarity of much of the Wharfe that while on one side the river's bed shelves very gently to the centre, on the other it

runs deep under a steep and generally curving
shore. Higher up the stream the woods raise
their richly plumed heads far towards the sky,
and you know that close at hand, concealed
behind the superabundant foliage, is the remnant
of what was once Bolton Abbey. This is why I
suggest you should lay aside your rod and rest a
space here, postponing acquaintance with the
grayling in favour of traditionary lore.

What say you, then? And now for the legend
of Bolton Priory.

Perhaps on second thoughts it will interest us
more if we stroll towards it and talk as we go.
The field we are now crossing, and whose fine
soft grass rebounds beneath our footfall as if it
were the turf of a well-kept lawn, was selected,
they say, for camping ground by Prince Rupert
on his way to Marston Moor, and if that impulsive
freebooter acted upon his customary principles he
looted yonder farmyards to a pretty good tune.
The old priory stands in the centre of a picture
which has been faithfully filled in by Whitaker in
his "History of Craven":—"But after all the
glories of Bolton are on the north. Whatever the
most fastidious taste could require to constitute
a perfect landscape is not only found here but in
its proper place. In front and immediately under
the eyes is a smooth expanse of park-like enclo-
sure, spotted with native elm, ash, etc., of the
finest growth."

(The "etc.," you will note, includes some
patriarchal beeches, oaks, aspens, poplars, and
half up the opposite slope, there are mountain
ashes that in the late autumn ever gleam a deep
crimson blaze on the hillside.)

"On the right, a skirting oak wood with jutting

H

points of grey rock ; on the left, a rising copse. Still forward are seen the aged groves of Bolton Park, the growth of centuries ; and farther yet the barren and rocky distances of Simon's Seat and Barden Fell contrasted to the warmth, fertility, and luxuriant foliage of the valley below."

Pursuing our way upwards, the woods on either side hem us in ; tinkling brooks and fairy-like glens appear ; the Wharfe, having assumed every shape of which a river is capable, henceforth consistently retains the characteristics of a mountain stream. Immediately above the priory its bed is full of large boulders; beyond, it runs still and deep; here it narrows, and there it widens—everywhere it has the bright bubbling charm of variety. This is what we have for two miles, and then we reach the Strid. At this spot—the Mecca of the Wharfedale tourist—the river gallops through a deep sluice between two rocks, so narrow that you may leap across it. Hence its name. And here it is the legend must be told ; after which let the grayling look out.

A certain fishiness about the story makes it quite appropriate at this time and place. One Lady Alice had a son who came to an untimely end in this madly-hurrying current, which, as we sit over it, roars in our ears. The story has been best told by Rogers, who shall, with the reader's permission, tell it again for our benefit. Wordsworth's version, though substantially the same, is, compared with Rogers's, even "as water unto wine." Says Rogers :—

> " At Embasy rung the matin bell,
> The stag was roused on Barden Fell ;
> The mingled sounds were swelling, dying,
> And down the Wharfe a hern was flying:

When, near the cabin in the wood,
In tartan clad and forest green,
With hound in leash and hawk in hood,
The boy of Egremond was seen.
Blithe was his song—a song of yore ;
But where the rock is rent in two,
And the river rushes through,
His voice was heard no more.
'Twas but a step, the gulf he passed ;
But that step—it was his last !
As through the mist he winged his way
(A cloud that hovers night and day),
The hound hung back, and back he drew
The master and his merlin too !
That narrow place of noise and strife
Received their little all of life."

So far all authorities are agreed, but an inspection of certain musty documents throws some doubt upon the sequel. The Lady Alice, according to Wordsworth's acceptation of the popular legend, was apprised of the lad's fate by a forester, who, with a tact and delicacy not unusual, pray observe, in those rude times, prepared the poor lady for his intelligence by asking—

"What remains when prayer is unavailing?"
Quoth the bereaved mother, "Endless sorrow."

" From which affliction—when the grace
Of God had in her heart found place—
A pious structure fair to see ;
Rose up, this stately priory."

That is Mr. Wordsworth ; but the version which seems, not only from documentary evidence, but from our knowledge of the parties interested, to be most likely, is that the monks and abbots of Embasy, up in the bleak fell district, tired of their lonely situation (and there being no fish handy), took advantage of the lady's grief to descend into the valley and remove their priory nearer the beeves and trout. Anyhow the priory was wealthily endowed, and in a short space of time the monks—self-denying souls!—possessed 2,193 sheep, 713 horned cattle, 95 pigs, and 91 goats.

The man sauntering towards us is the water keeper, and he will recommend us to retrace our steps. He tells us he has been trying all the morning to catch a dish of grayling for the Hall, but without success. Strapped to his back, in lieu of the orthodox creel, he carries a wooden box fashioned as closely as possible to imitate a fishing basket. He made it himself, and his rod and line were also the work of his own hands. They are heavy and rough, it is true, but in his grasp they can be made to do all that is necessary. He purposely uses a large heavy line, with which alone, he says, you can fish thoroughly against wind   It is astonishing to see how lightly, easily, accurately, and to what distance he casts his flies with that clumsy sixteen feet rod painted green, and that heavy horsehair line.

His casting lines are of a kind peculiar to the Wharfe, I believe. He uses nothing but horse-hair, beginning with four or five strands and gradually lessening the bulk until the last eighteen inches of the four yards are single hair. He never fishes with less than five flies, tied by himself.

> " He shakes the boughs that on the margin grow,
> Which o'er the stream a waving forest throw,
> When if an insect fall (his certain guide),
> He gently takes him from the whirling tide,
> Examines well his form with curious eyes,
> His gaudy vest, his wings, his horns, his size :
> Then round the hook the chosen fur he winds,
> And on the back a speckled feather binds ;

> So just the colours shine through every part,
> That nature seems to live again in art."

There is a grey pony in the neighbourhood, I am told, whose long tail has been quite a small fortune to its owner during the last fifteen years, and a local wag says the grayling give over rising the moment the animal which has contributed so long to their family death-roll comes down to the margin to drink. The keeper is not prepared to sign an affidavit in verification of this assertion, but he certainly has in his greasy pocket-book a large collection of long grey horse-hairs, and furs and feathers innumerable.

Do not be too haughty to believe that a few expeditions with a man like this are worth any quantity of mere theory, and that it is always best to follow his advice when once you are convinced that he is to be trusted. That is a principle I have never found to fail. You may be learned in pis-catorial lore, may be an old stager at the waterside, may be in all ways an adept admitted and proved ; but a practised native, though he reads not, neither can he write, will be your master on his own ground.

Thus, though my book contained the most ap-proved flies used in Herefordshire, Derbyshire, and Hampshire (all first-class grayling counties), I with-out hesitation took the keeper's queer spiders, and in the course of a few days proved by practical expe-rience the infinite superiority of his knowledge and wisdom. I fancy the best Wharfe fly-makers live at Otley. Their brown owl is a killing fly ; so is the little hackle termed a fog black. Partridge and woodcock hackles and a black gnat are favourites, and you never see a native's cast that does not pos-sess a hackle made of the under wing of the snipe with body of straw-coloured silk.

" Grayling are like women, sir—you never know what to be about with them," the keeper sagely remarked. By this our Yorkshire guide showed that he had studied well the character, not perhaps of the sex, but of the fish. They are undoubtedly skittish cattle (fish, and once more, *not* women), as we were that day and the next destined to find. One could almost fancy that they were cognisant of their rarity and value, and gave themselves airs in consequence. Cotton, has no high opinion of the grayling. His pupil exclaims—

" I have him now, but he is gone down towards the bottom. I cannot see what he is ; yet he should be a good fish by his weight ; but he makes no stir."

" Why, then," the master replies, " by what you say, I dare venture to assure you it is a grayling, who is one of the deadest-hearted fishes in the world, and the bigger he is the more easily taken. Look you, now you see him plain ; I told you what he was. Bring hither that landing-net, boy ! And now, sir, he is your own, and believe me, a good one, sixteen inches long I warrant him."

If the grayling thus described had brought an action for libel against Charles Cotton, of Beresford Hall, in the county of Derby, Esquire, a fair-minded jury must have found a verdict with damages. The grayling is in every sense by which a fish may be judged entitled to respect. Walton, who was as innocently credulous as a child in matters with which he was not practically acquainted, who would believe almost any story so long as it appealed to his quaint simple sentiment, and who probably knew less about the grayling than any other English fish, is inclined to place him on a pinnacle of honour. He reminds us that Gesner

terms it the choicest of all fish ; that the French,
who vilify the chub, term the grayling (or umber)
un umble chevalier. Without exactly endorsing
the statement, Walton retails with some unction
the Frenchman's dictum that the grayling feeds on
gold, and informs his readers that St. Ambrose,
" the glorious Bishop of Milan," calls him the
flower of fishes, and was so far in love with him
that he would not let him pass without the honour
of a long discourse.

Now the grayling, though not brilliantly marked,
like the trout, is, to my thinking, of gracefully pro-
portioned shape, and not by any means the craven
described by Cotton. Like the trout, the grayling
takes much of his character from the stream he
inhabits, and I found that the Wharfe grayling,
though not large, were of the most perfect sym-
metry, colour, and flavour. When the grayling
first leaves the water, nothing can be more beautiful than the almost impalpable lustre of royal
purple which shines over his silver undermail, and
the long distinct thin line running along the middle
of his side, from his bright lozenge-shaped eye to
his purple tail. His tapered snout and somewhat
round, elegant body, his white belly, with a
suspicion of gold along each side, the dark spots
about his sides, and the extraordinary dorsal fin,
increase the beauty of this high-bred-looking fish.

There is a dispute as to the smell of the grayling
in the first few moments of his capture, some argu-
ing in favour of thyme, and some saying the perfume is that of the cucumber. The fish has been
designated *salmo thymallus* in honour of the thyme
theory. Opinions upon this knotty point I think
will always differ. A fish taken from the Teme I
once thought had a decided smell of cucumber,

another from the Itchen was redolent of thyme ; the
first which the Wharfe yielded me smelt of something which the keeper said was cucumber, while
I equally maintained it was thyme. Very likely if
we had never heard or read of the alleged odours
the fancy would not have occurred to us!

Our Wharfedale experiences were those of every
grayling fisher who uses the fly. We were certain
of nothing. Roving and sinking as the anglers
practise it in Herefordshire with grasshopper or
gentle is probably the most certain way of catching
the grayling, who loves to lie close to the ground,
grubbing upon the sand or gravel, which he prefers
to any other bed. Even when he takes the fly,
which he will do at most times (not excepting the
winter frosts, if the sun should peep out for an
hour or two in the middle of the day) he rises swift
and straight from the deepest parts of the river,
and descends again with equal speed. His movements are indeed so rapid that the hesitation of an
instant on your part will be fatal. The fish loves
either the glide above, or tail of a current ; upon
being hooked he rushes for the stream, and as in
most cases your hook must be of the smallest, and
the grayling's mouth is remarkably tender, your
proportion of lost fish will be greater with grayling
than with trout.

"It is no good, sir," the keeper said, after we
had both carefully fished a mile of the Wharfe and
missed every fish that rose, each of which had been
faintly pricked ; "they are at their old tricks. I've
touched a dozen fish to-day and caught none, and
sometimes they go on like this all day long. We
shall get them between three and five this afternoon,
but not before."

He acted upon his own opinion and ceased ang-

ling, preferring to husband his strength for subsequent efforts, and watch me fish the rapids for
trout. It turned out in the afternoon as it had
been predicted. The grayling rose moderately,
but whereas, in the morning we both missed everything, we now landed all that we touched—eight
beautiful fish of about three-quarters of a pound
each.

When the sun began to touch shadow-land, and
the autumnal coolness of evening to succeed, the
grayling rose no more. This is their habit, and
their habit requires most careful study both as regards general characteristics and the peculiarities
of locality. No fish requires such careful watching
as the grayling, and when I hear him condemned
or spoken lightly of, I suspect that the fault lies
with the blamer rather than the blamed. So long
as I remained in Wharfedale and in the keeper's
neighbourhood, he would in the morning, as a first
and prime duty, look round at the sky, and then
at the water, and at the insects moving about, and
pronounce an opinion as to the probabilities of
sport ; and his general accuracy was surprising.

At Bolton the fish are not numerous : two or
three brace constituted a day's average sport : but
I met some fishermen who had for a fortnight been
unable to take a single grayling, although they had
caught a few small trout. Anglers differ greatly
in their estimate of a grayling's weight. One
Wharfedale fisher, when I told him I had seen a
Hampshire fish that scaled over three pounds and
a half, coughed incredulously, and said—

" Ah, that was a big one indeed. "

Plainly he did not believe me. It is rarely grayling so large as this are seen, and the monster I
quote was a supremely ugly fellow. A pound fish

is a good one, and though he will not fight so
desperately as a trout, he does not die without a
plucky struggle. Properly hooked, however, a
grayling ought never to be lost; but let the unsuccessful grayling angler be consoled with the reflection that many otherwise excellent fly-fishers
have never mastered the art of thoroughly hooking
this fish. The sun, except on frosty mornings, is
bad for grayling fishing—fog, frost, wind, rain, anything but sun may be tolerated, and unlike most
descriptions of fish the grayling is not to be met
with early in the morning or late in the evening.

My Wharfedale expedition, though not, I confess, productive of much in the way of pisci-slaugh-
ter, was never regretted; there was too much to
admire, too much to be interested about, and then
as to fish, one can always console one's self with
the anciently expressed comfort—

> "If the all-ruling Power please
>   We live to see another May,
> We'll recompense an age of these
>   Foul days in one fine fishing day.'

CHAPTER VII.

THE ANGLER IN IRELAND.

"The miles in this country much longer be ;
But that is a saving of time, you see,
For two of our miles is aiqual to three,
Which shortens the road in a great degree."

HETHER Ireland be a better salmon country than Scotland, or Wales the best trouting land, is not the question. Without any injustice to the bonnie Land o' Cakes, it may, however, I think, be taken for granted that the Emerald Isle is, on the whole, *the* Paradise of Anglers. Both Scotland and Ireland abound with beautiful streams and an abundance of fish, but in the latter country they are much more accessible to the passing stranger than in the former. It is more fashionable for the wealthy merchant or citizen to own an estate north of the Tweed than to possess one across the Irish Channel, and so it happens that rivers which in Ireland are absolutely free to the *bonâ fide* angler would fetch a high price and be jealously guarded in Scotland. Some day it may be that, in the revolutions of the whirligig which produces manners and customs, the fashion may run the other way, and then, while the bright charms of Ireland are rapturously acknowledged, its salmon and trout may have as heavy a price put upon their heads as have their finny brethren of North Britain at the present moment.

Indeed already there is a slow change in this direction, and each year, such is the increasing love of angling amongst Englishmen, some river hitherto open to all comers is added to the list of private profit-yielding preserves. The natives, debarred for the first time in the history of their fathers from liberty to angle, naturally for a while deplore the loss of another of the few privileges which the hard times have left them ; but happy, notwithstanding, are the people who have no worse grievance to groan under.

And there may, *in re* the Irish rivers, be added the consolation that many years must pass before any appreciable diminution can be suffered in the freedom which makes Ireland so desirable a ground for the angler who cannot pay a fancy price for his pleasures, or command an entire season of time in their leisurely pursuit. When driven from the plains he must flee to the mountains ; when forced from the rivers he must retire to the loughs. This generation, at any rate, is likely to pass away before such an extremity is reached. Even in instances of preservation of a pretty strict description, permission in Ireland is seldom refused, in moderation, to a stranger whose respectability is beyond question.

After fishing in lough and river under the freest of conditions in a certain district in Ireland, I once found myself whipping a burn in the south of Scotland, having obtained permission so to do from the agent of the nobleman who owned the land. It was a nice little stream for want of a better, and at times, I was told, productive of fair sport. Guided by a local guide whom I had attached to my service, I found myself in the course of my upward progress arrested by observation of the fern-covered grounds with woods beyond, a few Highland cattle cropping the herbage, a setter or two barking in the distance, birds of prey hawking here and there, and goodly mountains receding to a very distant background.

In the midst of my hearty enjoyment of the scene a youth appeared on the opposite bank, eye-glassed, knickerbockered, and haw-hawing. What right had I there? Where did I come from? What was my name? These and other questions, peremptorily demanded, were straightforwardly answered, and then sentence was pronounced. We were at once sent about our business by this lordly youth, who had talked of "my pwop'ty" until I assumed he was at the lowest a duke. Of course we shifted quarters immediately, and in trudging towards the boundary of what the young gentleman had called "the deer park,"—a strong stretch of the imagination, by the way—I discovered that our outraged landowner was the son of an English manufacturer who rented the place. No doubt he was a good son, and no doubt he had a perfect right to prevent any strolling vagabond from thinning out his troutlings; only, after some years' experience of Ireland, I cannot conceive it possible that any angler there, finding himself in a similar position (through another's error), and announcing his strangerhood, would have been made otherwise than courteously welcome, at least to finish the day he had begun.

Yet what an astonishing ignorance prevails respecting Ireland! "Is it safe?" once asked a broad-shouldered stockbroker of me, when with enthusiastic eloquence I told him of the rare sport to be had in that tight little island.

"Is it safe to trust yourself into those savage parts?" he demanded.

The man of Consols was reeling in his live bait as he asked me the question by the side of a very private sheet of water where I was lounging over an evening cigar, watching his efforts to get a "run." He admitted that he reserved £50 yearly for a month's holiday, not a farthing more nor a fraction less, and always spent it. He was a bachelor, and gloried in being unblessed with wife or child. He had "done" the Rhine because Tompkins had done it. He had accompanied Smith to Paris, Jones to Germany, Buggins to Florence and Rome, and on each occasion, so he protested, he had felt relieved when at length the last of his ten-pound notes had been changed. But Ireland? No: he had never ventured there. Was it safe?

By an almost superhuman effort I converted him, and saw him off by the Wild Irishman, with a magnificent angling outfit, resolved at last to risk his precious body amongst the Irish rivers and lakes. At first I believe he never moved out without a revolver. The weapon now lies buried, like his ignorance and prejudice, full fathoms five. He had been an enthusiastic fisherman for twenty-two years, but swears he never knew what real angling meant till then. The twenty-pound salmon that arrived while the last meeting of his club was being held was a little the worse for the journey from County Mayo to London, but it had been slain by his valiant self, albeit the members held their noses as they vehemently admired it. So long as our worthy friend lives you may take odds he will spend his fifty pounds—he says it is difficult to get through so much in those parts—in the country of which he will never more ask "Is it safe?"

The lakes of County Clare offer probably the best pike fishing in the United Kingdom, and trout and salmon in the streams; Kerry, with the waters of Killarney, is too well known to be more than mentioned; the Blackwater, Lee, and Bandon are sufficient of themselves to give Cork the highest reputation; and as for Limerick, why need go further than the Shannon?

"Oh Limerick, it is beautiful, as everybody knows,
The River Shannon full of fish beside the city flows."

The Shannon, speaking roughly, *is* full of fish, and except the famed salmon stretch between Killaloe and Limerick, is free. White trout, brown trout, and monster pike and perch abound in the Shannon waters. As long as I live I shall probably never see such a sight as—if I remember accurately—at Athlone. The train had stopped outside the station on the bridge over the river just as it was clearing after a flood, and bare-legged peasants were on the platform with trays of spoil, great trout and perch, by the hundred-weight, while below through the railings we could see the boats drifting down stream heaped up with recently caught fish. Take it all in all I doubt whether there is a river in the world for "all-round" angling to equal this splendid stream, which sweeps through Leitrim and the eight counties intervening between its source and the Atlantic Ocean.

Dublin is singularly unfortunate in its fresh-water fishing, but it is a mistake to suppose that the angler is there entirely at fault. It is not so very far from Powerscourt, with the romantic Dargle and its stores of merry little trout. There are pike and perch in the Liffey below the straw-berry gardens, and trout increase with your distance from incomparable Phœnix Park. The best spot I have always, however, found is under the Wick-low mountains near the source of the river. Kil-bride, though a long drive from Dublin, is a very pleasant trip, and often have I compassed it on a jaunting car. The trout are always small, but they make atonement in their extraordinary quantity, and the voracity with which they take the somewhat gaudy little flies by which they are tempted.

There are some events in life never to be for-gotten. You may not remember your first drub-bing at school, your first stand-up collar, your first shave, your first kiss, your first client, your first appearance in print, or the incidents, weather, and so on, of your wedding day ; but you cannot forget your first salmon. What a delicious remem-brance it is !

There was, to be sure, something a trifle curi-ous about mine. I was at Galway, as interesting a town as any in Ireland, and, as every one who has looked over the railings of the bridge must know, a regular show-place for salmon. The bottom of the river seems alive with them, and you may be amused for hours, when the humour seizes the fish, by watching their antics as they shoot and circle and leap as if in the performance of a dance on the up-the-side-and-down-the-middle principle. At the eventful time to which I am referring the salmon fishing was over, for the Galway river is not one of the late kind. The proprietor of the fishery, however, with the ready courtesy of his class, freely allowed me to try my best for a chance trout, and wished me luck. This wish was gratified to my heart's content, and the little lad with the net had for a time no opportunity of dropping asleep. In the middle of the stream there was a shallow and placid pool, surrounded by water rippling in the usual way over the stones. The fish below had ceased moving, and observing in the middle of this space the familiar expanding rings caused by a rising fish, I despatched my cast athwart.

"Tug, tug," was instantly telegraphed down the butt of the rod. Then there was a dull heavy strain.

Slowly at first, then at gathering speed, the small ebony winch made music. Straight across the pool, back again, here, there, and everywhere, the prey shot, churning the water into foam, and causing many another fish to leap into the air. Such a hullabaloo there never was. The boy shouted frantically. Workmen threw down their tools and rushed down, and in a few minutes a small crowd had collected. The fly rod was the lightest that could be made, the line finely tapered, the hook extremely small, so that when half an hour had gone, and the evening had begun to absorb the light, and the commotion in the water raged as before, hope of a satisfactory finale departed. Perseverance, however, gave me the victory, although the battle would probably have been on the other side had I not prevailed upon Tim to flounder into the water and net the fish as he ran. The wonder was how a five-pound salmon

I

could have created such a stir! Stooping to claim
him, I found out the cause : he had been hooked
in the dorsal fin with a small coachman! The
water was so low that in drawing the cast towards
me I had fouled him in that singular manner. And
this was how I caught my first salmon.

The fishing in Galway is excellent, but the best
has to be paid for at high rates, and the waters
are not allowed too much rest. The great lakes
—Corrib and Mask—contain all kinds of fish, but
the sport is uncertain. The district is most
interesting to the tourist, and the ride through
Joyce's country one of the treats of the island.
The circular tickets issued by the Midland Great
Western Company are a *bonâ fide* boon, saving
you trouble, insuring you comfort, and in every
way reducing the inconveniences of travelling to a
minimum.

Unless the waters are known to be in good
order I should not, starting from Galway, advise
an early halt for angling. The Spiddal, a river
about ten miles from the town, is a fair wet-
weather stream, and trolling in the lakes thereabouts is not to be despised : but on the whole
you had better let your rod lie undisturbed in the
well of O'Brien's roomy car, and enjoy your ride
through Connemara as an ordinary Christian.
Make the most of the Twelve Pins, envy Mr.
Mitchell Henry his house and fishing at Kyle-
more, and go into raptures with Killery Bay, for of
its degree you will meet with nothing to surpass it.
If you cannot make yourself at home at Westport,
in the hotel with the river and trees before the
door, your conscience must be in a parlous state.
You may be tempted here by what you hear of the
fishing in Lord Sligo's demesne, and the chances

of obtaining permission, but don't unstrap your
rods, or unlock the basket, until you find yourself
in due course at Ballina unless permission is
sure.

The Moy, as an open salmon river, has few
rivals, and the only fault to be found with it is the
general unhinging one suffers on reading every
week in one's English home a record of the fish
taken. It is impossible to settle down to the
duties of the day when, in the roaring Babel of
London, you read how Captain A. killed his five,
the Rev. B. his eight, and Sir John C. his ten fish,
weighing so many pounds ; and the most melancholy part of the business is, that you know it is
likely to be true. After two visits to the Moy I
am in a humour to believe almost any story of
fishermen's luck there. The proprietors grant you
permission for the whole season, fettering you
with conditions which are not only reasonable in
themselves, but such as every real sportsman will
rejoice to observe.

You are not required, as at some places in
Ireland, to take out your licence in the district—
of course there is no such thing as salmon fishing
without a licence—but you are requested carefully
to return the fry to the river, and to give up all
the salmon taken, with the exception of one fish,
as soon as possible after the capture, to the fishery
store. There are good seasons and bad seasons
on the Moy, as at the West End of London, but
it must be indeed a hopeless case if either in
the upper or lower waters, with a cast of friend
Hearn's flies and a " cot " well handled, you
cannot show trout or salmon as a reward for your
labours. You may not be able, as Hearns can,[1]

[1] He has since gone to his fathers.—W. S.

or rather could do, to pitch your fly forty yards
across the stream, or kill your hundred fish in an
easy month, as some anglers have done aforetime,
but something you can hardly fail to do.

Lough Gill is the most lovely lake in the north
of Ireland. I passed that way four years ago,
intending merely to sleep at Sligo and move on to
Enniskillen in the morning, but three days had
somehow gone before I called for my tavern bill.
Too late for salmon, or trout in any quantity, I
had some rare fun with the pike. The boatman
who took me in charge was a famous fellow for a
companion and "help," eager to please, glad at
your success, and sympathetic with your reverses
—in short, a model boatman for a long day's
work. I have no doubt in the world there are
pike of 40 lb. or 50 lb. in Lough Gill. A minute
account was given to me of a couple of young men
who had killed one of these giants, and who had
walked through the main street in triumph with
an oar passed through its gills; the handle and
blade resting upon their respective shoulders,
they thus unconsciously imitated the spies sent
out by Joshua, who according to the ancient
engravings which disfigure the pages of old-
fashioned Bibles, returned with a huge bunch of
grapes suspended in the same fashion as the great
pike of Lough Gill.

They—that is, both the fishermen and the fish
—are very fond of spoon bait on the lough, and a
careful fishing of the river communicating with the
lake will be no waste of time on your upward
pull. Keep pretty close to the left bank and look
out for the holes; from one little bend I took four
or five pike in five casts, and Pat, who, like all
Irish fishermen, regards every fish but salmon

as mere vermin, knocked them on the head and
consigned them to a locker in the fore part of the
boat as if they were so much lumber. The "jack
pike," as he termed pickerel of a pound or so, he
was more careful with, designing them for bait
by-and-by when we reached the lake.

Is there one amongst my readers who can
remember his state of mind when on some occasion he has been surrounded by the evidence of
fish, yet been unable to obtain one? That was
my hapless condition during a spell of midday
sun on the Garrogue River. It had stormed right
royally when, just previously, the pike in mad
succession took the glittering spoon, and then
large circles spread upon the water showing that
the trout were on the move. Even in Ireland,
however, where brown trout are not accounted of
high rank, you cannot in conscience meddle with
them at Michaelmas. Pat pointed to me the
direction of a deep pool, where in the spring, he
said, many a salmon was surprised, and where
now he knew there was a shoal of perch of the
genus "whopper." He had seen them the day
before, "yer honner, shoining loike bars of gowld
tied up with black ribbon, upon my sowl, sorr."

A phantom minnow should be in every wandering angler's case, and I should as soon think of
going to Ireland without one as without my pipe.
The phantom, however, carelessly handled played
me a trick which did not raise me in the boatman's estimation. A good perch was hooked,
brought to within a couple of yards of the boat,
and clumsily lost. I permitted him to approach
the top of the water before his time; there was a
pull-baker, pull-devil sensation, then a floundering
on the surface, a broadside flashing, and a sudden

disappearance. Pat had one or two provoking little ways with him. He had watched the whole business with positive eagerness, but the moment the misfortune happened he appeared unconscious of it, of me, nay, of himself, as, looking quite in another direction, he gazed musingly at the sky, softly whistling.

"Bad business that, Patrick?" I suggested, shame-facedly.

"Och, and did ye miss that same, yer honner?" he asked, with a magnificently assumed expression of surprise.

The salmon of Loch Gill are not as a rule large. The heavy trout, which take the fly well up to the end of June and July, are both good and numerous; perch of about half a pound weight the boys and girls catch by the bushel, by fishing over the boat with a simple piece of string and hook, weighted with a pebble, and baited with worms. The pike also are abundant, much too abundant to please the keepers, who in the spawning season shoot them without mercy. There were two parties of pike fishermen out on the day of my visit. I would not care to commit myself to details, but I should think each boat had not less than a dozen rods sticking over its gunwales, elevated at an angle of forty degrees into the air so as to allow of all the lines trailing without fouling. Every now and then we could hear the whizz of the winch, and would pause to see the pike hauled in hand over hand. We had a nice heap in the bottom of our own boat when we landed at Pat's cabin that night, but what was one rod amongst so many? Pat seemed to think I took too low a view of life. He wished me to try for a big fish, and nothing but a big one. He persisted in the wish. Now, I have one invariable theory on this head, and I gave him the benefit of it.

"Pat," I said, Johnsonianly, "I fish for sport, not gross weight. I would rather any day catch half a dozen moderately sized fish than one large one."

The man, it was plain, considered me an ass, but he merely looked up in his provoking way at the sky, and whistled again softly. At length, however, he was propitiated, for I proposed we should take a nip of "the craythur" for luck, fill our pipes for heart, and go in for the biggest fish in the lake. Then the good-humoured Patrick overhauled my spinning flights, selected one that would hold a shark, and adjusted it through and round about a "jack pike" of quite a pound weight. The plan was to trail it say forty yards at the stern of the boat, and I must confess that although it wobbled a good deal, and made a tremendous commotion in the water, it looked a most attractive mouthful for any pike-ish ogre that might be lurking near.

It so happens that Lough Gill is charged with fine scenery, and while the pickerel was wobbling steadily after our boat I forgot the chances of sport, and became lost in poetical contemplation of one of the sweet wooded islets that bestud the water.

The moralist tells you truly indeed that in beauty there is fatality. Had this been a mere Dagenham pond who knows what a contribution would not have been made to the South Kensington Museum?

My knowledge on this point is vague, but shall I ever forget that savage pull which bent the top of my rod swiftly into the water, or that mighty swirl far away in our wake when the giant, snapping my closely plaited silk as though it were cotton, went off with hooks, trace, and twenty yards of line, leaving me lamenting, and Pat a third time making astronomical investigations and screwing up his lips? It would have gratified me to have received a little consolation from my humble companion, but he was not going to belie his conscience for anyone just then. And that was what came of admiring the beauties of nature, and not perceiving that the line was carelessly entangled in the handle of the winch.

Let us now change the scene to another lough across the country, the largest lake in the three kingdoms, and one of the first four largest in Europe. In considering the angler's opportunities in North Ireland it were almost a sin to deal slightingly with the splendid lakes and rivers of Donegal and Londonderry, but there is such a thing as space to be thought of when your notions are to be put in type, and that thought will intrude itself at this moment.

As a skeleton guide to angling in Ireland I can with a very clear conscience recommend the inquirer to the chapter devoted to that subject in Murray's Guide; and this is a tribute one all the more gladly pays, as a set-off against hard words provoked by the vices of such literature on other occasions. The compiler of this guide to the angling waters in Ireland had the good common sense to aim at nothing more attractive than the imparting of reliable information, and this he has certainly succeeded in getting and giving. Shifting my responsibility to those unknown shoulders, I therefore turn to the waters of which I have had recent experience.

Randalstown, near Lough Neagh, comes first.
There is a choice of routes from England to
Belfast, and Belfast is well worth spending a day
or two in for its own sake. It is safest to purchase
your flies at Belfast, for they are of a particular
pattern, and the tackle makers there understand
precisely what kinds are suitable for existing
circumstances. A salmon licence may be obtained
either at Belfast or Randalstown, but by all manner
of means do not forget to include wading stock-
ings and brogues in your kit, else a beautiful piece
of the river which, by stopping at the O'Neill Arms,
you are at liberty to fish in the grounds of Shane's
Castle, will be altogether beyond your reach.

The O'Neills have been mighty kings in Ulster,
and their emblem, the red hand, will often meet
the eye in Antrim. There are two inns well
known to anglers visiting this part of Ireland, and
they are both O'Neill Arms, the one being at
Randalstown, and the other at Toome Bridge ;
and the angler who cannot make himself at home
at either ought to be kept on short commons until
he comes to his proper senses. There is a delicious
sense of freedom and coming pleasure on entering
the passage of an angler's hotel, and being greeted,
not by bagmen's trunks and sample boxes, but
salmon and trout rods neatly ranged on the rack,
and landing nets occupying every spare corner.
What a thrill of anticipation passes through one
when the landing net is damp from recent use, and
bugled with the silver scales of the last captive !
There is no inn in the world so comfortable as an
honest angling house—a statement which holds
equally good in the Highlands, by the waters of
Ireland, among the mountains of Wales, or on the
banks of the English rivers.

The fishing in Lough Neagh is mostly a matter of nets. I heard a few sly whispers of what was done sometimes on windy days by cross fishing, and saw evidences (of which no more) which rather set at nought the fisherman's ruling that little, if anything, can be done with a fly on that one hundred and fifty-four square miles of fresh water. At the O'Neill Arms at Toome Bridge I saw, with my own individual eyes, a magnificent lake trout of sixteen pounds taken that morning by net from the lake, and in the recess of one of the coffee-room windows, there lies under a glass case a stuffed specimen of the same family, labelled "26 lb." Trolling and spinning are the best methods of angling for the Lough Neagh trout and pike.

The fishermen do a great deal with night lines baited with scraps of pullan, the fresh-water herring which abounds here, and which one boatman told me was often found on the cross lines. This must be a very exceptional circumstance, seeing that the flies used in this poacher's contrivance are almost as large as salmon flies. The lake is famous for delicious eels, and hundredweights of them are despatched to England by an English lessee who has purchased the fishery.

At Antrim a river known as the Six Mile Water runs into the lough. Other streams feed the lake, but only the River Bann, a capital salmon river, carries its waters to the sea. I made my first bow to Lough Neagh from the Antrim end, and in that same Six Mile Water there should be, unless the shrewd lad who witnessed my loss has since recovered it, a derelict Canadian spoon-bait which caught a snag instead of a fish. The fishermen use a stiff open boat that carries a good press of sail, and if you can catch a mild breeze a trip across to the opposite shore should be unfortunate for the pike and an occasional trout. The Six Mile Water used to be an excellent salmon and trout stream, but it has been poisoned time after time by mills and factories, and is now in its lower portion scarcely worth the trouble of fishing.

An idle day—that is to say, a day on a boat on Lough Neagh, with a couple of spinning baits to take care of themselves, the glamour of sunshine over the woods and shores, and a sweet bell-like voice reading softly to you (as the incense of the meerschaum slowly ascends into the clear atmosphere) about the legend of Shane's Castle, and the traditions of the lake and land—is a penance one would risk not a little to suffer. After three days' conscientious whipping and wading at Randalstown or Toome Bridge a right-minded man should find it quite bearable to be petted and read to for a few hours while reclining lazily in the roomy stern-sheets of a Lough Neagh fishing boat.

The Main is a river after the angler's own heart, especially in September and October. Visit it in August, and your execrations are likely to be as deep as the rolling Zuyder Zee. The flax plant is an interesting object no doubt, and useful withal. In June when the pretty blue flowers are in blossom you may become even sentimental over it; in July the ripe crop may give joy to the farmer, and satisfaction to Dorothy his wife. But the angler has another tale to tell. It will be years before I shall reconcile myself to Irish linen, so deadly is my hatred of the flax water of which I had painful experience. All Ulster anglers curse the flax water if they curse nothing else, and if they do not speak their condemnation they think it.

The cut flax is placed in water pits to soak, and the filthy trenches being drained off when the soaking is complete, the rivers become discoloured, the air is polluted with a stench to which that of a tanyard is otto of roses ; the fish are sickened to death's door.

Luckily they do not die under the infliction, but they never move or feed, and the experienced angler at once puts his rod on the rack. The only fish that affects unconcern at the appearance of flax water is the impudent little samlet, which bolts a fly as big as its own head, and worries you incessantly at all times.

The Main river is noted for heavy trout. When I crossed the bridge on my way from the railway station my heart gave a bound at what I saw. A lad was sauntering homewards dangling, with his fingers thrust into the gills, a trout of some four or five pounds ; a young working man drifting with the stream in a boat checked by a pickaxe slung over the bow was taking trout on an average at every third cast ; further up on the meadow banks I saw the well balanced figure of the trout fisher. Eager as the traditional war-horse is said to be for the battle, I hastened to the river side, sniffing carnage as I went. It was at the close of a day's rain, the first that had fallen for a month, and the river, though slightly coloured, was in superb order. It ran by in stately measure, broke out like a Christmas carol upon the scours, tussled and fought round the big boulders, and postured like a dancing master round the curve of the pools.

And how the fish rose for one little hour ! Old Tim in the potato garden over the way, young Mick knee-deep in water, Squire Brown in the rushes, the doctor under the weir, the captain in the quiet part of the stream—one and all kept up a pretty hoorooing while the game lasted. The stranger, latest arrived, although his flies were all wrong, and he had in his blind haste got in the teeth of the wind, shared in the general good fortune, and wet, muddy, and tired returned to the inn at dark with the strap of his creel cutting into his shoulder. It was a carnival of trout, large and small, brown and yellow.

On the following morning it must have been highly amusing to the non-angling spectator to see the blank countenances of the expectant sportsmen who at daybreak went down to the waterside. A turbid, ochre-tainted flood had arisen during the night, and, too vexed to speak, they returned without adventuring a solitary cast. Allowing a week of fine weather to interpose, I again went to Randalstown, expecting naturally to find the flood abated. So it was, but there was a dark umber stain in the water which I could not understand until I was informed that this was the flax pollution, and that I might as well attempt to fish in a water butt. The warning was amply justified, for after nine hours' severe labour I was the richer by about three ounces of trout.

On my next visit I was more fortunate. Rumours of half a hundredweight of salmon in one day caught by one rod, exaggerated though no doubt they were, might still be true, and for salmon I tried heart and hand. About two miles up the river the Fates whispered me good omens. The stream, running sharply across from a pretty coppice, swept in a long, deep, semi-circular pool under a steep rock-shelved bank, and feathered away in a foamy tail. A cloud went across the sun, the wind ruffled the dark water, and the favourite claret fly dropped

down upon the precise square inch that would bear
it in natural motion into the current.

> " Let the proud salmon gorge the feather'd hook,
> Then strike, and then you have him—He will wince :
> Spin out your line that it will whistle from you
> Some twenty yards or so, yet you shall have him.
> Marry ! you must have patience—the stout rock
> Which is his trust hath edges something sharp ;
> And the deep pool hath ooze and sludge enough
> To mar your fishing—'less you are more careful."

Doubtless ! But we *are* careful, though twice
twenty yards are run out in one jubilant fanfare
from the click reel before there is time to think of
patience, or sharp edges, or anything else but the
pleasant tingling which the taut line has communi-
cated to every nerve. The gallant fish evidently loves
the shade, for he has shot up to the plantation's
edge, cleaving the water as he took the narrowest
part of the channel.   He is partial to gymnastic
exercises too, for into the air he purls, sending
one's heart into one's mouth for fear.   But he is
too well hooked, and being closely followed he
returns back again to the pool, to yield up the
ghost perhaps in sight of a comrade who may by
his fate take a salutary warning.   I don't say an
eight-pound fish was much to brag about, but with
only an ordinary trout rod and a landing net, which
you must perforce use yourself, it did not come
amiss to the captor.

It is, however, as I have before said, in
September and October that the best sport is
obtained in the Main river.   Great trout up to
twelve and fifteen pounds then run out of Lough
Neagh, and salmon also ; and there is a numerous
congregation of anglers from all parts of the
country so long as the sport lasts.   But the Main

is not what it was, and a bare-legged peasant woman confidently told me why. A few years since a gentleman from London came and took out certain fish, from which he extracted the spawn, and returned them again to the stream. For a couple of days, she said, there were strange disturbances in the pools, as if the fish were sitting in conference on the business. The end of it was that on the evening of the second day, as she was leading her goat to new pasture, she observed a movement on the surface as if an orderly procession were passing down the middle of the river. It was not for her to judge, she concluded, but her private belief was that the fish so summarily deprived of their spawn had, in dignified resentment, retreated into the lake, never more to return.

At Toome Bridge there is a beautiful stretch of trouting water. The waters of the lough, broad and clear here, tumble over a weir forming the vigorously rocked cradle of the River Bann. Not only can you take fish close under the fall, but by bringing your boat to within a foot of the uproar, you may cast your flies into the lake itself, and frequently hook a blithe two-pounder within a yard of the edge. Whether you land him or not is another business, for as he has a habit of projecting himself over the weir, the chances are more in his favour than yours.

This river must be fished from a boat, and it sometimes swarms with trout. Using fine tackle and small flies in favourable weather you may easily take three or four dozen fellows ranging between half a pound and a pound, with once now and then larger fish. It is a distinct specimen from the lake trout, which cuts as red as

a salmon and has a salmon flavour ; these yellow
river fish are neither so well coloured nor
flavoured.

On my last evening at Toome I saw a most
wonderful sight.   In the west, over the mountains, looking almost ethereal in the fading light,
the sun was sinking into a world of golden cloud-
architecture, at which one looked with a feeling
akin to awe.   Turrets were piled upon turrets,
their tops gilded with a reddish hue ; there were
seas and mountains and forests in that mystic land
of shadows, and they all melted into thin air like
a dream.   Directly eastward, on turning from this
glorious pageantry, I found the moon rising full
and weird out of a bank of dark purple clouds
which brooded over that portion of the lake.   The
moon-rising was as wonderful in its way as the
sunset, and appeared, indeed, to be in sympathy
with it.   It seemed as if the Queen of Night had
resolved to emulate the God of Day, and, from
the dusk, carve out another such city as that which
had faded in the western sky ; but the attempt
was not successful, and the moon, as if observing
it, gave up the contest, and broke into a genial
smile, which was reflected in ripples of silver all
over the lough.

CHAPTER VIII.

PIKE-FISHING.

"He headlong shoots beneath the dashing tide,
The trembling fins the boiling wave divide :
Now hope exalts the fisher's beating heart ;
Now, he turns pale, and fears his dubious art ;
He views the trembling fish with longing eyes,
While the line stretches with th' unwieldy prize."

HE *bonâ fide* angler knows no season but that prescribed by the laws of fence, and the pike-fisher is the hardy annual of sportsmen. When others lay themselves, like ships out of commission, high and dry in dock, he is on the alert. There is this to be said in his favour :—When on a dark gloomy November day he sallies forth to the slushy water meads he has nothing but his love of sport to sustain him. Enthusiastic adorers of the beauties of nature may venture upon stretching a point to unusual limits, but they would overstep the mark sadly if they sought to glorify or find anything to laud in the month of short days and foggy nights.

K

" Who loves not Autumn's joyous round,
When corn and wine and oil abound?
Yet who would choose, however gay,
A year of unrenewed decay? "

Who, indeed? Not the pike-fisher. Tourists
have come home like birds to their roosts; the
Michaelmas daisies, in their pale funereal lavender, have had their day; the chrysanthemums
have brilliantly brought up the rear of the year's
floral march, the first fire has been kindled at
home, and our lamps are trimmed for the winter
campaign. Most people have cast aside thoughts
of out-of-door delight, and settled down to ordinary pursuits till spring. But the pike-fisher
suffers no interruption in his favourite pastime;
rather, after Michaelmas he looks forward to four
or five months of prime sport.

He has, supposing he began in August, seen
the corn embrowned by the sun; has, standing
by the river-side while the pike is taking its time
in gorging the live bait, observed the reapers
thrust in their sickles, and the women and children gather up the sheaves; has, while trudging
through the lane that offers the shortest cut to the
station, been compelled to turn into a gateway to
give room for the passage of the harvest-home
wain, from which he has plucked half-a-dozen
ears of golden grain to bear away as a trophy;
has seen the walnut tree thrashed, and the orchard
grass glowing with pyramids of mellow fruit; has
noticed the bright patches of pale yellow in the
branches of the elm-tree, and the rapidly changing
hues of the chestnut—first signs of the coming
leaf-fall; has on the thatched roof in the villages
marked the assemblage of the swallow tribe,
marshalling day by day until the final flight

darkens the air; has, in the fields and hedgerows, observed the wild flowers reduced to a few stragglers fretting mournfully in the wind to follow the gaily-uniformed main army; has looked upon the quaker-like drab of the meads, the burning crimson of haw and hip, the bead-glimmering blackberry; has noted the rapid gradations of the bracken and fern from boldest green to faintest primrose; has admired the sturdy oak keeping up an appearance of russet vitality long after its compeers have succumbed, until with a few plucky withstandings of the blast itself gives in, shivering and heartbroken.

All these have been marshalled before his review, and he concludes that on the whole, though the autumn in its ripeness may be more enjoyable and beauteous than the uncertain spring and too hot-blooded summer, he would certainly not vote for a year of unrenewed decay; he knows that when the waterweeds begin to rot and drift away from their roots the fish move into deep water and are more amenable to piscatorial discipline than they were in the days when cover was plentiful.

Let us, therefore, court practical thought of the sport which yet remains when all else worth troubling about has been suspended. By November the last salmon and trout, to which we have aforetime borne good will and faithful testimony, have fully retired into winter quarters and winter occupations, and the best that remains for the angler are the fresh-water shark and the grayling. Roach, dace, and perch are in good, some think the very best of condition in the late autumn months, but bottom-fishing in the cold and damp, while a fair test of devotion and hardihood, will reign over a comparatively limited constituency, since there are—to adapt a simile from an old Puritan—hosts of fair-weather anglers as well as fair-weather Christians. Pike-fishing, therefore, stands first on the catalogue of winter opportunities.

Even that sportsman who sneers at humbler members of the craft, condescends occasionally to make advances to the pike, and many are the country-houses where a Brobdingnagian specimen is encased as proof of the prowess of the squire, the captain, or his lordship. In their condemnation of "Cockneys" the upper ten of the angling world do not include the wielder of trolling or spinning rod, though they may look askance at a bait-can. The pike, more even than salmon or trout, touches the fisherman nature, and makes us all kin. And this for several and obvious reasons.

The fish is the largest of the coarser denizens of our waters, and as such appeals to the sportsman who likes to kill something that cannot be whisked like a minnow over his shoulder; and there is always the possibility, although experience generally reduces the probability to a minimum, of a great prize to be remembered as long as one lives and handed down to posterity as a sacred heir-loom. The pike is, moreover, a heartless scoundrel who sticks at nothing. The laws relating to infanticide he regards not, and if some of the legends of our boyhood's books are truth, he is an ogre more atrocious than the late Fee-fi-fo-fum, who, we have been assured, drove a thriving trade in the bone-grinding business. He is the enemy of all other fish, and rests not until he has worried and pouched everything within his reach.

He is much more artful than some persons suppose him to be, and has to be captured with a considerable amount of guile, and if taken in a sportsmanlike manner (of which more presently) battles fairly for his life.

A ferocious fish of prey, he merits no mercy, for he gives none, and is of the class that is doomed to perish by the weapon by which it lives. He is furthermore abundant in most waters, especially in England, and the Government as yet have not protected him with licence. Finally, to stop short in an enumeration which might easily be extended, he is, numerous assertions notwithstanding, worthy of respect as an article of food. It might be urged that his appearance, his cruel eyes and sharkish jaws, are against him; but what would become of us, good reader, if we were each and all judged by our looks? Besides, I have said enough to prove how and why the pike should be every angler's game.

Think kindly of *Esox Lucius,* if only for the quaint stories—ay, and truly wonderful stories— to which he has from time immemorial given rise. It has been said that he is bred from weeds by the help of the sun's heat ; that men and maids have been attacked by him ; that he has lived through two generations ; that he flies at mules coming down to drink, and maintains a bull-dog grip until, dragged out, the animal's owner takes him off; that he has fought duels with otters for carp captured by the latter ; that he possesses a natural balsam or antidote against all poison; that a watch with a ribbon and two seals attached has been taken by an astonished cook out of his capacious maw ; that in a pool about nine yards deep, which had not been fished for ages, a pike was, amidst hundreds of spectators, drawn out by a rope fastened round his head and gills, which pike weighed *one hundred and seventy pounds,* and had previously pulled the clerk of the parish into the water ; that fox cubs and waterfowl have been received at one fell bolt into his ravenous gullet.

This and more also, is it not written in the chronicles of the craft ? And it is hard to say what is true and what false when the voracity of the pike is the question under consideration. Stories almost as marvellous as any of the above you may hear to the present day, vouched for as true by modern anglers. At the first blush you laugh to scorn the narration which gives the weight of a pike at 170 lb.—a pretty sensational return as things go ; but judging from the rate of growth, constitution, and general character, there is no reason for drawing the hard and fast line at say forty pounds. I have perfect faith in the oft-repeated assurance that in Holland, Germany, and Ireland fish up to sixty pounds may be—of course as exceptional examples—met with. Still, if the pike-fisher can *average* captives of eight pounds he has no reason to complain, and from what I have seen during the last year or two I suspect there are far too many anglers who are not ashamed to take and exhibit jack amongst which a miserable two-pounder is the premier sample.

Not the least source of pleasure to the pike-fisher is the opportunities which now and then fall in his way of visiting the parks of English landowners where the waters are strictly pre-served. Such water usually takes the form of ornamental lakes, placed where it shall add new charm to the tall ancestral trees of the fair estate. I have in my mind's eye at the present moment one of these sheets of water where the abounding sport is not less enjoyable than the beautiful scenery and interesting historical associations. On one side the trees not only grow by the water-side, but hang over the lake in dense foliage always mirrored in the surface, and always lending new colour to it. Opposite stands an ancient rookery, from which, before the tender May leaves have become too fully developed, many a young cawer is tumbled out by a party of sportsmen, mostly farmers and tradesmen from the nearest town, who are permitted on two given days every year to hold a rook-shooting festival. A little to the rear of a level bright-green lawn, smooth as a billiard-table (when newly mown by the noisy machine), half-hidden by hoary-trunked beeches, stand the ruins of a castle that was in its heyday in Queen Elizabeth's time, and whose remains are now picturesque and covered by luxuriant ivy. Owls dwell there, bats in the summer time wheel in and out of the dusky remnants of goodly arches.

Pull your boat into the middle of the lake, and look away to the south-east. Look beyond the home park as soon as you have ceased to admire that peerless herd of Channel Islands cattle, whose representatives have worn red, blue, and yellow ribbons at famous agricultural shows. They *are* cattle, although you may be deceived by their sleek beauty into believing them to be deer. The deer are the specks that dot the green slope beyond the moat and fence which keep them to their own haunts, and on the crest, crowned by forest trees of every kind, is the spot I wish you to observe. This is where Oliver Cromwell is said to have surveyed the ground and planned his

attack ; and not far from yonder boat-house is a
bit of broken ground where he planted his rude
cannon and pounded away with partial success
upon the castle.   For a mile the lake thus extends
amidst the scenery characteristic of English country
life, scenery which cannot be matched in the wide
world,—the scenery of an English gentleman's
hereditary estate.

I linger over this scene because it is typical of
hundreds of similar pictures scattered over our
lovely English shires with such variations as
history and locality enforce ; and in each there
will be some fascinating link with the past, some
special charm, artificial or natural, to assert itself.
Nor do I forget that in and out of yonder alleys
two centuries ago there walked a great hero
musing upon the strange adventures of his life and
the temporary cloud which hung over his brilliant
prospects.   Probably we have been walking over
the precise spot where Raleigh sat and wrote, and
capturing the lineal descendants of the fish upon
which he commented in the following :—

> " Here are no false entrapping baits
> Too hasty for too hasty fates,
>   Unless it be
>   The fond credulity
> Of silly fish, the worldlings who still look
> Upon the bait, but never on the hook."

Were I owner of such a fair piece of water as
we find in every English park, or proprietor of a
fishery to which anglers were admitted on pay-
ment, each recipient of permission to fish, friend
or stranger, should be bound strictly to certain
rules : for example, there should be no pike-fishing
till the 1st of September; all fish under three pounds
should be returned to their native element ; and

very positively no gorge hooks, for either live or
dead bait, should under any circumstance be
allowed. This last, I am aware, would appear to
be a severe rule, but it would apply to every one
alike and would be absolutely necessary if the
smaller fish are to be returned to the water.
Snap-fishing is the fairest and most sportsmanlike
way of capturing pike ; and though it would be
too much to say that it is the only method a real
sportsman would adopt, it is certainly the artistic
thing to do.

It may appear strange after this—but what is
there in this inconsistent world more inconsistent
than human nature ?—to sing the praises of trolling
with the dead gorge, and to confess that in eight
expeditions out of a dozen it is the mode to which
I used to give preference. In this I am dealing
only with rivers governed by no such rules as the
above. If the gorge hook were prohibited no one
would more cheerfully adhere to the regulations
than myself, but where the majority of anglers use
it in one of its two possible forms, it would be an
unnecessary self-denial to place oneself at a disadvantage with one's fellows. It can scarcely be
gainsaid that trolling is the pleasantest if not surest
winter form of pike-fishing. It is pleasantest because it offers the advantage of perpetual motion
with the minimum of toil ; it is surest when you
cover all ground and go to the fish instead of
leaving the fish to come to you.

Many experienced men maintain that more fish
are taken by spinning ; on the whole, however,
and taking one day with another, this I have not
found to be the case. There are times when the
fish lie close and lazy in holes and nooks where
the spinning flight passes above them, or at too

great a distance to tempt them, in their then state of mind, from their shelter.

The dead fish dropped carefully, and worked in an artistically up and down movement, to their own level and immediately before them, leaves no time for reflection. Their sharklike instincts prompt an instantaneous dart, and the murderous jaws snap in a moment across the middle of the bait. True, after being retained and run hither and thither, you may be mortified to find your free gift rejected and returned to your hands mangled, but you have had the excitement of the "run," which is not the less exciting because it is succeeded by the blank of disappointment. You may, and you naturally do, condemn yourself into thinking that, had you been spinning, the fish would have been all the same yours ; why not, in the absence of proof to the contrary, console yourself with the reflection that he lay *perdu* between two banks of weeds either of which would have caught your triangles, to your loss of time and perhaps property ?

There is in one sense more variety in the old-fashioned art of trolling than in the modern science of spinning. To spin at all successfully you must keep up a certain uniform speed, and where there are weeds (the normal condition of pike waters) you cannot work very near the bottom. The troller has therefore more to study, and must regulate the rate at which he moves his bait by the colour of the water, the strength of the current, and the force of the wind. He may pause now and then to look about him, and dawdle in his employment. The spinner must slacken not, neither must his eyes wander long. Take a couple of men who have been pursuing the different methods during the day, and examine the right hand forefinger of each, and it will be strange if the spinner cannot produce certain red, raw diagonal stripes as witnesses to the truth of my argument.

Sometimes you will find it necessary to let the bait at every cast touch and for a moment rest upon the bottom, at others you may impart to it a half spinning action. Trollers often make the mistake of working with too much haste, and others fall into the opposite extreme. The middle course here, as in most human affairs, pays best. Trolling has many of the advantages of fly-fishing. With your bag to your back and your gaff stuck into your girdle, you may move through the enemy's country unencumbered with baggage, free to come and go, to keep on or to halt, as inclination may suggest and occasion require. Booted to the thigh in trolling equipment, with nothing more than your trace hook, bait box, bag, and waterproofs over the shoulder, there is nothing after fly-fishing so pleasure-giving as to wander by the side of a river with a light trolling rod in your hand.

In some parts of the Midland district the anglers use a singular rod of not more than nine feet long for trolling. It is quite stiff, but the owners can throw an immense distance and quite accurately with it. The chief objection to this weapon is that it is useful for nothing else except fishing with the gorge.

And how conveniently that little interval when the "run" is under weigh comes in ! The angler never fills his pipe so proudly, so serenely, so full of hope and determination as when, satisfying himself that the line is free in the rings, and the

winch handle clear of twigs, grass, and other
obstacles, he lays down the rod to allow the candidate for his gaff to pouch in undisturbed confidence.
If the run comes to nothing he does not give up in
despair.   Perhaps the points of the hook have not
been rank enough, perhaps too rank, perhaps the
lead has been felt and the fish rendered suspicious.
He therefore tries him a second time with a brighter
bait, and should he still refuse thinks no more of
the matter.

There are a few primary conditions which may
be insisted upon in pike-fishing at all times, and
more particularly as regards trolling.   The tail of
the bait should be closely tied and the protruding
spines cleanly cut off.   A slovenly angler loses
half the battle.   The veteran jack-fisher whose
pupil I was proud to be, and who has sworn by
trolling as against spinning for half a century with
unfailing success, would never fix loop to swivel
until the gills also were neatly tied under the
shanks of the hook, and certainly if the slight
amount of extra trouble this gives does little good,
it can do no harm.   But I have met with several
instances where, for want of this little nail, the
shoe has been lost.

Again, never treat the pike family as if they
were arrant fools.   We take it too much for
granted that anything will do for pike and perch.
Thus it is amazing to behold the clumsy gimp and
massive tackle used, fair weather and foul, by men
whom you would reasonably expect to have more
discretion.   In clouded water use anything that
comes uppermost, but under unfavourable circumstances as much care should be taken as with the
more wary tribes of fish.   Walk along close to the
edge of a pike water and see how at your approach

the fish rush away. Instead of assuming that the pike fears and cares for nothing, act always as if he were as shy as a carp, and you lose nothing, while the certainty is that you will be a frequent gainer.

To keep as far from the water as possible, at first at any rate, is a precaution I would recommend to every one. Begin with a cast that is really no cast at all; that is to say, noiselessly drop—not throw—the bait as near the bank as you can, then begin to cast in successive lengths at will. The man who thus approaches water which has been unapproached on the same day stands an excellent chance of making acquaintance with the prowlers who lie under the overhanging banks. More pike in an ordinarily deep river are taken in this way within six feet of the shore than further afield.

Then as to gorging. Very whimsical are the notions prevailing on this head. I know of many persons who literally take out their watches at the first signal of a run, and be the movement of a fish what it may, strike home as soon as ten minutes have elapsed. A very old young gentleman I could name gives precisely fifteen minutes' grace. Now, it is indisputable that if the fish has gorged there is no danger of losing him, but at the same time I would submit that this waste of time in a short winter's day is quite unnecessary if the habits of the creature be sufficiently studied. It is every pike-fisher's experience that quantities of fish are lost by striking too soon. Most experienced trollers I think will agree with me that if the gorging process be not complete in a quarter of an hour it will never be effected, since *Esox Lucius* is only making sport of you, instead of you

of him ; also that at times the fish are in no haste
to close the transaction.

Live baiting is a deadly operation sometimes,
and an exciting one if the bait is affixed to snap-
tackle.   On lakes, or broad rivers where a thirty
yard cast is desirable, it requires not a little skill
to haul in the line until you have the requisite
tautness for striking, because striking at these
times must be sharp.   This style of fishing in a
narrow river abounding with deep holes which
can be brought nearly under the point of the rod
gives wonderfully good sport, and is figuratively
as well as literally above board.   Dace for live
baiting, as for spinning and trolling, are immea-
surably beyond roach, gudgeon, or trout as baits,
and next to dace a large gudgeon will be found
most lively and hardy.

The use of the live gorge hook threddled under
the skin suits the idle man, or the unskilful, to the
letter.   Open confession compels me to admit that
I often fall back upon it, but never without the
guilty feeling that after all it is next door to
poaching, and that I am for the time a mere
trimmer-fisherman.   No pot-hunter should be, or
ever is, without it.   There is small skill connected
with a process where the fish does all the work.
It has not the excuse of trolling, in which the
chief art is how to find your fish.   The live bait
wriggles and swims, the jack comes from near or
far, and, after inspection, takes it.   After the
lapse of the usual time you haul in and lift him
into the boat.   Compare his feeble attempts to
escape with the play given by a fish hooked only
in his horny, prickly mouth.   There is no com-
parison, and when you hear men lamenting that
in this sort of live baiting they have been " broken

away "—that is the regulation phrase—you need not be perplexed if you are somewhat unable to estimate their skill as anglers.

Assuming that every pike-fisher deserving the name subjects his line, traces, swivels, and hooks to a smart testing strain before he begins, and that they are of ordinary strength, it is difficult to conceive how a pike with a couple of hooks deep in his gullet tearing at his vitals can, with ordinary patience, break violently away. Grant the fellow time, and he may be turned up like a log.

Once more let me confess to preaching what I do not always practise. On one Allhallows Day I had the opportunity of fishing a small lake under the Chiltern Hills. There had been a remarkably sharp frost for that time of the year, and there was, over the narrow mouth of the reservoir, ice a third of an inch thick, which took full half an hour to cut through with a punt. The morning was a simple blank. Dace on the best spinning flights to be procured were useless. Artificial gudgeon and minnows, and spoon bait, were tried, and there was not a sign of success. The luncheon hour found us weary and despairing : a live roach was then tried with the usual gorge hook, whose gimp was passed from the shoulder under the side skin, out of the back not far from the tail. Before the cold meat was fairly removed from the napkin, the float went off like an arrow, and this proved a keynote to which a rattling tune was played for the rest of the day.

Not only was the afternoon's sport good, but the surroundings were themselves most delightful. The keeper was out with his dogs and punt seeking wild ducks, and as the birds took a good deal of shooting, and the fowler did not stop until he

had four couples, besides two or three coots, there
was plenty to look at between the disappearances
of the great crimson float. Another source of
observation was the effect of the frost upon the
trees.

> " It shook the sere leaves from the wood
>   As if a storm passed by."

The wind was a mere breath, and that at fitful
intervals, but whenever the breath came, like a
passing sigh, the rustling of the leaves which had
been stricken by the frost, and the tremor and
haste of their flight to the ground, were most
curious to behold. In the morning the bit of
lawn between the keeper's house and the landing
steps was bare : in the evening it was ankle deep
in the dark brown dead leaves shed by the horse-
chestnut trees. Of my "take" I will only say
that a new rush basket had to be purchased to
convey it to town, and that some unknown friend
thought it worth a paragraph in the columns of a
certain sporting journal. During the day, at
another end of the lake, a party of merry gentlemen had been laughing and shouting and singing,
so much so that it never occurred to me that they
could be prospering much with their rods. They
had scarcely moved from one spot, but they came
in at dusk with seventy pounds of fish between
them.

Spinning demands, last, but as I have already
suggested, not least, some notice. Many high-
class anglers disdain to fish for pike in any other
way. There are several kinds of flights recommended as superior to all others, but so long as
the bait spins, and there is something dangerous
at its vent—there or thereabouts—it does not

signify much. A large strong triangle at the end of a short length of gimp, passed into the vent and out of the mouth of the bait, is used at all times by various friends of my own, who declare it surpasses every invention that has been devised. Others give the palm to a succession of the most terrible triangles; others use nothing but artificial baits. There are inventions by Francis, Pennell, Chapman, Wood, Marston, and Otter, and I know not how many others, and they are all good, and all worth a trial.

The pike-fisher's box should contain two or three flights for natural bait, a spoon, a large phantom minnow, and a medium-sized artificial dace; having these he need not remain at home because the live-bait can has returned empty from the tackle-shop. Spinning from boat or bank does not require the extreme length of line supposed by some to be necessary, and young beginners may to an erroneous conception of what is here essential trace the inextricable tangles which act so prejudicially against the temper, and which send their bait round about their ears instead of twenty yards off as they had fondly hoped.

Let it never be forgotten that a short line cleanly cast, and a bait splashing little, and spun back well under hand, are more effective a hundred times than a sensational hurl into space; also that to clear your way as you go, and render yourself able to stand close to the edge of the water, a preliminary cast right and left about a yard from and parallel with the bank should be essayed. Where rushes fringe the river this precaution should never be omitted. Time and practice alone make a good spinner, and there are veteran anglers who, chiefs at trolling, are in the last rank as spinners. On the other hand, a masterful spinner is more likely to be an effective troller.

Spinning may not be the pleasantest or surest, but there can be no hesitation in pronouncing it the most artistic method of pike-fishing. But there is spinning and spinning, and many men delude themselves into the fancy that their clumsy splatter-dashing is the correct thing. The best spinner is he who, like Caleb Plummer, goes as near to nature as possible. Spinning with the artificial contrivance makes you independent of the bait nuisance. Procuring bait, dead or alive, is, as many of my readers will ruefully admit, frequently a more formidable undertaking than getting the pike, and to travel a distance either in train or dogcart, on foot or on horseback, with a can full of splashing fish that will give up the ghost unless the water be continually changed, is a penalty and not a pleasure.

The various spoonbaits, phantom fish, shadowy fancies, and well made imitations of a more substantial nature, are so numerous and cheap, and answer the main purpose of sport so well, that the spinner may laugh at contingencies which give infinite trouble to trollers and live baiters. The fish angled for—which, after all, is not a totally disinterested party—has a better chance also, and the fisherman having arrested his prisoner is able to exercise a very summary jurisdiction upon him. However, on the question of pike-fishing, opinions will always differ, and pike-fishers, touching the respective methods which this sketch has suggested, will, let me hope, agree to differ and object, if it shall so please them, with that urbanity and gentleness of spirit which from the beginning has characterized their fraternity.

A serio-comic incident which occurred to me once upon a time while spinning I cannot forbear recounting. Hearing that in the small reservoirs attached to some print works near Manchester there were pike, I soon procured the manufacturer's permission, and started off from the metropolis of cotton-dom with nothing but an artificial trout as bait. It had never been remarkable for its perfection, and after long use had become battered out of shape and colour. All the reservoirs but one were carefully spun over with the unlikely machine to no purpose. In the last a fish beyond doubt struck at it four times in succession, and mightily puzzled was I that nothing more productive had resulted.

An inspection, however, showed that the loose triangles over the shoulder had not a sharp point between them, and it became necessary with a bit of thread, and in a very rough - and - ready manner, to substitute for them a more prickly set of hooks. At the next spin I hooked my gentleman—a long, gaunt, wretchedly-coloured fish, with a body as thin as a hake's. Not another "touch" was received during the remainder of the afternoon, and I departed with my famine-stricken wretch in the basket.

Three months later at a junction railway station in Lancashire I fell into conversation with a homeward bound party of artisan anglers whose rods and baskets I considered sufficient warrant for self-introduction. By-and-by I told the story of the starved pike, starved as I was now able to say, for I had dissected him to discover the cause of his preternatural lankiness.　A middle-aged man broke forth into lamentation—

"Eh! mon, and wur it thee that tuk it?　Aw looved yon fish gradely, that aw did."

To the end of my days I may not forget the pathetic melancholy of that man's tone and countenance.　After he had mourned in silence awhile I brought him round—by the aid of the refreshment counter—and the murder came out.　In one of his fishing trips at holiday time he had captured a pikelet while angling for roach, had brought it home, deposited it in the "lodge," and fed it tenderly.　The pike throve, and, according to his narrative, some intimacy sprang up between them; he saddened as he remembered how the fish would come to the side to be fed, and firmly believed that it knew as well as he did when the Easter and Whitsuntide holidays, and a consequent glut of gudgeon and minnows, drew near.　By-and-by the man lost employment, and in his absence his wife, who had always personally disliked "t' varmint," left it to its own resources.

During that unlucky interval my ruthless and fatal hand robbed the reservoir of its one inhabitant, and that inhabitant of its miserable life.　The scant comfort left to Tim Bobbin was that the dark uncertainty as to its fate had been removed from his mind by my casual appearance on the junction platform.

NOTE.—When this chapter was written, the largest modern pike of which we had authentic account was the 35 lb. fish netted from Rapley Lake.　At the Fisheries Exhibition there were, however, larger specimens taken in angling by Mr. A. G. Jardine, one of our most famous pike fishermen.　To my request for particulars of his principal captures, that gentleman has kindly supplied me, for the purposes of this edition, with the following memoranda :—

"January 24th, 1877, was a windy day ; in fact, it was blowing a gale. Fishing a lake of fifty acres near Rochester I had already caught several pike by spinning, when I put a large dace of 8 or 9 oz. on live snap-tackle, and casting out into fifteen feet of water, tried the profundities of the lake. In a few minutes my invitation to lunch was accepted by a large fish which gave me most exciting sport for the space of twenty minutes or half an hour. It frequently took sixty or eighty yards of line off the reel in its efforts to escape. When gaffed and in the boat it gave me much trouble by lashing and floundering about, upsetting my tackle-case and live-bait can. A lively morris-dance of the smaller fish took place around the large one before I could get it securely placed in my fish sack. It was a female of handsome shape and fine condition, and weighed 36 lbs., was 46 inches in length and 25 inches in girth. Frank Buckland made two casts of it. One is in his museum at South Kensington, the other H. L. Rolfe painted for me. This and the taxidermal specimen I exhibited at the Fisheries and the Fish-cultural department of the Health Exhibition, with others of large size. In addition to the above-mentioned 36 lb. pike, my catch included twenty-eight others, of which I kept seventeen, weighing together 83 lbs.; also some perch, from 2 lbs. to 3 lbs. each.

"On another stormy day, November 11th, 1879—large pike are always on the move, and feed best in a gale—I had permission to fish a lovely sheet of water of about fifteen acres, in one of the home counties. After being in a small punt in the centre of the lake for some time, and the gale increasing to such an extent that I was shipping water, I hauled up anchor, and made for the lee-side of an island where, in ten feet of water, I suspected I should discover the cruising ground of a monster pike which I had seen smash up the rod and tackle of a friend who was fishing there with me on the 4th of March of that year. I tried with a ¾ lb. roach on snap-tackle, fishing deep in an open space between the weeds. The tempting morsel induced this aldermanic pike to take a bite, when it met with the surprise of a triangle in its jaw. In the first mad rushes the fish ran out nearly all my hundred yards of line, and leaped some feet out of water. Its size and strength showed me that I had formed an attachment of a most delicate nature. My Nottingham line was fine but new, and my trace of salmon-gut. Moreover, I could not follow the fish, for the punt was anchored, and I had no assistance, the keeper having gone to feed his pheasants. But upon his return I had gaffed, and had her pikeship (for this too was a female) safe in my punt. It measured 47 inches, was 25 inches girth, and weighed 37 lbs.

"February 24th, 1882, was very boisterous, and just the right sort of a day for successful pike-ing. I was fishing in Sussex, and had capital general sport. The rule was to return fish less than 4 lbs. weight to the water. My largest pike weighed 30½ lbs., was 44 inches long, and 24 in girth. It took a *very* small dace on paternoster, and consequently on that kind of tackle—single hook on gut trace gave splendid sport before it was sufficiently mastered to be gaffed. It was one of the best pike for shape and beauty I have ever caught, and one of the handsomest specimens at the Fisheries Exhibition. In addition, I kept fifteen other pike, weighing together 89 lbs.

"January 22nd and 23rd, 1884, were favourable for pike-angling—plenty of wind, and just enough frost to make fish keen for food. Fishing on those days with a friend in the West of England, our catch consisted of fifty-three pike. My companion's best was a fine fish of 18¾ lbs., and he lost one much larger while I was playing from the same boat, at the same time, another which must have weighed over 20 lbs. I also caught four others, the largest one of 23 lbs., and the united weight of these six fish turned the scale at 120 lbs. Four of the largest were preserved by Sanders (who has stuffed all my specimens), and exhibited at the Health Exhibition.

"Query? How is it that all the largest pike are females? In January and February, when pike have paired previous to spawning, on catching a large female, say of 20 lbs., and "going for" her mate and catching him, I have generally found him to be about 12 lbs. Indeed, I have never known a large male but once, and that came from Lord Normanton's water, and weighed 28 lbs. He was a very handsome fish.—A. G. J."

I once saw half-a-dozen pike, the largest 13½ lbs., which had been taken by Mr. Jardine in the Thames, during a pea-soup flood. The peculiarity of the sport was that the fish were caught by ledgering, with live dace for bait. The angler had moored his punt for luncheon over a rush-fringed eddy, into which the pike had, no doubt, shunted out of the current. He probably took every fish of that flood-bound company.—W. S.

· CHAPTER IX.

FRESH AND SALT.

"Night came, and now eight bells had rung,
 While careless sailors, ever cheery,
On the mid-watch so jovial sung,
 With tempers labour cannot weary."

THE great advantage of sojourning near
the sea-shore is that if fresh water fails,
you have plenty of salt close at hand.
Fresh-water fish may, and too frequently do, take offence at adverse winds, and
lose their tempers and become sullen because of a
little clouded water ; your salt-water denizens, on
the contrary, are above (*below* perhaps I ought to
say) such trifling considerations as atmospheric
changes and an odd storm or two in the upper air.

The Norfolk Broads when they do yield sport
do so in no stinted measure ; they bless you in
basket and store. But they are uncertain as the
idle wind which you respect not. The rivers
Waveney and Yare contain roach, rudd, eels, and
pike, with cartloads of bream in the summer,
but they, too, are unusually capricious in their
behaviour.

After some days of paltry sport, do not blame

me if I tire of the district and everything associated
with it.   I have had a turn at three of the fourteen
Broads a few miles inland from the Norfolk coast;
have pulled through the watery lanes bounded by
walls of bulrush and sedge, and tried my hardest
under the blazing sun in the open water; have
fumed and fretted, and have been only comforted
with the reflection that the liggering parties [1]
whom I had seen drinking bottled beer, and
singing songs on the water, had not caught a fish
between a score of them.   Perhaps if I had gone
to Buckenham or Cantley it might have turned
out differently, for on my return to town a friend
compared notes with me, and I learned that on
these very days he caught four pounds short of a
hundredweight of roach at the former place, where
the tide flows faintly and where the fish happened
to be on the feed.

   "Patience that lasts three days," think I, looking out at eventide upon Yarmouth market-place,
"has a right to get rusty at last ; and to-morrow,
behold! I pack up my effects and flee on the
wings of the morning."

   Then it was that there flashed into my despondent mind the grand discovery recorded in the
first sentence of this chapter; then it was I started
forthwith to Gorleston to hold conference with a
good motherly matron who owned a good fatherly
husband, who, in his turn, owned a good weatherly
fishing vessel ; and thus it was that I spent a night
with the Herring Fleet, to give the salt water an
opportunity of courteously recompensing me for
the deceptions and coquetry of the rivers and
Broads.

   [1] Liggering has been, fortunately, prohibited on the
Norfolk and Suffolk district.

" You'll find it rough accommodation on board the *Seabird*, sir, but we'll make you as comfortable as we can," I am told next morning on appearing alongside, according to arrangement.

And what more can I expect ? Beggars, says the proverb, are not precisely in the position of choosers, and I have begged from the owner of the *Seabird* the privilege of a passage during one of her herring-fishing excursions. The worthy owner was once sailor boy, sailor man, and skipper himself, and he is too close a stickler for the proprieties to grant the cheerful consent which trembles on his lips until he has obtained the ratifying approval of the *Seabird's* commander. It is not every shipmaster who will be pestered with a useless landlubber on his busy deck. But the captain of the *Seabird* with a broad smile speaks his welcome, and superadds the warning couched in the above remark.

The herring season is in full swing, for the middle of October has arrived, and in the bountifully furnished market-place, which visitors to Yarmouth will well remember, the poulterer's stalls are laden with Michaelmas geese. Huge baskets of ripe blackberries are also exposed for sale, and pyramids of delicious outdoor grapes add their testimony to the lateness of the season. Should other witnesses be required, you may find them on the bits of cardboard in the lodging-house windows announcing empty apartments, and a consequent scarcity of visitors. When these signs and tokens appear, you may be sure the herring season is in full swing. While the undoubted summer lasts, Yarmouth is one of the most popular resorts of middle-class London, but about the period when "the hunter's moon" begins, the visitors smell the east wind and take flight. Then, about the second week in September, the herring boats are ready for the great harvest of the sea, which is expected to last till the end of November.

The *Seabird*, therefore, has already seen a month's active service. There she lies in the turbid tidal river which gives Yarmouth its name, resting awhile that her crew may enjoy a few hours' respite. Yesterday she came in with a cargo of fish ; to-day she is moored idle in the bend of the river, within gunshot of Gorleston Pier ; to-morrow she will again spread her wings of dusky canvas and make sail for the fishing-ground in yonder offing. Her little flag—a white square on a ground of scarlet—flutters jauntily on the mizen-truck. The aft companionway, the hold, and the forecastle, are fastened down with padlock, and no careful watch patrols the black, solidly-patched, service-worn deck. Truly the skipper indulges in no mere affectation when he suggests that the *Seabird* is not exactly a floating palace.

To-morrow comes with the brightest of sunshine and the most musical of Sabbath bells. The crew arrive in twos and threes, swinging themselves down upon the damp decks, and if one or two lads seem to be suffering from that common malady in these parts—a Saturday night on shore—there is, let it be charitably said, little wonder. For three weeks until yesterday the *Seabird* was hard at work outside of the harbour, and it would be expecting too much from human nature, especially human nature in a sailor's guernsey, to demand that the strapping young able-bodied fellows, who are as yet not half awake, should not make the most of their very brief holiday after the manner of their kind.

At length here we are on board—skipper, mate, cook, crew, and cabin-boy, eleven souls, with a stranger on what we may term the quarterdeck to make the complement a dozen, all told. The Hams and Peggottys of the village lounging on the quay above our heads make facetious remarks to the *Seabird's* crew touching their " first-class passenger," who somehow manages to survive these trials, and keeps close to the skipper at the helm, while the crew, with a lusty " Heave-ho!" chorus, warp the *Seabird* out, and run up the big mainsail and jib.

Favoured by wind and tide the *Seabird*, in a few minutes, has ploughed through the yellow flood past Gorleston pier-head and is cleaving blue water, crushing, as it were, millions of diamonds out of her sun-gilded track as she goes. The church bells make fainter and fainter melody, the low shore land becomes lower, the people and buildings on the beach dwindle, dwarf, and fade. It is an old-fashioned iron handle which the skipper at the helm grasps, and this suggests inspection, which reveals that the *Seabird* herself, if not old-fashioned, may without defamation of character be described as a homely sort of craft. The Yarmouth herring fleet may have more comely vessels, but not many of heavier tonnage than the *Seabird*. She was once a smack, but has been latterly converted into a " Dandy," that is to say a yawl-rigged concern of some five-and-twenty tons. As a rule the Yarmouth herring boats are lugger rigged, and the largest are not more than five-and-thirty tons.

It is a day of peace on land, but these east coast toilers of the sea, I soon discover, are wroth with a keen grievance. What is uppermost in the mind will speedily be proclaimed by the tongue, and the sight of a small half-decked fishing boat, of not a third our size, inflames the more inflammable of our men. The grievance is, broadly stated, the presence of Scotch fishermen in Yarmouth and Lowestoft waters, and very bitter are the feelings of the English on the point. This is a Scotch boat making for land, and as she passes us within half a cable's length, our young men discharge a broadside of jeers and taunts at her handful of men.

"Pretty fellows these Scots to brag that they never profane the Sabbath by handling rope on that day, and yet to be skulking about like this," shouts one.

"They can live upon barley-meal without a morsel of meat from week-end to week-end, can these miserable Sawnies," cries another. The cabin-boy facetiously rubs himself against the capstan-head and blesses the Duke of Argyle ; the cook—unkindest cut of all—flourishes aloft the leg of pork he is preparing in the caboose. To these demonstrations of derision the Scots answer never a word, but keep on their way to the river's mouth.

Our skipper is a fair-complexioned man. You often meet with this blonde type of men and women on the Yarmouth coast, inclining you to lend a serious ear to the disputed tradition which teaches that Cerdic the warrior, or some other antique Saxon, settled here and planted a race with hair as yellow as the sands upon which they landed. Our skipper is a Saxon in every feature, and he stands beside the helm ; but, unlike the gentleman who occupied the same position on board the schooner *Hesperus,* his mouth is pipeless, smoking being unentered upon his list of small vices. He goodhumouredly listens to his subjects as they growl about the Scotchmen, smiles, I fear approvingly, and with a cheery hail gives the order —

"Now, my lads, bend nets. Look alive, bo'!"

The latter adjuration is for the cabin boy, who is dreamily employed in washing a tub full of potatoes for the mid-day meal, and whose occasional glances towards the dim line of coast the watchful skipper has noticed. The "Bo'," a pale-faced, silent youth, who confides to me that he doesn't like the sea, grins in a melancholy manner, and looks alive as directed.

Bending the nets is an initiatory operation which must not be omitted. The bulk of the nets are neatly stowed away in the hold, but here lies a pile of recently repaired articles that must be tied together with strong twine. The patriarch of the crew, acting as storekeeper, assists the mate in cutting the fastenings into requisite lengths, another man passes them on to the tyers, and another clears away the work when it is done. Thus early the orderly method by which alone herring fishing can be prosecuted becomes apparent, and everything forthwith goes on with a precision and discipline which, from the rude appointments of the boat and rough-and-ready manner of the crew, you would not have considered probable.

Away on the starboard bow some one descries an object in the water—a cask, perhaps, or a chest. Our world, you must observe, is very limited in its area, and it is astonishing what importance trifles assume in it. We become quite excited as our skipper luffs up and steers for the prize, while all rush to the windward bulwarks and lean over the rail with undisguised interest. It is only a small rough box, but it is fished carefully up, and for the space of half an hour all the probabilities which human ingenuity could suggest as to the origin and history of this bit of woodwork are advanced. Talk about an "exhaustive debate," you should have heard the crew of the *Seabird* before they had dismissed this six-pennyworth of white deal from their hands and minds.

About the hour when the people on shore are walking home from their churches and chapels the *Seabird* has reached the fishing ground, and has taken her station as one of a very numerous family. The sun has become obscured, the sea rises with the wind, and the skipper prophecies "a breeze." To the crew this is a matter of positive indifference. They must remain here until a certain quantity of herrings are in the hold—it may be one day, it may be three—but the weather is a consideration which never troubles them. Since the sun was beclouded we can see nothing of land, but ships of all sizes are continually passing, proceeding up or down with an adverse wind.

The *Seabird*, it appears, will drive with the tide all night, and I make apparently careless, but really anxious, inquiries with the view of ascertaining what the chances are of being "collided." Are herring boats ever run down? Oh, yes, run down sometimes. A lugger, for example, was cut in two last year—no, the year before—and seven out of eight men went to "the locker." This is the way in which death by drowning is spoken of—very familiar, it struck me, as well as slightly disrespectful to the Davy Jones commonly associated with the metaphor.

The person who was facetiously described by
the shorelings as the "first-class passenger" soon
makes a disagreeable discovery. Deeming himself a very good sailor, he has gone to some
trouble to enter upon this expedition ; solely in
expectation, however, of being perpetually under
sail. Movement is life. Movement on the sea,
so long as it is decidedly progressive, is life in a
not unpleasant form. Now I hear the order given
to take in sail, and am informed that for the next
twelve or eighteen hours the *Seabird* will drift
with the flood—perhaps a dozen miles north and
then a dozen miles back again : but always and
entirely at the mercy of the waves.

Verily circumstances alter cases. The billows
which, while we were careering seawards with a
stiff breeze on the beam, dashed over the bows,
were welcome and delicious to the *Seabird ;* and
to the passenger who, having nothing else to do,
was able to enjoy the motion. To be tossed like
a balk of timber on the said billows, and yet be
like the caged squirrel whose perpetual wanderings never raise him an inch higher, is a vastly
different thing. Yet this is the prospect ; and I
find it out, when too late, that the trawler, and not
the herring boat, should have been the object of
my wooing. However, there is no help for it ;
out here there is no shore boat to hail.

The small sails are taken in, and the topmast
struck. The mainsail follows, and, as if to remove
all hope, the mainmast is lowered backwards, as
the river steamers lower their funnels when passing under a bridge. The spar drops into a crutch
upheld by a stout piece of timber about twelve
feet long, fitted into the deck, somewhere about
the centre of the vessel. Brought for the moment

broadside to the waves, the *Seabird* wallows and rolls furiously and helplessly, until she is, by the small sail on the mizenmast, brought up to the wind. The rolling then ceases, but there supervenes a very lively game of pitch and toss, which threatens to become livelier as time wears on. This, then, is to be our condition for the night; and the only comfort we can snatch is that there are fully half a hundred boats in similar plight within ken, looking for all the world like disabled craft whose spars had been carried away in a hurricane. The *Seabird* is now technically "driving;" the movement, if any, being astern.

Mugs of hot tea, solid ship's biscuit, and, when called for by an epicurean member of the crew, a herring fried very brown to cover it, having been handed round, the word is given to "shoot nets." Every member of the crew but the cook and cabin boy engages in this work, which requires care and occupies considerable time. The dark brown nets lie stowed away in the hold, and the first work is to bring them to light.

It will simplify the description to explain at once that the drift net is nothing more than a wall of netting extending from the bows of the boat to a distance of about two miles, sunk by means of a cable nine or ten yards deep, and kept near the surface by small kegs called "bowls" and by a plentiful employment of large corks along the upper part of the net. The herrings swim in shoals, run their unsuspecting heads into the net wall, and become entangled in the meshes. This, however, is anticipating. The nets, or to be strictly accurate, the series of nets, tied together in an unbroken length as before explained, are not yet shot.

The skipper and three "hands" receive the nets, which glide freely over a roller from the hold ; a lad takes up the "seizing," a short length of rope attached to every thirty yards of net, and walks with it to the bows, delivering it to a man who is paying out the stout cable, which, in addition to its function of keeping the bottom line of the nets fairly sunk, sustains the frail fabric as a connected whole. Sometimes vessels passing across the line of nets tear them asunder, and but for the cable the dissevered portion—perhaps a mile in length—would be destroyed. A trusty man is therefore placed in the bows to affix the seizing to the cable with thoroughness.

As the *Seabird* drives astern and the shooting proceeds the bowls ride ahead of us like huge black floats, growing smaller and smaller until they are mere spots on the wave. Already, before the nets are fully shot, three brigs, a French fishing smack, and a barque reaching over towards land, pass across our line, doing more or less damage, one may be sure. The process of shooting keeps all hands in action for a couple of hours, and then, sitting as best they may on deck, with a service that gives little trouble, and appetites that require no caviare, the men dine. Potatoes (such red kidneys the mate, who had grown them in his garden, swears never were before) cooked in their jackets, a grand leg of pork boiled to a turn, pudding, *alias* "duff," biscuit hard and wholesome, and a *petit verre* of highly perfumed Jamaica rum, constitute the sole bill of fare. Each man is his own carver, waiter, toastmaster, and speechmaker, and the music of the spheres leaves nothing to be desired in the way of orchestral accompaniment.

M

"Nightfall on the sea" is not a bad notion for a warm drawing-room, brightly lighted, and with the soft presence of women to give savour to the salt of home. I could in this paragraph draw a vivid portrait of a being who watches the footsteps of nightfall one after another upon the water on a Sunday evening about four-and-twenty miles east of Yarmouth, with a dismal sense of the falsity of poetical pictures of things pertaining to the maritime profession.

He sits shivering and ill at ease, overcome by qualms with which conscience has nothing to do ; a limp object on a sail behind the tiller handle, feebly noticing that the bow of the vessel is sometimes high in the air and the next moment down at the end of a slippery incline. Through his heavy head scraps of sea balladry are blown like flakes of foam by the blast. He vows never again to perpetuate the heresy contained in the fiction, "Rock'd in the cradle of the deep." He scoffs at the bard who found something to sing about in "the odour of brine from the ocean." He grins with ghastly expression when, noticing the lowered mainmast, the pretty words, "he climbs the mast to feast his eyes once more," are shaken uppermost. He is especially hurt to think that even the oblivion of actual sea-sickness is denied him. Such a sketch I might limn for the amusement of the callous ; but I forbear.

The herrings have not behaved as we had fondly hoped. At eight o'clock a few fathoms of our two miles of net wall are hauled in, just as the moon struggles out of a bank of clouds, but there it no encouragement to proceed further. Then the men disappear down the aperture of two feet square into the small dark closet around which their berths are hidden. The skipper, kind and thoughtful as a mother to his first-class passenger, insists upon offering him the use of his bunk, and spreads him a brand new Union Jack for blanket. On deck the two lights prescribed by law have been hoisted on the mizen-stay, and the watch has been set. The two lanterns are a signal to trawlers and passing vessels that the herring fishermen are out, and would prefer the gift of a wide berth, lest their nets should be broken. The sea seems alive with double warnings, and from some of the boats turpentine lights—yclept "flare ups"—are perpetually flashed.

Pitching and driving, you feel a queer sensation when a full-rigged ship, phantom-like, seems to be bearing down upon you, and somehow all the stories of collision you have heard, read, or written, crowd in procession through your mind, as you earnestly keep your eye on the approaching monster, resolving, should the worst come to the worst, to hoist yourself on board the destroyer by the bowsprit rigging. The monster passes half a mile ahead; but only think what might have happened.

The fisherman sailors sleep in their clothes, and are contented with their lot. Theirs is a co-operative system; they are paid by results. The more fish the more pay. Called up on deck at twelve, and again at two o'clock, they rub their eyes and go, and return again if they are not immediately wanted. At four o'clock, however, a genuine cry rings down into the darkness.

"Haul ho, boys! Haul ho!"

Now we turn out in earnest, for "Haul ho!" means herrings, and who knows but that it may mean herrings in such quantities that to-morrow, instead of pitching and driving tediously, we may be able to hurry to harbour? The men encase themselves from head to foot in oilskin, and in the cold starlight prepare to haul in their two miles of netting.

The cable, or warp as the men term it, is brought in by the capstan worked in the old-fashioned manner with bars. Some of the Boulogne boats have small steam-engines to do this work, which requires the incessant labour of four or five hands until the hauling is at an end. To the landlubber prone upon the flag of his country in the skipper's bunk, the tramp, tramp of the men on their ceaseless round is as the march of an army, and it is their preliminary circuits that have recalled him from an uneasy dreamland, and brought him into the keen morning air to watch his shipmates deal with the herring. Two men stand about six feet apart in the middle of the boat on the starboard side to haul the net upon deck. At the bow the sailor who was perched there in the afternoon is perched there again to unfasten the seizings he had then tied to the warp.

A man takes his post in the hold to stow away into the smallest compass, and in regular layers, the nets with bowls attached. The other men are "scudders," which, being interpreted, signifies that they seize the net as it is passed over the bulwarks, and by violently shaking it, jerk the fish out of the meshes. In a little while we are all speckled with scales, like harlequins, in silver mail; there are scales everywhere, high and low; scales in your beard and scales in your pocket— ay, in the tobacco-pouch in your pocket.

Thus the herrings are scudded on the deck for the space of five hours, and when the neighbourhood is too much cumbered with fish, they are shovelled into a separate part of the hold through holes formed for the purpose. The fish are mostly exhausted from their struggles to be released from the net, and many of them never move after they are shaken from the toils. Others, on the contrary, leap about the deck vigorously ; but it is soon over. The proverb "dead as a herring" seems to cast a reflection upon the vital powers of this little fish, and there is ground for it. Herrings speedily yield up the ghost when taken out of the water. They are most exquisitely tinted at first with a hue of faint rose-pink, but the mere contact of one herring with another is enough to strip it of its beautiful vesture.

The majority are caught by the gills ; a few, I notice, have thrust themselves more than a third of their length through the mesh, and they retain the impression of the cord in a girdle cut round the body, though it does not fracture the skin. The position of the bulk of the fish on one side of the net shows which way the shoal moved, and the common direction they took. A few now and then have been captured while swimming from an opposite quarter, waifs and strays probably. Here comes a cod caught somehow in the gills, and already drowned ; for him and his kindred a long-handled landing net is kept near. From first to last the nets bring up a dozen mackerel and half as many whiting.

The other boats near us are hauling in concert, and over the line of nets of a lugger that two days later, alas ! is doomed to founder in the tempest, whose vanguard gusts are sweeping the *Seabird's* decks, a horde of buccaneer fowl, gannets, gulls, and whatnot, are hovering, dragging the nets out of water, and robbing the fishermen of their hardly won spoil. The sun rises on the sails of many of the herring fleet homeward bound. Some of them have been driving out here for two or three days, and are returning with fewer fish than have fallen to our share in one night. It is still undecided whether the *Seabird* shall take flight or linger through another day and night. There is nothing to complain of in the "take," but every man and boy can remember when, in very exceptional hauls, ten times the quantity have been taken. Not this year, however. They all agree that the good old times have gone, and that the herrings are neither so numerous nor so prime as they used to be. Several boats are mentioned, while the herrings are being shaken out of the nets and the scales are discharged around in volleys, which have earned hundreds of pounds less than in the previous year.

After five hours of hard work the last bowl is seen tossing on the crest of the waves and disappearing in the troughs; the skipper takes the hatch from the well in which the fish are stored, pronounces the haul to be "a last"—nominally 10,000, but actually 13,200 fish—and laconically orders the crew to make preparations for getting under weigh. A wise skipper this! Instead of smothering his dainty herrings with salt, as many of his compeers are doing, and staying for another chance, he determines to hie for port and save the fresh-herring market.

A rude, laborious life my comrades of the *Seabird* must have. In all weathers, and for nine months in the year, they pursue the double avocations of sailor and fisherman ; fishermen first, perhaps, and sailors afterwards. At times a gale suddenly rises before the hauling begins, and it is a point of honour with the east coast fishermen never to forsake the nets. They make everything snug, and so long as the craft can be kept head to wind they ride out the storm, buffeted and tossed, while we at our firesides little wot of their hardships and perils. The herring season over, the *Seabird*, for example, becomes a trawler, and scours the North Sea in the teeth of the winter weather. Every available inch of space below decks is required for stowage, and there is scarcely room for comfort. The trawlers remain on their distant fishing ground for weeks together, fast cutters visiting them daily to convey the fish to shore ; and many a fisherman is washed overboard during the transfer of the fish to the carrier smack.

The *Seabird* has heels in the morning as she heads for land. Each added sail causes her to throb with delight ; the crew, after their long spell of toil, are light-hearted too, and even the forlorn object who sat on the sail abaft the tiller handle last night shares in the prevailing gaiety. "Homeward bound" after all is a better tune than "Nightfall on the sea." There must be no stoppage till the *Seabird* ranges alongside Yarmouth fish wharf; the herrings must be sold at Billingsgate before the town is fairly astir tomorrow morning, and the *Seabird* to-night must once more shoot her nets a score of miles at sea. At the mouth of the river a tug answers our signal ; takes two other new arrivals in tow, and drags us with a rush past Gorleston on the one side and South Denes on the other, to the wharf.

Here the well-known scenes are repeated. The fish are taken away in "swills," placed on the wharf, and sold by auction. The *Seabird*, with her genial skipper and jolly crew, having had the last herring emptied into the "swill," is tugged out into the stream, and from the pier where the boys are hauling up small codlings and whiting, an hour or two before sunset I can spy afar off the little flag with a white centre and red ground voyaging in company with other boats, two at least of which never more return to land.

CHAPTER XI.

UNLUCKY DAYS IN WALES.

" 'Tis not in mortals to command success,
But we'll do more, Sempronius ! We'll deserve it."

MONGST the full tale of unlucky days that have fallen to my share the three most unlucky were in the Principality. Number one was a February day on the Usk; number two a Whit-Monday on Lake Ogwen; and number three a half-holiday on Llangorst Pool.

When you are the fortunate holder of an invitation to fish a stream worth the fishing to an extent which makes the invitation equal in your eyes to its weight in gold, you naturally rejoice, and prepare to live up to your privileges. Placed in circumstances which make it doubtful whether such an opportunity will for many a long day again be offered, wind and weather are not likely to stand in your way. Yet, if there is anything more absolutely hopeless than the prospect of inducing a trout to look at a fly on a frosty morning, not five days beyond January, with ice on the puddles, and a thick garment of hoar upon the shoulders of the mountains, I should like to hear what that prospect is.   The opening of my February day on the Usk was enough to make one exclaim with cynical Byron :—

> " No—as soon
> Seek roses in December, ice in June ;
> Hope constancy in wind, or corn in chaff ;
> Believe a woman, or an epitaph ; "

—as hope to deprive a trout of life on such an objectionable fishing day as it in every respect was.

But if only for the fun of the attempt we resolved to make the best of the inevitable, and, donning our warmest ulsters, departed on our eight mile drive to the river.   Cowper indited a quantity of interesting lines on " A Winter's Walk at Noon ; " had I a Cowper's muse I might have sung the charms of " A Winter's Ride at Morn."   Not that the captain, my genial host and companion, was of a poetical turn of mind ; but he could handle the reins, and also the whip, with the reservation that long familiarity with the fly rod led him to impart an involuntary whipping motion to the weapon, and make everlasting casts at the chesnut's ear.   The captain was not poetical, probably because it is not a way they have in the army, but he had a poet's love for the beautiful, and uttered many neat remarks in praise of the mountains along whose side we journeyed.

Wales is rich in valleys, and that which lay beneath us was perfect in all the features that should compose a clearly defined vale.   Never exceeding a mile in width, never too narrow to obstruct the view, it stretched across from one range of hills to another, level as a lawn, and brightly green.   Down the middle flowed a trout stream ; farms and cottages, like decorations on a

courtier's bosom, shone in the strengthening sun.
It wound about under the hills enough to give
repeated changes of landscape, yet not abruptly to
spoil the gracefulness of the general idea, which
was that of a succession of sweeping vistas, leading
to something still more beautiful beyond. In the
distance bolder summits than any immediately
overshadowing the valley lifted their brows,
wrinkling with fantastic rapidity as the sun-
beams smote the frost and thawed the whiteness.
Nearer at hand we had incipient furze blossoms
and hedges heavy with glittering hoar.

The keeper was waiting for his young master,
with a question in his eye which it was unnecessary
to translate into words. "Oh yes, we'll try certainly, as we have come so far," answered the
captain, divining his thoughts, "but there is not
the ghost of a chance."

"'Deed there's not, sir," replied the man.

Cheering ourselves thus we made ready in the
fishing lodge and walked across the meadow armed
cap-à-pie; flies—a March brown, blue dun, and
February red. There are not many streams in
the three kingdoms that will repay for whipping
in the second month of the year, but the Usk, and
other smaller rivers in that part of South Wales,
are fairly and legally open to the rod at the beginning of February. Excellent sport is sometimes
had on warm days as the month draws on ; March
and April are indeed accounted the best months in
the year. The Mayfly brings no harvest to the Usk
as to other trout streams, the stock flies throughout
the early months of the summer being the March
brown, blue dun, and coch-a-bondhu, with slight
variations of shape and size according to the
altered conditions of the water.

The Usk at the portion we attempted is sparkling and lively, but plays no unseemly antics, as it
flows along its level bed, meandering freely around
oft-recurring bends, and seemingly proud that the
mountains standing sentinel over it must in honesty
place it in a different category from those descend-
ing brooks that babble their business to the whole
country side.   The banks are not encumbered with
trees ; the angler perceives this and keeps in the
back-ground, for, as the Poet-Laureate truly warns
us :—

> " If a man who stands upon the brink
> But lift a shining hand against the sun,
> There is not left the twinkle of a fin."

The captain generously gave me the pick of the
streams, and if he was generous I was grateful,
and not at all disinclined to take him at his word.
Soon an amazing thing happened : I hooked a
trout, though the thin ice was crackling under the
feet as I stood to play him—hooked, played, and
nearly lost him through the well-meant endeavours
of a friend who was commissioned to put the net
under him.   That which ends well, we are assured
by ancient proverb, is well, and it may save the
reader some anxiety of mind to tell him, by anticipation, that the trout was ultimately safely bagged.
The captain stood in the stream and made the
welkin ring with laughter at our bungling.   My
volunteer assistant was, physically, as fine a man
as you would wish to see, and handsome in the
bargain : at least, so the Welsh damsels told themselves, and—him.

But the landing net was not dreamt of in his
philosophy, nor had his burly form been framed
for bending low over a steep bank.   His innocent
but determined attempts to smite the fish off the

hook as soon as it came within range, his bewilderment when requested in angry tones to sink the net, his beaming pride when by a lucky accident the trout, escaping a vicious prod he had aimed at its head, ran into the net, were very mirth-inspiring to the captain.   And after all this fuss, command, entreaty, and (I fear me) abuse, the fish might have weighed half a pound.

The second trout was a beauty, of nearly three times this size ; with it no trifling could be permitted.   Our friend, therefore, repeating his dangerous assaults, was instantly deprived of the landing net, and the angler became his own assistant.   If the truth must be wholly told this anecdote is introduced to pave the way for a morsel of advice. Keep your landing net and gaff in your own hands as much as possible—you will be more independent, less likely to lose fish by trusting to inexperienced strangers, and better able to cope with a sharp emergency when it arises, as sooner or later arise it will.

A third trout completed my bag on this early February day on the Usk.   My own London-made March browns, upon which I had with reason prided myself, were, as so often happens, useless : it was a large and unpretending fly given me by the keeper which performed the trifling transactions that I had been able to carry through.

When the fish are rising, and one's stay by a good river is restricted, all the feeding encouraged during the day should be left to the fish and such like small deer.   The keen sportsman cannot afford to throw away half-hours upon knife-and-fork.   But on a February day, appetite sharpened by the frost, and hopes blighted by two hours without a rise, asceticism does not commend itself to the pilgrim's

affections.   Man, after all, is a gross animal.   It
is humiliating to chronicle the admission, but it is
true, that the feature of that particular day which
stands out most boldly in my recollection is—not
the drive along the mountain side, not the yellow
furze blossoms and silvered branches, not the genial
companionship of my gallant young guide, not the
rescue of the trout from the evil attacks of Adonis,
not the sight of a comely Usk trout safe in the
depths of the net, but the homely table in the
fishing lodge garnished with a leg of real Welsh
five-year-old mutton fed on the home farm and
roasted artistically.   Man, I repeat, is a gross
animal ; but for all that, mutton when it is Welsh,
when it is five-year-old, when it is well roasted
from knuckle to blade, is not to be put aside in
terms of contemptuous indifference.

   The afternoon passed principally in an inspection of the pools for salmon, of which we saw
several.   The keeper had hooked one which he
pronounced an "old Turk," and set at liberty,
not because of its oriental attributes, but because
it was not in season ; the captain also had turned
one over, and I had scared a small fellow from the
water's edge.   The Usk is as late a river for salmon
as it is early for trout.   When was the Usk not
famous for its salmon?   Poets wrote about it in
1555 :—

> " In Oske doth sammon lye,
> And of good fish, in Oske, you shall not mis ;
> And this seems strange, and doth through Wales appere
> In some one place are sammons all the yeere.
> So fresh, so sweet, so red, so crimp withal,
> That man might say 'Loe' sammon here at call."

Coming from the sixteenth to the nineteenth
century it is not difficult to furnish a convincing

proof of the abundance of Usk "sammon." Not
many seasons since a gentleman, who himself related to me the circumstance, counted on a bend
of the river not more than 200 yards long thirty-
nine old or spent fish that had perished while
waiting for floods to take them to the sea. The
late Mr. Robert Crawshay, the iron king, rented
a large section of the Usk, and was one of the
most enthusiastic of its anglers. On the 22nd of
October, 1874, he himself—other members of his
family also killing fish—caught nine salmon—a
male of twenty-two pounds hooked in the pectoral
fin, a female of sixteen pounds at the same time
and place, also caught by the pectoral fin, a female
of nineteen pounds hooked in the side, and the remainder—all hen fish—taken in the ordinary way
—thirteen pounds, ten pounds, eight pounds, five
and a half pounds, four and a half pounds, and
four pounds—total 102 pounds.

To the recreation of angling Mr. Crawshay
added that of photography, as frequenters of our art
exhibitions will remember, and he made the one
wait upon the other in a manner very interesting
to the pisciculturist. The whole of the salmon
taken on the day specified he photographed for
scientific purposes. The three largest were photographed separately on an extended scale and
partly opened, so as to show the precise condition
of the fish in spawn. The roe in the nineteen
pounder appears ingeniously exposed in its natural
position ; it weighed three pounds ten ounces, and
as the number of ova in one ounce is 380, the eggs
in this one salmon numbered 22,040.

Frost in February is not out of the course of
nature, but what say you to a Whit-Monday hailstorm ? Was that the reception the mountains of

North Wales should have given to a confiding man who had travelled two hundred and thirty miles to pay them (and their water-basins) due homage? Yet even so it happened. On the Saturday previous I had diligently fished up the meadows of Nant Ffrancon, or the Beaver's Hollow, content with a satisfactory basket of small trout, revelling in the wild loneliness of the valley, and almost happy; the drawback was a herd of Welsh cattle which, led on by a scoun-drelly little bull, chased me with most malicious intent, and interfered sadly with the peace of mind which would otherwise have invested me like a mantle. For skirmishes of this nature the angler in North Wales must be prepared; they are much too generally part of the sport.

Llyn Ogwen as the *bonne bouche* had been reserved for a long day. They never fish on Sun-days in Wales, but the quarrymen take long walks into the country, and come home in the evening with something moist in their handkerchiefs. On Whit-Sunday, walking up to reconnoitre, and order a boat, I myself saw a few movements by Ap-Evans, Ap-Jones, Ap-Williams, and Co., which fully explained the odour of fried fish that pervaded Bethesda at night. A lovelier day than this never dawned; the wild hyacinths, primroses, buttercups, and daisies, bloomed fresh and fair in the private grounds through which you are per-mitted to cut off a long turn in the high road; the birds sang out of the fulness of their holiday heart; the fleecy clouds ran lightly before the wind over the hills; the air, soft and amorous, cooled you with a fan of balmy perfume.

The craggy mountains and stupendous rocks at the upper end of this valley seem made for storm and gloom only, but they did not take this clear June sunlight amiss, and made no opposition to its beams searching out and revealing weird clefts and chasms said in legend to be the abode of devils and imps; one precipice by Llyn Idwall was and is believed by the superstitious to be the main entrance to Satan's kitchen, and is named Twlldduaccordingly. The fish in Lake Idwall, says Welsh tradition, were, in memory of the murder of a prince by his ruthless guardian, for ever doomed to the loss of one eye; the guide books tell you that, as there are no fish left in the lake, it is impossible to verify the legend. Unfortunately for the unity of this touching narrative—one does not like to have one's idols shattered—Lake Idwall on this Whit-Sunday was considerably dimpled by the rising of fleshly trout, and one fish leaping a somersault out of the water to all appearances was not the victim of optical defect. Still it is a horribly gloomy pool, dark and remote amongst the mountains, and frowned upon by savage rocks.

Lake Ogwen is more open, and more easily accessible, and there is one house tolerably near. You fish the lake from a boat, and in the absence of an oarsman—and there is no such thing in the locality—you heave a block of granite attached to a rope over the windward gunwale, and let the shallop drift.

On the Whit-Monday morning with which we are now concerned the mountains were hooded as if with gigantic masses of cotton-wool, curling slowly into fantastic figures, dispersing and gathering, stealing down towards the valley, trailing over the faces of the rocks, and performing a thousand weird movements. The wind began to

N

blow from the gorges, cutting you like a knife.
Having pulled the clumsy dingy furlongs in the
eye of the wind, I was not slightly provoked to
find the quickening blasts converting me, as I
stood waiting for a lull, into a sail, and the boat,
notwithstanding the granite drag, hastening back
at a prodigious rate, and threatening shipwreck
upon a cluster of serrated crags at the lower end.
The affair ended in an hour's furious gale, to
which the hapless angler was exposed, there being
no possibility of pulling ashore, and no cover
under the mountain, at whose lee-foot the boat
lay partly beached.   Then the gale, quickly running down the chromatic scale of Boreas, whispered itself seaward.   The sun at last came out,
not with the open and frank countenance of a
friend, but with the pallid cheeks of a con-
spirator.

Now, or never, was the time to put off once
more, and soon the flies, five in number (as you
may make them on this weedless water), were
tripping lightly to and fro.   Thirty minutes of sun,
even if feeble, and sport, even if in moderation,
are helps to endurance, and sets off against a
drenched skin.   In that space I had caught fifteen
trout of a peculiar kind—very yellow, very thin
for their length, very greedy after the fly, very
stupid when hooked, very slippery when handled.
If I add that the fish weighed three pounds gross
weight, there will be no injustice done as between
man and trout.

The last fish was being played, when as an effective *finale*, a hailstorm burst.   I had been too intent
upon fishing to notice it brewing overhead, but it
speedily gave me a taste of its quality.   Of course
the boat was the farthest possible point from land;

of course I was the longest possible time in hauling in the granitic contrivance ; of course the wind
mastered the oars ; of course everything went
wrong. The discharge of the Storm-King's extra-
sized small shot caused acute pain to face, hands,
and neck, and drove me huddled and heedless
into the bottom of the boat, which went whither-
soever it listed, and this, to sum up the catalogue
of woes, was on the rockiest part of the foreshore.
Ten minutes' peppering with large hailstones
seemed a whole day of pain and discomfort, and
there was an accompaniment of thunder and
lightning that added an element of awe to the
warfare. This was a holiday not to be forgotten :
though I did shorten it as soon as the storm abated,
and sought shelter in the cottage.

Through its green glass window panes, long
after comparative serenity had succeeded to our
elevation, we could see the pale blue forks cleaving the clouds far down the valley, and every
token of a repetition of the commotion which had
visited us. The masses of cotton-wool, no longer
white, brooded henceforth slate-coloured and sul-
lenly over all the hills, and bird and beast had
vanished from sight and sound when the homeward walk was, in dampness and shivering, prosecuted.

The main result of my visit to Llangorse Pool
was to induce a deep-rooted scepticism on the
subject of waterproof clothing, and sincere pity for
two unoffending friends whom I had tempted
from the hotel fireside with exciting promises of
sport, and positive assurances that the weather
would be fine, and the scenery observable under
the most favourable auspices. This, to be sure,
was a daring thing to do in February, but the

weather-glass in the hall, and the weather-glass aloft, to say nothing of the head boots, backed me in my honestly-meant persuasions. And we departed at noon, and took train to Tallybont station.

Merthyr Tydvil is a metropolis truly, but it is the metropolis of coal and iron. Even when the grimy workers are contentedly toiling, the town is the reverse of cheerful of aspect; when they are on strike, when the great blast furnaces are blown out, and trade is stagnant, it cannot be said that additional liveliness has been secured. But down the valley through which the Brecon railway has been laid you very quickly reach fine scenery, which you appreciate all the more, perhaps, because of distant views of chimneys belching forth serpent coils of dense smoke. This I pointed out to my trusty and, alas! trusting companions, with the laudable desire to divert their attention from numerous ugly appearances overhead. For the turn of noon was stealthily lowering a curtain, first of gauze, then of more thickly spun veilwork, till hill and vale, streamlet and lake, were alike hidden from view.

A little local knowledge, or any improvised plausibleness that will pass as such, is a boon under such circumstances, though one is apt to find out that a little knowledge is, as forsooth it has been, from the time of Adam, a dangerous thing. All I know of Llangorst Pool I nevertheless place at the disposal of my companions, but my data, even when drawn out like a thin wire, do not go far. The Welsh name of this water, is Llyn Savaddon; it is three miles long, and a mile across at the widest place. Although there are numerous legends connected with it, the only one

I can recall, now that of all times they are needed,
is that the waters rest upon a deeply-buried city.
One of my companions has heard the same story
of an Irish lake, and makes game of the whole
pretence.

He gets more interested at the stores of eels,
perch, and pike, which I vouch have roamed the
pool since the days of the good monks of Llan-
thony, and becomes almost hopeful when informed
that the place is credited with pike of any size up
to 50 lb. He remembers, he says, a paragraph
not a fortnight since in a London paper recording
the capture of one of 24 lb. from Llangorst; hopes
I have been careful to bring the gaff; thinks if my
bag is too small, we may borrow or purchase a
market-basket or potato-sack.

Dissembling, however, could be continued no
longer. It began to rain hard and straight, and
I was weatherwise enough to be sure that it
would rain for the rest of the day. Better have
told those young men to wait in the warmth of
the station refreshment room till I came back;
better even have myself taken the next returning
train. But hope springs eternal in the human
breast.

"Fifty pounds, I think you said?" observed the
friend who knew all about the Irish lakes, as he
resolutely tucked up his trousers.

It was this phantom that inspired him to follow
us through those sodden meadows and slippery
marshes into the rain-beaten village nearest the
pool. The other friend bore up manfully till he
reached the tavern settle, and then he brought up
to his moorings under a wharfage of smoked bacon,
wishing us luck, and requesting to be awakened, if
he slept, when we returned with the game.

" Fifty pounds is a fine fish, old fellow," the
more hopeful companion said as we trudged
through mire and rain. He could think of
nothing but that. Sympathy I could tender him
none, having just discovered that a new water-
proof suit warranted to stand fast, let in water
like a sieve, and being mentally engaged in debat-
ing whether there is anything in the world so
thoroughly illustrative of "adding insult to in-
jury" as a waterproof garment that assists the
rainfall to saturate you.

A brave little Welsh boy, as we stand lingering
shivering on the brink, offers to pull us out into
Llangorst Pool. His offer is accepted, and I work
like a galley slave with the rod and spinning
tackle. There are two other water parties, but
they are coming in, and without waiting to be
asked they tender the tidings " Not a touch to-
day." The assurance from one gentleman who
had given over fishing and was dangling his spoon
over the stern, to the effect that the pool was full
of pike, and that he had caught ten prime fish
yesterday, was not received with that genial
delight one sportsman should feel in the prosperity of another. My friend, couched under the
umbrella in the bows, surveyed me with grim
speechlessness, and smiled. Thank goodness, he
referred no more to the abnormally high maximum
I had given him to represent the weight of the
Llangorst monsters. Yet I had read the same in
honest printer's type.

The afternoon, in short, was the deadest of
blanks; it rained incessantly. The road by
which, at the expense of an additional half mile,
we avoided the terrors of mead and bog on our
return, was more unpleasant than our former

route ; the trains were late ; the whole prospect blurred and blotted. I have a vivid remembrance of that unlucky Saturday ; for I ruined a new hat, caught a severe catarrh, found out that the water-proof man had cheated me, and have reason to believe—no friendly communication having been received from him since—that I mortally offended an intelligent and useful acquaintance because of that fifty pound pike.

CHAPTER XII.

OUR CLOSING DAY.

" Should auld acquaintance be forgot,
And never brought to min'?
Should auld acquaintance be forgot,
And days o' lang syne?
We'll tak a cup o' kindness yet
For auld lang syne !"

OT to the waterside at all must the reader—kind, intelligent, and indulgent, of course—be now transferred, but to a warm, well-lighted apartment to which he has been aforetime introduced. On the last night of March, it may be remembered, a united family, not ashamed to avow themselves followers of quaint, pure-hearted Izaak Walton, whose nature was eminently unselfish, assembled amidst their piscatorial trophies on the eve of their " opening day."

Since that occasion three of the four seasons have sped their allotted course. It was an occasion for the putting on of harness, just as the present is the time when the waterside warriors have met to lay it aside, and, so to speak, place their weapons on the rack. The twenty-eight pound pike, that great perch, the bellows-shaped bream, the dark fat tench, the burly-shouldered chub, and the handsome trout maintain their fixed expression upon the walls. The hand of change touches them not. Two, however, of the angling brotherhood have for ever laid down the rod since the year opened, although both were merry and hale on that 1st of April expedition by the water-side. Though their places have been filled, our departed friends are not forgotten ; on the contrary, as we stand in informal groups around the fire, awaiting the expected summons, their good qualities are lauded and their skill is sadly remembered.

In due time the cloth is removed, and preparations are made for "a night of it." We are very old-fashioned and conservative here, as we have been any time these last fifty years. A few of the very young brethren have incurred the pity of the majority by drinking claret during the feast, and they now are given up as hopeless because they produce elegant cigar cases, and talk of Partagas and other fashionable brands. Rare old brown sherry, port with real bees' wing, and ripe, fragrant Madeira have been circulated amongst the veterans, and now nothing but the longest of churchwarden pipes, artfully twisted spills quite a yard long, tobacco on small trays, and an open line of glimmering night lights posted down the centre of the mahogany, with mighty bowls of punch such as this generation seldom sees, will satisfy the traditions of past gatherings, and the tastes of present feasters.

We are very practical. The president raps the table with an ivory mallet and says "Gentlemen, 'The Queen.'" We rise and say "The Queen," sip, and sit again. "Gentlemen, the secretary will make his annual statement," says the president. Thereupon we are informed that the past season, like the season before it, was a miserable time for anglers. Last year there was too much rain ; this year there had not been enough. The fly-fishers who had travelled far and wide had found the trout streams barren and dry: the bottom-fishers had been scorned by the roach, put to shame by the perch, and left in the lurch by the barbel. The pike-fishers still lived in hope, but until sharp frosts cut down the weeds, and floods washed them away, the angler could not be said to have a fair chance.

"Gentlemen, pipes," laconically, and formally rising, now observes the president. This is tantamount to the military "stand at ease," and clouds arise and tongues are loosened without a moment's delay. Every member is required to contribute to the entertainment of the general body, beginning with the oldest and proceeding down the incline of seniority. Thus no time is wasted in profuse excuses or affected apologies. You may sing, or perpetrate a speech, or recite, or stand on your head, but you must do something, and bring your contribution within a hard and fast compass of five minutes.

The fence-line of three score years and ten has been passed by our patriarch—the dear old man of whom we are all so proud, who was never known to lose his temper, to do his fellow an evil turn, or to pass the bottle ; who this very autumn sent up from the Shropshire streams a fine dish of grayling caught by himself, with flies of his own making. He is a "character," and has an unfaltering belief in the old times.

"I'm an old-fashioned fogey," he tells us, "but

I don't think you youngsters are as jolly or genuine as the anglers of my early days. You are over-wise in your own conceits, bless your hearts; but it's only theory. You read more, but you modern anglers are not half as good naturalists as your fathers were. You can give the scientific name of a polecat, but you never saw it, and if you met one walking down Regent Street you wouldn't know what it was. Now, when I was a young man I shot a polecat in the very copse some of you know so well at the back of the osier-bed. I doubt whether you know a hawk from a handsaw."

Here our gay comrade, who is nothing if not Shakespearian, interposes "Hernshaw, not handsaw." General laughter succeeds, in which the patriarch joining, continues:—

"There you are. It's precisely what I mean—you youngsters know too much. I say handsaw, and stick to it. But there, it isn't your fault altogether; the world moves on and things change. The time is past when a kingfisher perches in confidence on the rod of an angler, as I have known it to do. But it's all right, and I'm delighted to be here once more. I can't throw a trolling bait any longer, and I've as much as I can do to see a rise a dozen yards off if there's a ripple, but I enjoy my summer outings and the soft winds as much as any; and if I can't wade in a swift stream or do a day's spinning, I can nick a grayling with the best of you." And indeed he can; and the old man hopes that God will bless us all, and that when we are in our seventy-second year we shall be as hearty and happy as he is. To which we add an internal "Amen" in the midst of the applause.

The next gentleman would make a splendid

backwoodsman, if six feet two of straight lissome framework and an unquenchable love of field sports count for anything. Yet he has a gentle soul in that long muscular body, and says the tenderest things in a wonderfully sentimental voice. The voice lifted into song is sweet as the pipe of an Arcadian shepherd. Though essentially a town-suckled, town-bred, and town-loving man, he thus warbles :—

Give me the brook at the foot of the mountains,
  Where cool, sparkling waters spring fresh from the hill :
Give eddying scours, cascade-hollowed fountains,
  And rills rushing down through the glen to the mill.
There's a maid at the mill ; there's a trout in the stream ;
For the trout will I whip ; of the maid let me dream.

Ah ! tell me no more of glory or duty,
  Of vict'ries of peace, or triumphs of war ;
My mountain-born fish, my mill-nurtured beauty
  Are the only delights that tempt from afar.
Yes ; the maid of the mill and the trout of the stream
Where'er I may roam ever rise in my dream.

The trout it is said loves bright summer weather,
  And merrily plays at the opening of day ;
So stroll I to where the brooks join together,
  And wrong would you be should you tauntingly say
'Tis the maid at the mill, not the trout in the stream,
That hastens my footsteps at dawning's grey gleam.

My first cast falls on the hurrying water,
  An old casement creaks 'neath the time-honoured eaves—
A miss ! and thy fault, O miller's fair daughter,
  Peeping out from thy bower of dew-covered leaves.
Witching maid of the mill ! Lucky trout of the stream !
The angler fares ill who of maidens will dream.

Lo ! here by this spot, where merry trout gambol,
  At noon lies the only protection from heat :
At evening, perforce, I hitherward ramble—
  Is not the quick flash of the water-wheel sweet ?
Hush ! The maid of the mill walks forth by the stream ;
Shall I follow ? Or still idly angle—and dream ?
      *   *   *   *   *

Given is the brook at the foot of the mountains,
  Where cool, sparkling waters spring fresh from the hill ;
Given eddies and scours, and cascades and fountains,
  For they all rush down through the glen to the mill—
And I live at the mill, whipping trout from the stream :
I followed, was hooked, and need nevermore dream.

To the sentimental backwoodsman succeeds one
who, instead of a prosy conveyancer, should have
been, as nature intended him, something in the
comic line of life. He does not sing a comic song
now, however, since he knows he will by-and-by
be called upon willy nilly to repeat certain old
favourites of that ilk. The truth is he has for a
week been preparing a string of wretched puns,
which he thus runs off the reel, drolly emphasizing
the words italicized : " Gentlemen, I hope no one
will *carp* at what I'm about to say, or think my
remarks an enc-*roach*-ment. Is it not a fact in
natural history that *every Jack has his Gill?* It is
not every *acute angle*-r who can *keep a pike*, or say
with the *judicious Hooker*,

> " 'I had a bream, a whacking bream,
>   I dreamt that I had three.'

Before sitting down I should like to state my
in-*tench*-ion of presenting to you, though not by
any means as an *eele*mosynary affair, a copy of
Mrs. Barbel's ' Dace abroad and evenings at home,'
bound in *gut*-ta *perch*-a ; also to observe that the
true motto for every angler is *I'm a float.* The
fact is "——

The fact was that the company would have no
more rubbish of this sample, though the word-
torturer subsequently confided to me that his most
effective abominations were unsaid. We, however—the conveyancer's cheap wit must be the
excuse for the simile—only jumped from the

frying-pan into the fire, inasmuch as the next three entertainers were terribly dull dogs. One of them floundered (why did not the conveyancer try to work in the *flounder?*) through two sentences, and broke hopelessly down; the other recited a soliloquy on "The chief purpose of man"; the third, who had a voice like a saw-sharpener, dashed into "Where the bee sucks," screeching in the most excruciating fashion the long run on the last word in the Bat's back line.

At this stage of the proceedings there was a universal desire for a melody in which a chorus-singer might hear of something to his advantage, and the member whose turn came next happened to be just the fellow for the crisis. Swinging his pipe, and looking round with a now-then-all-together air, he roared in stentorian harmony :—

" Now Johnny the angler's a jolly lad—hurrah ! hurrah !
He's never disheartened and never sad—hurrah ! hurrah !
He's out of the racket of trouble and toil ;
He's king of the water if not of the soil :
    And light is his step when Johnny comes marching home."

There were eight verses of this home-spun material, the last stanza containing the inevitable moral, in which the author suggested that there could not be a better all-round bait for the angler than contentment, and laid down the indisputable axiom that "Fair-play is a jewel for fishes or men." Probably this was the most roughly constructed song sung during the evening, but nothing could exceed the gusto with which the " responses " were taken up, or the fine effect produced by the raps dealt out to the table as a suitable accompaniment to "hurrah ! hurrah !" Another member chanted in a sort of Gregorian the story of poor " Cock Robin," and at the end of every verse the whole

company, taking their parts like a well-trained
choir, gave a pretty melancholy refrain :—

"All the birds in the air fell a sighing and a sobbing
When they heard of the death of poor Cock Robin."

True, sobbing according to usage does not strictly
rhyme with Robin, but we were not fastidious, and
were not tired, although the verses were just as
numerous as the birds, beasts, and fishes who were
concerned with the tragic decease and touching
interment of the defunct Redbreast. The late Mr.
Weiss himself could not have sung the "Village
Blacksmith" better than it was given, and there was
one who came so close to reality in his imitation
of the veteran Ransford that it was necessary to
look a second time to decide whether it was not
that splendid interpreter of Dibdin who sang and
acted "Tom Tough." Next to the Cock Robin
chant in popularity amongst the chorus-singers
was a singularly quaint and catching slave song,
brought by a young member from Carolina, where
he had heard it sung by the plantation hands. The
general burden of the solo I have forgotten, but
the chorus printed itself upon the memory at once,
and I fancy it gives a pretty clear notion of the
rest :—

"There's a good time coming and it's almost nigh,
    It's a long, long time on its way.
Then go and tell Elijah to hurry up Pomp,
And meet us at the gum-tree down by the Swamp,
    To wake Nicodemus to-day."

There are aggrieved anglers as well as pa-
rishioners, and our aggrieved member carried the
meeting entirely with him on introducing the great
live-bait question. This, he maintained, was the
question of the day, and though he hesitated to

commit himself to a definite statement, he broadly hinted that government must sooner or later take it up. Giving head to the righteous indignation which rippled through his voice he graphically depicted the mingled horror, disgust, and disappointment suffered by honest anglers who were unable to secure live-bait for love or money. A pretty state of things, forsooth! Here were hundreds of fine fellows who spend the Sunday meditating calmly by the murmuring river, and innocently angling, who must be robbed of their enjoyment if the fishing tackle shops could not procure live-bait. If there were laws against the capture of small fish let the laws be altered; what was the use of Government if the wants of the people were not supplied? The author of these ideas of political economy worked himself into such a passion that his five minutes had expired before he could arrive at the one or two practical suggestions he intended to make.

The gentleman next in order trolled a song (written by Mr. G. Manville Fenn) which was twice encored, for it was new and bright and capitally rendered :—

THE FISHING PHILOSOPHER.

" To tramp the wet turnips, and pepper a bird ;
Or butcher tame pheasants to me seems absurd :
Give me the soft streamlet meandering by,
Where I can take trout with a well-chosen fly:

" And my rod light and limber, my line true and fine,
My creel on my back, and a scrap when I'd dine ;
Sweet Nature around me ; the world's troubles far ;
Believe me we fishers philosophers are !

" With beagle, or greyhound, go hunt puss, the hare,
Or chase, in gay scarlet, the fox to his lair ;

Give me my roach tackle ; of ground bait a heap ;
A fig for all else, be the stream swift and deep :
   " For my rod light and limber, &c.

"You may shoot, you may hunt, you may stalk the red deer;
Let me list to the music of some falling weir,
While I tempt the sly chub, the fat barbel, and jack,
Oh ! I envy no king if I bear a few back :
   " With my rod light and limber, &c.

That gallant acquaintance, the gay comrade, was observed closely, and his friends knew by the dignified reserve ennobling his brow that that tempered brain had prepared for us an intellectual treat. He had dealt with what may be termed the melodramatic aspect of the recreation to which we were all devoted. He poured out his soul in recitation, thus :—

I greet thee, friend, upon this autumn day,
And give thee welcome to this sheltered lake.
Here for a season let us haply stay,
Of this good weed—Returns—I pr'ythee take.
So gaze we now upon the tinted leaves
Which mix their colours by their own good law.
Breathes there the man who in his heart believes
That Providence is not above us? Psha !
Fill up thy pipe, thou tall, thou goodly youth,
And strike a light upon this roughened edge.
See'st thou the float ?
         Alack in naked truth
It still bobs pikeless near yon fringe of sedge.
Now let us therefore our discourse resume.
Another light ? With pleasure ; strike it low ;
(The worst of fusees is their—well—perfume)
Those drifting clouds are white as driven snow.
What is the theory of wind, of heat, of cold ?
Why points the needle to the northern pole?
To deal with these a man must needs be bold.
   Pray sink the bait-can in that nearest hole,
Else will those gudgeon prematurely die,
Nor roach nor dace their little span will save.
   I'll give my bait, I think, another shy ;
E'er saw'st thou pike so cowardly behave?
Mark now these thirty yards; how neat they show,

O

Coiled carefully upon the level ground—
One, two, three—swish—call'st thou not that a throw?
That should a good fish take, if one's around.
Have you the papers seen? or *Punch?* or *Fun?*
It doesn't matter; only one gets dull
On hours of waiting.
            Look! by Jove, a run.
Down goes the float. See how the pike can pull.
This is as it should be. I dare would bet
A heavy jack is running out the line
Into deep water, into deeper yet
Before he gives a pause.
            Let us combine
To drink his health. Unscrew thy silver flask
And sip we lightly the ambrosial tap:
Now turn with caution to the genial task.
In grass or sedge should we our capture wrap?
Prepare the gaff with care, else do I vouch
Our prize may vanish at the nick of time.
A little moment further shall he pouch;
To strike in haste is piscatorial crime.
Haul in the line with very cautious hand:
Thus the requirements of the case are met.
I'll show you how a captured pike should land,
And you, the lesson learned, will not forget
I gently strike soon as the line is taut,
Though the barbed hook has doubtless done its work:
The bending rod denotes a good fish caught,
The plunging top betrays his angry jerk.
He's spent, I ween, as warily he's drawn,
Reluctant, but not hostile, to the shore.
The winch revolves. Here on this grass-grown lawn
Shall lie the prey, to murder fry no more.
   The float appears from the pellucid deep,
Then comes the knot that fastens line to trace;
A moment yet and you may snatch a peep
Of the hooked *Luce*, now winching in apace.
About five pounds would be a shrewdish guess,
If one may judge from shoulder, fin, and tail,
Which he betrays—maybe a little less.
Ah! hapless fish, useless it is to sail
To right, to left, with that indignant stroke.
This trusty gaff was never known to fail;
You'll shortly find it is no passing joke,
Though gainst your plight 'tis not for me to rail.
So so: your yellow side is upward turned:

As good you are as numbered with the slain,
And you, good friend, the lesson well have learned—
Begad, he's off ! the gimp has snapped in twain."

By the time that the Waltonian brotherhood rose, crossed hands, and pronounced that fine bene- diction, "Auld Lang Syne," they had thoroughly gorged—not the meat and drink, to which they had, nevertheless, sensibly done justice, but—that bait, Contentment, which had been recommended to them by the Boanergesian soloist.   So at peace with the world were they that even the Home Secretary, at whose new mandate the party was prematurely dissolved, was pardoned as a victim rather than condemned as a persecutor.   With all their hearts they wished each other health and happiness, abundant sport by the waterside, pros- perity at home, and no missing faces at the next merry meeting.

CHISWICK PRESS

C. WHITTINGHAM & CO

October, 1884.

LOW'S BIJOU CATALOGUE:

A SELECT LIST

FROM THE

CATALOGUE

OF MESSRS.

SAMPSON LOW, MARSTON, SEARLE, & RIVINGTON,

188, Fleet Street,

LONDON.

SAMPSON LOW & CO.'S COMPLETE CATALOGUE of Works in Travel, Biography, Fiction, Belles Lettres, School Books, Geographical Research, &c., may be had on application to the Publishers, 188, Fleet Street, London.

Ask to see the CHRISTMAS HARPER'S *at your Bookseller's.*

Printed by WM. CLOWES and SONS, Limited, Stamford Street and Charing Cross.

"AN EXTRAORDINARY SHILLINGSWORTH."

HARPER'S MAGAZINE.

1885	Sunday	Monday	Tuesday	Wednes.	Thursd.	Friday	Saturd.	1885	Sunday	Monday	Tuesday	Wednes.	Thursd.	Friday	Saturd.
Jan.	...	...	...	...	1	2	3	July	...	...	...	1	2	3	4
	4	5	6	7	8	9	10		5	6	7	8	9	10	11
	11	12	13	14	15	16	17		12	13	14	15	16	17	18
	18	19	20	21	22	23	24		19	20	21	22	23	24	25
	25	26	27	28	29	30	31		26	27	28	29	30	31	...
Feb.	1	2	3	4	5	6	7	Aug.	...	...	...	...	...	...	1
	8	9	10	11	12	13	14		2	3	4	5	6	7	8
	15	16	17	18	19	20	21		9	10	11	12	13	14	15
	22	23	24	25	26	27	28		16	17	18	19	20	21	22
Mar.	1	2	3	4	5	6	7		23	24	25	26	27	28	29
	8	9	10	11	12	13	14		30	31	...	...	...	...	...
	15	16	17	18	19	20	21	Sept.	...	...	1	2	3	4	5
	22	23	24	25	26	27	28		6	7	8	9	10	11	12
	29	30	31	...	...	...	...		13	14	15	16	17	18	19
Apr.	...	...	...	1	2	3	4		20	21	22	23	24	25	26
	5	6	7	8	9	10	11		27	28	29	30	...	...	...
	12	13	14	15	16	17	18	Oct.	...	...	...	...	1	2	3
	19	20	21	22	23	24	25		4	5	6	7	8	9	10
	26	27	28	29	30	...	...		11	12	13	14	15	16	17
May	...	...	...	...	...	1	2		18	19	20	21	22	23	24
	3	4	5	6	7	8	9		25	26	27	28	29	30	31
	10	11	12	13	14	15	16	Nov.	1	2	3	4	5	6	7
	17	18	19	20	21	22	23		8	9	10	11	12	13	14
	24	25	26	27	28	29	30		15	16	17	18	19	20	21
	31	...	...	...	...	...	...		22	23	24	25	26	27	28
June	...	1	2	3	4	5	6		29	30	...	...	...	...	...
	7	8	9	10	11	12	13	Dec.	...	...	1	2	3	4	5
	14	15	16	17	18	19	20		6	7	8	9	10	11	12
	21	22	23	24	25	26	27		13	14	15	16	17	18	19
	28	29	30	...	...	...	...		20	21	22	23	24	25	26
	...	...	...	...	...	...	...		27	28	29	30	31	...	...
	...	...	...	...	...	...	...		...	...	...	...	...	...	...

HARPER'S CHRISTMAS NUMBER, 1884.

VOL. 70, No. 415.

PRICE ONE SHILLING.

HARPER'S MAGAZINE for December, 1884, beginning the Seventieth Volume, *will be especially a* CHRISTMAS NUMBER.

Among the attractions of the Number will be:—

With Six Full-Page Engravings printed separately on Plate Paper.

(3)

A BIT OF NEW YORK.

HARPER'S MAGAZINE, 1885.

THE Publishers of HARPER'S MAGAZINE respectfully invite public attention to some of its leading attractions for the coming year. Their enterprise, aided by the co-operation of the best writers and artists, has been abundantly rewarded by the increased success of the Magazine, which has to-day an American circulation larger than it has ever had before, and which will enter upon its new year with an edition for England alone of over fifty thousand copies. They will endeavour to maintain its position as the best magazine for the home, always fully abreast of the times, and always advancing its standard of literary, artistic, and mechanical excellence.

NEW SERIAL NOVELS, &c.

' The January Number will contain, *inter alia*, 1. The first instalments of Two New Serial Stories, (*a*) AT THE RED GLOVE, with illustrations by Reinhart. (*b*) EAST ANGELS, by Constance Fenimore Woolson, author of "Anne."—2. MEZZOTINT ENGRAVING, by Dr. Seymour Haden, illustrated by his etchings.—3. "SHE STOOPS TO CONQUER," with illustrations by Abbey.—4. Professor Ward's article on WYCLIFFE, with illustrations. —5. AMERICAN POLITICAL IDEAS, by Prof. John Fiske (first of three articles).—6. THE PRINCE OF WALES, by Dr. W. H. Russell, with illustrations.

HISTORY AND BIOGRAPHY, &c.,

Will be as fully represented in the forthcoming numbers as in the past. Amongst other articles is one on The House of JOHN MURRAY, with illustrations; on JOHN RUSKIN, with Portrait, his Lake Home, &c.; on English and American Railways.

(4)

HARPER'S MAGAZINE, 1885
(continued).

SPECIAL ILLUSTRATIONS.

Apart from the illustrations for descriptive articles and stories, which will be engraved in the best style, our readers may expect frequent reproductions of the finest works of art executed by the old masters and by living artists; also, original drawings from E. A. Abbey and Alfred Parsons, illustrating the works of English poets.

DESCRIPTIVE PAPERS.

" AN ENGLISH AUTUMN," illustrated by Parsons, Corbauld, and others. NORWICH, by Miss Lillie, fully illustrated. THE LONDON SEASON, by Jennings, illustrated by Corbauld, Woodly, Gregory, &c. BALMORAL, illustrated; &c., &c.

SHORT STORIES AND SKETCHES.

In this field the forthcoming volumes will present features of unusual interest. ;

OLD FEATURES EVER NEW.

The *Editor's Easy Chair* and *Editor's Drawer* have become household words. The former has for thirty years been conducted by GEORGE WILLIAM CURTIS, and its every paragraph bears the stamp of his earnest thought—eloquently and gracefully expressed—on all subjects of current social interest. The *Editor's Drawer* is conducted by CHARLES DUDLEY WARNER. His own contributions and those accepted by him will greatly enhance the entertainment of this unique miscellany of humorous anecdote.

(5)

THE TOLL-BRIDGE.

Ready October 15th, with numerous Illustrations, Demy 8vo., cloth extra, price £1 1s.

A SKETCH OF THE

LIFE AND TIMES

OF THE

Rev, SYDNEY SMITH, M,A,

Rector of Combe-Florey; Canon Residentiary of St. Paul's.

Based on Family Documents and the Recollections of Personal Friends.

By STUART J. REID.

The book contains more than fifty unpublished Letters, and several unpublished Essays and Poems. It is illustrated by a new Portrait of the Rev. Sydney Smith, engraved on steel, from a miniature on ivory, the property of his granddaughter, Miss Holland. The volume is enriched with numerous Illustrations specially executed for its pages, and also one of great interest, drawn in 1840, by Mrs. Grote, whilst Sydney Smith's guest at Combe-Florey. There is also a facsimile of an autograph letter—now in possession of Sir Michael Hicks-Beach, M.P. —addressed to Mrs. Beach, of Nether Avon. It also contains a considerable amount of fresh information concerning the life of Nether Avon, Edinburgh, Foston, and Combe-Florey; and the author's endeavour has been to illustrate, by an appeal to facts, Sydney Smith's fidelity to duty at every stage of his career, the practical benevolence which marked his private life, and the courage with which he used his great gifts for the public good.

(6)

A PRINCIPALITY. [From Gibson's "Highways and Byways."]

NEW WORKS OF TRAVEL.

New Work by

JOSEPH THOMSON,

The African Explorer.

MR. THOMSON has just returned from Eastern Africa, and is preparing an account of his recent most adventurous journey in the **MASAI COUNTRY**, opening up an entirely new, shorter, and healthier route to THE VICTORIA NYANZA. MR. THOMSON has been extremely fortunate in being the first to exploit an ENTIRELY UNIQUE REGION—ethnographically and geographically—a region teeming with interest, containing such features as snowclad extinct volcanoes rising to a height of 19,000 feet, and one seen for the first time; magnificent mountain ranges reaching 14,000 feet in altitude; plateaux at an elevation of 9,000 feet. Another feature discovered was the existence of a curious narrow meridional Trough containing a series of beautiful lakes.

Of this interesting country Mr. Thomson traversed over 1,000 miles entirely new to geographers, and if the country is interesting, the people are more so. He has visited five new tribes, and of these three are in a sense new to ethnology differing from any tribes hitherto described; their customs are of the most astonishing description. Mr. Thomson had a lively time amongst these tribes. They are the most dreaded people of the whole of East Africa. Caravan after caravan has been annihilated by them, and it was only by a series of lucky accidents that he got through them. Besides these he discovered a tribe inhabiting a series of enormous caves.

Mr. Thomson's personal adventures have been of a perilous character many times charged by rhinoceroses and buffaloes while hunting; once tossed into the air and nearly killed, and at another time in the midst of a herd of elephants.

The work will be fully illustrated from Photographs taken by Mr. Thomson *en route* and it is hoped will be ready for publication in One octavo volume before Christmas.

(7)

WESTWARD HO!

Second Edition, demy 8vo., cloth extra, with numerous Illustrations and Map,
price One Guinea. A THIRD EDITION is in the Press.

THE KING COUNTRY;
OR,
EXPLORATIONS IN NEW ZEALAND.

By J. H. KERRY-NICHOLLS.

Being a Narrative of 600 Miles of Travel through Maoriland.

SOME OPINIONS OF THE PRESS.

The *Saturday Review* of Aug. 28 says:—" Such Englishmen as think it rather a matter
of shame than of boastfulness to be ignorant of one of the noblest and most promising of
their possessions, will find in Mr. Kerry-Nicholls' bulky but delightful volume the
wonders of a forbidden land displayed before them with a vividness of portraiture which
only a master-hand can produce. . . . One of the pleasantest books of travel ever written."

" The whole interest of this most interesting of volumes lies in the dash and daring of
the author, in the difficulties he surmounts, and in the new and infinitely varied, but
always fascinating, character of the scenery he traverses."—*St. James's Gazette.*

" Mr. Kerry-Nicholls has made a very successful journey, and has placed the result
before the world in a graphically-written volume, valuable for its scientific data, and
amusing to the general reader on account of its lively sketches of little-known tribes and
store of humorous anecdote. Of special interest are the descriptions of a journey
through the marvellously interesting region familiarly known as the wonder-land of
New Zealand, and the exploration of the king country."—*London Daily Telegraph.*

" The result of this exploration is given in a clear vivid manner, and as our author had
already visited not only the Alps but the Himalayas, had seen the beauties of Fusiyama
and the Yosemite Valley, the glades of Ceylon and the grandeur of Niagara, he possesses
considerable qualification for judging of the scenes he describes. . . . His account of the
well-known terrace of Te Tarata and Te Otukapurangi is well worth attention. . . . So
life-like are his descriptions that the reader can almost imagine himself a visitor to the
various places, and a participator in the risks. . . . We can heartily commend the book."
—*Athenæum.*

" So far as the 'King Country' is concerned, Mr. Kerry-Nicholls will satisfy any
reasonable thirst for information in those who for the first time devote their attention to
the matter, while to those who are already acquainted with the history of Maoriland so
far as it has been ascertained, his narrative of explorations in that far-off region will
be of especial value. . . ."—*Morning Post.*

" Mr. Kerry-Nicholls has written a very interesting and useful book, . . . he writes
with grace and freshness, has a genuine love for Nature, and a cheery spirit in the face
of real hardship; he uses his scientific knowledge to good purpose, and has filled a
copious appendix with botanical, zoological, and linguistic information of interest and
value."—*Pall Mall Gazette.*

" The incidents of every day's journey are set down with fidelity without tediousness,
and vividly without any effort to 'make a point,' or, in other words, to sacrifice truth
merely to picturesque effect.......Mr. Kerry-Nicholls supplies us with many interesting
facts regarding the habits, language, and social condition of the Maoris......."—*Observer.*

(8)

A GLIMPSE OF MONTREAL.

IN THE PRESS.

New Work on the Great North-West by STAVELEY HILL, Q.C., M.P.

FROM HOME TO HOME;

BEING

AN ACCOUNT OF TWO LONG VACATIONS SPENT AT THE FOOT OF THE ROCKY MOUNTAINS.

By STAVELEY HILL, Q.C., M.P.

One Volume, demy 8vo., fully Illustrated by Woodcuts and Fifteen Photogravures after Photographs and Drawings by the AUTHOR and Mrs. STAVELEY HILL.

" From Home to Home "—from my old home of Oxley Manor in Staffordshire, to the New Oxley in the foot hills of the Rocky Mountains—it seemed at first a long step, a great migration; but distance really lies in the completeness of separation, and this completeness of separation each year diminishes or destroys. . . . My tale is of much that had been seen, but also of much in which the trail of any preceding traveller was but faintly marked, if traceable at all. It is of a land of which the new life is but just breaking for mankind, a land of many hopes and much promise; a land where, if the toil of life be boldly faced, its responsibilities manfully taken up, and its duties faithfully discharged, the search after the new home will, I doubt not, be found amply to reward even those who at first turn with the deepest regret from the old one left behind, indeed, but in no way deserted or forgotten. But we must not talk of that which is left behind; nowhere more than in the North-West is the bidding of the Master more fraught with meaning, that he who has put his hand to the plough may not look back. Our ploughman has a long furrow before him; let him stick to it, it will lengthen every season, and will bring with its increasing length an increased source of wealth and comfort.

(9)

Notice.—MR. HENRY M. STANLEY'S NEW WORK ON THE CONGO, about which we have numerous inquiries, will probably not be ready for publication until the beginning of next year.

In One Volume, demy 8vo., about 400 pp., Sixteen full-page Chromo-lithographs, and Fifteen Lithographs, beautifully executed by C. F. Kell, after the Drawings supplied by the Author. Price One Guinea.

THE SNAKE-DANCE OF THE MOQUIS OF ARIZONA.

Being a Narrative of a Journey from Santa Fé, New Mexico, to the Villages of the Moqui Indians of Arizona; with a Description of the Manners and Customs of this peculiar people, and especially of the revolting religious rite, the Snake-Dance; to which is added a brief Dissertation upon Serpent-worship in general, with an Account of the Tablet-dance of the Pueblo of Santo Domingo, New Mexico, &c. By JOHN G. BOURKE, Captain Third U.S. Cavalry.

In One Volume, royal 8vo., cloth extra, 21s.

THE HUNDRED GREATEST MEN.

Portraits of the One Hundred Greatest Men of History, reproduced from Fine and Rare Steel Engravings.

WITH GENERAL INTRODUCTION BY RALPH WALDO EMERSON,

AND INTRODUCTION TO

SEC. I. BY MATTHEW ARNOLD.	SEC. V. BY A. P. STANLEY.	
„ II. BY H. TAINE.	„ VI. BY H. HELMHOLTZ.	
„ III. BY MAX MULLER AND	„ VII. BY J. A. FROUDE.	
R. RENAN.	„ VIII. BY PROFESSOR JOHN	
„ IV. BY NOAH PORTER.	FISKE.	

(10)

BASE OF THE ALBERT MEMORIAL, SOUTH KENSINGTON.
[From Conway's "Travels in South Kensington."]

Artists at Home,

Photographed by J. P. MAYALL, and Reproduced in Facsimile by Photo-Engraving on Copper Plates. Edited, with Biographical Notices and Descriptions, by F. G. STEPHENS.

Imperial folio, cloth extra, price 42s.

CONTENTS:

Sir Frederick Leighton, P.R.A., D.C.L., LL.D.—William Calder Marshall, R.A., H.R.S.A.—Thomas Webster, Hon. Retired R.A.—Valentine Cameron Prinsep, A.R.A.—John Everett Millais, R.A., D.C.L.—Samuel Cousins, Hon. Retired R.A.—George A. Lawson.—Marcus Stone, A.R.A.—Lawrence Alma Tadema, R.A.—Richard Redgrave, Hon. Retired R.A. —John Pettie, R.A.—Frank Dicksee, A.R.A.—George Frederick Watts, R.A., LL.D.—W. Hamo Thornycroft, A.R.A.—William Frederick Yeames, R.A.—John MacWhirter, A.R.A.—Sir John Gilbert, R.A.—Philip Hermogenes Calderon, R.A.—Briton Riviere, R.A., M.A.—Joseph Edgar Boehm, R.A.—Edward John Poynter, R.A.—Thomas Oldham Barlow, R.A.—Robert Walker Macbeth, A.R.A.—George Adolphus Storey, A.R.A.— The Right Hon. W. E. Gladstone, M.P., Professor of Ancient History in the Royal Academy.

(11)

Dedicated by permission to the Queen.

NEEDLEWORK AS ART.

By LADY MARIAN ALFORD.

With over a Hundred Woodcuts, Photogravures, and other engravings.
Royal 8vo., cloth extra.

TO THE QUEEN.—Your Majesty's most gracious acceptance of the
Dedication of my book on "Needlework as Art," casts a light upon the
subject that shows its worthiness, and my inability to do it justice. Still,
I hope I may fill a gap in the artistic literature of our day, and I venture
to lay my work at your Majesty's feet with loyal devotion.

MARIAN M. ALFORD.

RECOLLECTIONS OF FLY-FISHING FOR SALMON, TROUT, AND GRAYLING.

With Notes on their Haunts, Habits, and History. By
EDWARD HAMILTON, M.D., F.L.S., &c. Illustrated by a
Mezzotint Engraving by FRANCIS SEYMOUR HADEN, Esq.,
and other woodcuts. Small post 8vo., printed on handsome
paper by Whittingham, cloth extra, 6s.

. Also, a Large Paper Edition of which *only* 100 *copies have been
printed*, and each Copy being numbered from One upwards; 10s. 6d.

AN AMATEUR ANGLER'S DAYS IN DOVE-DALE.

Being an Account of My Three Weeks' Holiday in July
and August, 1884. Printed by Whittingham, Chiswick
Press. Imperial 32mo. Fancy boards. 1s.

. Also, a Large Paper Edition, printed on hand-made paper, parchment
binding (100 only printed), price 5s.

FRENCH AT HOME AND AT SCHOOL (First Book).

Containing the Accidence; the most indispensable part
of Syntax; Useful Sentences for Conversation; the Regular
and Irregular Verbs, &c., &c.; and French-English and
English-French Vocabularies of all the words contained
therein. By F. JULIEN, French Master of the King Edward's
VI.'s Grammar School, Five Ways, Birmingham; Author of
"Petites Leçons de Conversation et de Grammaire"; "First
Lessons in Conversational French Grammar"; "The
English Student's French Examiner"; "Phrases of Daily
Use and Practice"; and "French Conversational Reader."
Square crown 8vo., cloth, price 2s.

(12)

IMPORTANT WORK ON THE HISTORY OF MUSIC.

Preparing for Publication.

A HISTORY OF MUSIC

From the Earliest Times to the Present.

By W. S. ROCKSTRO,

Author of "The Life of Handel," "The Life of Mendelssohn," "A History of Music for Young Students," "Practical Harmony," "The Rules of Counterpoint," etc.

In One Volume, Demy 8vo, of about 450 pp., cloth, 14s.

SYNOPSIS OF CONTENTS.

SECTION I.

MUSIC IN THE EARLY AGES.

SECTION II.

MUSIC IN THE MIDDLE AGES.

SECTION III.

MUSIC IN THE SEVENTEENTH CENTURY.

SECTION IV.

MUSIC IN THE EIGHTEENTH CENTURY.

SECTION V.

MODERN MUSIC.

SECTION VI.

FUTURE PROSPECTS.

IN PREPARATION.

RUSSIAN CENTRAL ASIA:

INCLUDING

KULDJA, BOKHARA, KHIVA, AND MERV.

WITH APPENDICES ON

The Fauna and Flora of Russian Turkistan.

With Map, Photograph, and upwards of 60 Illustrations.

IN TWO VOLUMES. OCTAVO.

By HENRY LANSDELL, D.D., M.R.A.S., F.R.G.S.,

Author of "Through Siberia."

A journey of 12,000 miles by rail, river, horses, and camels, through Western Siberia to the Ili Valley at Kuldja; thence through Russian Turkistan and the Kirghese Steppes to Tashkend, Khokand, and Samarkand. Crossing into Bokhara, the Author travelled through the Khanate as guest of the Emir, floated 300 miles down the Oxus to Khiva, and then continued by a new route across the desert to the Caspian. One of Dr. Lansdell's objects (as before in Siberia) was the distribution in prisons and hospitals of the Scriptures, on the Patriarchial and Persian customs of which the work throws occasional light. In upwards of 70 chapters, the book treats more or less fully of all parts of Russian Turkistan; describes many hundreds of miles of country not previously visited by an English Author; gives 4,600 species of fauna and flora in about 20 lists, with introductions to each, and adds a bibliography and an index.

THE

NORTHBROOK GALLERY,

EDITED BY LORD RONALD GOWER, F.S.A.

A Descriptive and Historic Account of the

COLLECTION of the EARL OF NORTHBROOK, G.C.S.I.

Illustrated by Thirty-six Permanent Reproductions taken direct from the Paintings of Crivelli, Fra Bartolommeo, Raphael, Giorglone, Sanchez-Coello, Murillo, Petrus Christus, Van Hemessen, Holbein, Dürer, Cranach, Janet, Van Dyck, Hals, Mieris, Berck Heyde, Schalcken, Delaroche, Gainsborough, Stanfield, Webster, Mulready, and other celebrated Masters. Handsomely bound in cloth, with gilt edges. Impl. 4to.

Price £3 3s. 0d.

An ÉDITION de LUXE, limited to Fifty Copies, printed on hand-made paper, half-bound in Morocco. Royal folio.

Price £5 5s. 0d.

(14)

THE MOST IMPORTANT AND BEAUTIFUL WORK ON ORIENTAL ART EVER PUBLISHED.

*** Parts One and Two are already published. Part Three will be ready in December next; and Part Four, completing the work, will be ready in the ensuing Spring.

THE ORNAMENTAL ARTS OF JAPAN.

Illustrated with One Hundred Plates—Seventy in Colours and Gold, and Thirty in Monochrome—with General and Descriptive Text.

By GEORGE ASHDOWN AUDSLEY.

PROSPECTUS.

The purposes of the present Work, entitled "THE ORNAMENTAL ARTS OF JAPAN," are twofold. Firstly, it is compiled with the view of illustrating the more important branches of the Art Industries of the country, and placing in the hands of Art lovers a comprehensive series of Plates, representing truthfully, in colours, gold, &c., the finest examples of Japanese Art Work preserved in English, American, and Continental Collections. Secondly, it is so arranged, and its Plates are so richly supplied with ornamental accessories, that it forms an exhaustive work on JAPANESE ORNAMENT AND DECORATION, of the highest value to Designers in all branches of Art Manufacture. Artists will find the Work of the highest interest, and a veritable storehouse of most original and suggestive material.

The Arts which are fully described and illustrated, are Drawing, Painting, Engraving, and Colour Printing, on paper, silk, wood, &c.; Embroidery on silk; Ornamental Weaving, in silk and gold; Application, Incrusting, and Inlaying, in various coloured material; Lacquer Working, on different materials; Carving in wood and ivory; Metal Working in gold, silver, bronze, and iron; and Cloisonné Enamelling. Architecture, Keramic Art, and certain minor Arts are touched upon so far as they are related to the Arts above enumerated, but are not illustrated.

"THE ORNAMENTAL ARTS OF JAPAN" will contain ONE HUNDRED FOLIO PLATES (measuring 16 inches by 11¼ inches), seventy of which are to be in colours, gold, and silver, produced, directly from the original objects, by the most talented and skilful chromolithographic artists in Paris, under the personal direction of the Author. The remaining Thirty Plates are to be in Monochrome, produced from Japanese Indian-ink Drawings, Wood Engravings, Metal-Work, Ivory Carvings, &c., by photographic printing processes, by which absolute fidelity is secured.

In addition to the Introductory and General Text, all the Plates will be attended by Descriptive Notices, giving the names of the collectors in whose possession the objects are.

CONDITIONS OF PUBLICATION.

The work, forming Two handsome Folio Volumes, will be issued in Four Parts enclosed in ornamental cloth portfolios, at intervals of about six months. The First and Second Parts are now published. Part Three will be ready in December.

The entire Edition for the sale in ENGLAND and the COLONIES is strictly limited to 690 copies. The Author and Publishers bind themselves neither to print further copies nor publish any smaller edition.

THE WORK WILL BE SUPPLIED TO SUBSCRIBERS ONLY, at the following prices prior to the issue of Part III.:—

ARTISTS' PROOF COPIES, printed on finest Japanese paper, numbered and signed by the Author—*ONLY FIFTY COPIES PRINTED FOR SALE* £21 0 0

NOTICE.—The entire English Edition of Artist's Proof Copies of "The Ornamental Arts of Japan" is subscribed for, and the list is closed.

GENERAL COPIES, printed on finest plate Paper. *Only* 640 copies printed for sale in England and the Colonies . £15 15 0

Note—On the issue of the Third and succeeding Part, the Price of the General Copies will be raised to all subsequent Subscribers.

(15)

In one volume, large Imperial quarto, size of page 16¼ by 11¼ inches, cloth extra, gilt edges.

Preparing for publication early in the Spring. The price has not yet been decided, but it will probably in the first instance not exceed £8 : 8 : 0.

IMPORTANT WORK ON JAPANESE ART.

THE PICTORIAL ARTS OF JAPAN.

Illustrated with One Hundred and Fifty Plates, Sixteen in Colours, and Gold. With General and Descriptive Text.

By WILLIAM ANDERSON, F.R.C.S.,

Late Medical Officer to H.M.S.'s Legation in Japan, Medical Adviser to the Naval and Home Departments of the Japanese Government, and Member of the Council of the Asiatic Society of Japan ;

Author of " A Descriptive Catalogue of the Collection of Chinese and Japanese Pictures in the British Museum.

PROSPECTUS.

The recent acquisition by the Trustees of the British Museum, of the Anderson collection of ancient and modern pictures by Japanese and Chinese artists, cannot fail to invest the subject with a new interest for every student of art in all parts of the world.

This collection, which was made by Mr. William Anderson during a long residence in the capital of Japan, is the largest that has ever been brought to Europe. Upon it has been based a series of investigations, the main results of which it is now proposed to publish under the title of " The Pictorial Arts of Japan."

The whole of the information offered in this work has been gathered by the author from the most trustworthy native sources, and is *for the first time* placed within the the reach of European and American readers. Its comprehensive nature is sufficiently indicated in the following abstract of contents to obviate the necessity of a further summary.

The plates, which are to be executed in the highest style of art, will constitute an important feature of the volume. They will comprise about forty reproductions, in chromo-lithography and monochrome, of the most representative of the Pictures in the National Collection ; about eighty woodcuts by the best Japanese engravers ; several photographs taken for the author from famous art treasures in different parts of the country ; and a large number of other illustrations having reference to the subject-matter of the text

ABSTRACT OF CONTENTS.

SECTION I.—GENERAL HISTORY.
SECTION II.—TECHNIQUE OF PICTORIAL ART.
SECTION III.—FORMS AND APPLICATIONS OF PICTORIAL ART.
SECTION IV.—CHARACTERISTICS OF JAPANESE ART.
APPENDIX.—Native Art Criticism.—Sketch of Chinese and Korean Art.

An Edition de Luxe, of ARTISTS' PROOFS, printed on larger paper, will also be issued.

*** THE ÉDITION DE LUXE will be strictly limited to *One Hundred Copies,* and every copy will be numbered, and supplied to subscribers in accordance with receipt of order.

☞ Order Forms and full Prospectus will be sent on application.

PREPARING FOR IMMEDIATE PUBLICATION.

THE STORY OF THE LIFE AND ASPIRA-
TIONS OF KOOLEMANS BEYNEN, a Young Dutch Naval Officer. One volume, crown 8vo., cloth extra.

BIB AND TUCKER, being the Recollections
of an Infant-in-Arms. By ELSA D'ESTERRE-KEELING, Author of "Three Sisters." Imperial 32mo., fancy boards, 1s.

" To my horror, 'Hang me,' fairly shouted the old doctor, ' if the little beggar isn't winking ! ' "

Popular Edition, now ready, price 6s.

HENRY IRVING'S IMPRESSIONS OF
AMERICA, narrated in a Series of Sketches, Chronicles, and Conversations. By JOSEPH HATTON, Author of "Clytie," "Cruel London," "The Queen of Bohemia," "To-day in America," "Journalistic London," &c., &c.

ROUND THE WORLD. By ANDREW CARNEGIE,
Author of "Four-in-Hand in Great Britain," Demy 8vo., cloth extra.

By the same Author.

AN AMERICAN FOUR-IN-HAND IN
BRITAIN. 1 Vol., 8vo., with an Autotype Illustration. Price 10s. 6d.

" A genial, jovial, almost rollicking record of a trip in a four-in-hand from Brighton to Inverness ; and the high spirits and good humour of the writer infect the reader."—*Truth*.

Also a cheap Popular Edition, in fancy boards, crown 8vo., price 1s.

MY COMFORTER, and other Religious Poems.
Selected and Edited by the Compiler of "The Changed Cross," "The Shadow of the Rock," &c. 16mo., cloth gilt, gilt edges, price 2s. 6d.

THE WOMAN QUESTION IN EUROPE. A
Series of Original Essays. Edited by THEODORE STANTON, M.A. With an Introduction by FRANCES POWER COBBE. Demy 8vo., cloth. Price 12s. 6d.

DEDICATED TO THE RIGHT HONOURABLE THE MARQUIS OF LORNE, K.T., C.M.G., &c., &c.

ENGLAND AND CANADA: a Summer's Journey
between Old and New Westminster. With some Historical Notes. By SANDFORD FLEMING, C.M.G., LL.D., M. Inst. C.E., F.G.S., &c., lately Engineer-in-Chief of the Intercolonial and Canadian Pacific Railways. One Volume, with Map, crown 8vo., cloth extra, price 6s.
(17)

ETCHED EXAMPLES OF PAINTINGS OLD
AND NEW. With Notes by JOHN W. MOLLETT, B.A., Officier de
L'Instruction Publique, France; Author of Lives of Rembrandt,
Wilkie, Watteau, and Meissonier, in the "Great Artists" Series, &c.
Royal folio, cloth extra, gilt top, price £1 11s. 6d. Large Paper
Edition, £3 3s.

THE ACCURSED LAND; or, First Steps on
the Waterway of Edom. By Lieut.-Col. H. E. COLVILE, Grenadier
Guards, Author of "A Ride in Petticoats and Slippers." Crown 8vo,
cloth extra, 10s. 6d.

A STRUGGLE FOR FAME. By Mrs. RIDDELL.
Small post 8vo., cloth, 6s. Forming the new volume of Low's
Standard Novels.

NOW READY.

MARCUS AURELIUS ANTONINUS. By PAUL
BARRON WATSON. With Frontispiece Portrait. Demy 8vo., gilt
top, cloth extra, price 15s.

NOW READY. Royal 8vo. half-morocco, price 18s.

INDEX TO THE ENGLISH CATALOGUE
OF BOOKS. Vol. III. January 1874 to December 1880. Compiled
by SAMPSON LOW.

CATALOGUE TITLES and INDEX ENTRIES.
Hints by CHARLES F. BLACKBURN. Royal 8vo., 14s.

ALL ROUND SPAIN. By Road and Rail,
with a Short Account of a Visit to Andorra. By F. H. DEVERELL.
Crown 8vo. cloth. [Nearly ready.

THE FATE OF MANSFIELD HUMPHREYS,
WITH THE EPISODE OF MR. WASHINGTON ADAMS IN
ENGLAND AND AN APOLOGY. By RICHARD GRANT WHITE,
Author of "England Without and Within." Crown 8vo. cloth, 6s.

CHASING A FORTUNE, and other Tales. By
PHIL ROBINSON.

TIGERS AT LARGE, and other Tales. By
PHIL ROBINSON.
These are the titles of two new little works by the Author of that
charming work "In my Indian Garden." They will form the first of a
series of little 32mo. prettily printed shilling volume .

(18)

Small crown 8vo., cloth extra, 112 pp., price 2s.

THE CHAIRMAN'S HANDBOOK. Suggestions

and Rules for the conduct of Chairmen of Public and other Meetings, based upon the Procedure and Practice of Parliament. By REGINALD F. D. PALGRAVE, the Clerk-Assistant of the House of Commons.

SIXTH AND ENLARGED EDITION, with Additional Chapters on the Duties of Chairmen of Board and Shareholders' Meetings, and the Practice of Committees.

THE ALGONQUIN LEGENDS OF NEW ENG-

LAND. Myths and Folk-Lore of the Micmac, Passamaquoddy, and Penobscot Tribes. By CHARLES G. LELAND, Author of "The Gipsies," &c. With Illustrations from Designs scraped upon birch bark by an Indian. One volume. 12mo. 8s.

A SCHOOL BOOK OF ELECTRICITY. By J. E.

H. GORDON, B.A., M.S.T.E., Member of the Paris Congress of Electricians, 1881; Author of "A Physical Treatise on Electricity and Magnetism," "A Practical Treatise on Electric Lighting," "Four Lectures on Electric Induction," etc.; Manager of the Electric Department of the Telegraph Construction and Maintenance Company, Limited.

FOOD FOR THE MILLION. A Guide for starting

Public Kitchens. With Statistical Tables, Calculations of the Prices of Thirty-six Dishes. Statement of the Starting Expense, the Yearly Current Expenditure, the Gross and Net Profits of a Public Kitchen, and a Ground Plan. By Captain M. P. WOLFF, Author of the "Proposal for the Improved and Cheap Supply of Cooked Food to the Working Population on Self-supporting Basis." With a Preface by the Rev. H. R. HAWEIS, M.A. Small post 8vo., price 4s. 6d.

Crown 8vo., cloth, with several Maps, price 7s. 6d.

OUR HANOVERIAN KINGS. A Short History of

The Four Georges, embracing the period, 1714–1830. By B. C. SKOLTOWE, M.A. [*Nearly ready.*

THIRD AND CHEAPER EDITION. Crown 8vo., cloth, price 3s. 6d.

THE PUBLIC LIFE of the Right Hon. the

EARL OF BEACONSFIELD, K.G. By FRANCIS HITCHMAN. With Portrait.

SOME HERETICS OF YESTERDAY. By S. E.

HERRICK, D.D. One vol., crown 8vo. 8s. CONTENTS:—Tauler and the Mystics; Wickliff; John Hus; Savonarola; Latimer; Cranmer; Melancthon; Knox; Calvin; Coligny; William Brewster; John Wesley.

(19)

A BICYCLE RIDE AT WILLIAMSTOWN.

Nearly ready. Crown 8vo., price FIVE SHILLINGS.

MARY HARRISON'S COOKERY BOOK.

THE SKILFUL COOK. A Practical Manual of
Modern Experience. By Miss MARY HARRISON, First-class Diplomée
of the National Training School for Cookery, South Kensington.

*** The aim of this book is to present a Useful Collection of Approved
Receipts, framed according to the most recent Experience—the various
Dishes being accompanied by clear Practical Directions. A Selection of
Menus is given—adapted to Dinner Parties of varying size and cost.

THE HOME KITCHEN. A Collection of Practical
and Inexpensive Receipts. By MARION HARLAND. 366 Menus and
1200 Recipes of the Baron Brisse. In French and English. Crown
8vo. 5s.

THE ROYAL COOKERY BOOK. By JULES
GOUFFÉ. Fully illustrated. Coloured plates, £2 2s. Domestic
Edition, 10s. 6d.

OUR DOMESTIC BIRDS. A Practical Poultry-
Book. By ALFRED SAUNDERS. Demy 8vo. 6s.

Now ready. Demy 8vo., with Illustrations, ornamental cloth, price 16s.

PLANT LORE, LEGENDS, AND LYRICS.
By RICHARD FOLKARD, JUN. Embracing the Myths, Traditions,
Superstitions, Folk-Lore, Symbolism, and Language of the Plant
Kingdom.

NEW NOVELS.

JACK'S COURTSHIP, MR. CLARK RUSSELL'S New
Three-Volume Novel, will be ready for publication towards the end
of October.

ENSLAVED. A Novel. By ROBERT J. LANGSTAFF DE
HAVILLAND, M.A. 3 vols. crown 8vo., 31s. 6d.

(20)

"COME, LET'S GOE A-MAYING." [From Abbey's "Herrick."]

ILLUSTRATED HANDBOOKS OF HISTORY OF ART.

Each volume contains about Sixteen Illustrations, including a Portrait of the Master, and is strongly bound in decorated cloth.

ENGLISH PAINTERS.

Sir Joshua Reynolds. By F. S. PULLING, M.A. 3s. 6d.
William Hogarth. By AUSTIN DOBSON. 3s. 6d.
Gainsborough and Constable. By G. BROCK-ARNOLD, M.A. 3s. 6d.
Sir Thomas Lawrence and George Romney. By Lord RONALD GOWER, F.S.A. 2s. 6d.
Turner. By COSMO MONKHOUSE. 3s. 6d.
Sir David Wilkie: A Memoir. By J. W. MOLLETT, B.A. 3s. 6d.
Sir Edwin Landseer: A Memoir. By F. G. STEPHENS. 3s. 6d.

ITALIAN PAINTERS AND SCULPTORS.

Giotto. By HARRY QUILTER, M.A. From recent investigations at Padua, Florence, and Assisi. 3s. 6d.
Fra Angelico and the Early Painters of Florence. By C. M. PHILLIMORE. 3s. 6d.
Fra Bartolommeo, Albertinelli, and Andrea del Sarto. By LEADER SCOTT. 3s. 6d.
Ghiberti and Donatelo. By LEADER SCOTT. 2s. 6d.
Mantegna and Francia. By JULIA CARTWRIGHT. 3s. 6d.
Leonardo da Vinci. By Dr. J. P. RICHTER. 3s. 6d.
Michelangelo Buonarroti. By CHAS. CLEMENT. 3s. 6d.
Raphael. By N. D'ANVERS, 3s. 6d.
Titian. By R. F. HEATH, M.A. 3s. 6d.
Tintoretto. By W. R. OSLER. 3s. 6d.
Correggio. By M. COMPTON HEATON. 2s. 6d.

SPANISH PAINTERS.

Velazquez. By E. STOWE, M.A. 3s. 6d.
Murillo. By ELLEN E. MINOR. 2s. 6d.

TEUTONIC PAINTERS.

Albrecht Dürer. By R. F. HEATH, M.A. 3s. 6d.
The Little Masters of Germany. By W. B. SCOTT. 3s. 6d.
(21)

THE YOUNG IDEA.

ART BOOKS—*continued.*

Hans Holbein. By JOSEPH CUNDALL. 3s. 6d.
Overbeck: a Memoir. By J. BEAVINGTON ATKINSON. 2s. 6d.
Rembrandt. By J. W. MOLLETT, B.A. 3s. 6d.
Rubens. By C. W. KETT, M.A. 3s. 6d.
Van Dyck and Hals. By P. R. HEAD, B.A. 3s. 6d.
The Figure Painters of Holland. By Lord RONALD GOWER, F.S.A
   3s. 6d.

FRENCH PAINTERS.

Claude Lorrain. By O. J. DULLEA. 2s. 6d.
Watteau. By J. W. MOLLETT, B.A. 2s. 6d.
Vernet and Delaroche. By J. RUUTZ REES. 3s. 6d.
Rousseau and Millet. By W. E. HENLEY. 2s. 6d.
Meissonier: a Memoir. By J. W. MOLLETT, B.A. 2s. 6d.

ILLUSTRATED HANDBOOKS OF ART HISTORY OF ALL AGES AND COUNTRIES.

Architecture: Classic and Early Christian. By R. SMITH and
   J. SLATER. 5s.
Sculpture: Egyptian, Assyrian, Greek, Roman. By G. REDFORD. 5s.
Architecture: Gothic and Renaissance. By ROGER SMITH and
   EDWARD POYNTER. 5s.
Painting: Classic and Italian. By E. POYNTER, R.A. 5s.
Painting: German, Flemish, and Dutch. By H. J. W. BUXTON
   and E. J. POYNTER. 5s.
Painting—Spanish and French. By GERARD W. SMITH, Exeter
   Coll. Oxon. Crown 8vo. 70 Illustrations. Cloth extra, 5s.

ELEMENTARY WORKS ON ART.

Elementary History of Art, Architecture, Sculpture, Painting.
   By N. D'ANVERS. 200 Engravings. Crown 8vo. Cloth 10s. 6d.,
Elementary History of Music. By N. D'ANVERS. Crown 8vo. 2s. 6d.
   (22)

AGAINST STREAM.

RECENT BOOKS
OF
TRAVEL AND VACATION READING.

VOYAGES OF DISCOVERY IN THE ARCTIC AND ANT- Arctic Seas and Round the World. Portraits, Maps, Charts, and numerous Illustrations. By Deputy-Inspector-General ROBERT McCORMICK, R.N., F.R.C.S., Chief Medical Officer, Naturalist, and Geologist to the Expedition. 2 vols., royal 8vo., cloth, £2 12s. 6d.

TEMPLES AND ELEPHANTS; or, Narratives of a Journey of Exploration through Upper Siam and Lao. By CARL BOCK. With Coloured Plates and numerous Woodcuts. 8vo, cloth extra, 21s.

THE RIVER CONGO, FROM ITS MOUTH TO BÓLÓBÓ; with a General Description of the Natural History and Anthropology of its Western Basin. By H. H. JOHNSTON, F.Z.S. With numerous full-page and other Illustrations, and a new Map of the Congo from its mouth to Bólóbó. Demy 8vo., cloth extra. Price One Guinea.

ACROSS CHRYSE; from Canton to Mandalay. By ARCHIBALD R. COLQUHOUN. With Three Original Maps and about 300 Illustrations. Second Edition. In 2 vols., demy 8vo., cloth extra, £2 2s.

WANDERINGS IN A WILD COUNTRY; or, Three Years amongst the Cannibals of New Britain. By WILFRED POWELL, F.R.G.S., &c. Illustrations, 8vo, 18s. Also Cheap Edition, price 5s.

THE HIGH ALPS IN WINTER; or, Mountaineering in Search of Health. By Mrs. F. BURNABY. Cr. 8vo, Portrait of the Author, 2 Maps, and several Illustrations from Photographs, cloth gilt, 14s.

THE NEVER NEVER LAND; a Ride in North Queensland. By A. W. STIRLING, F.R.G.S. With Map and Illustrations. Crown 8vo., cloth extra. 8s. 6d.

A VOYAGE ROUND GREAT BRITAIN, with Short Glimpses of Aberdeen, Edinburgh, Stirling, St. Valéry-en-Caux, and Paris. By Capt. T. HARGREAVES. Crown 8vo., cloth 5s.

(23)

EGLANTINE.

BOOKS FOR HOME READING.

QUEEN VICTORIA, HER GIRLHOOD AND WOMANHOOD. Told for Girls by GRACE GREENWOOD. Illustrated. Crown 8vo. 6s.

FREDERIC THE GREAT and MARIA THERESA. By the DUC DE BROGLIE. 2 vols., cloth, 30s.

PETER THE GREAT (THE LIFE OF). By EUGENE SCHUYLER. 2 vols., demy 8vo. 32s.

"FROM YEAR TO YEAR." By Rev. E. H. BICKERSTETH. 16mo. Cloth, 3s. 6d. Roan, 5s. and 6s. Calf or morocco, 10s. 6d.

THE DIARY AND LETTERS OF THOMAS HUT- CHINSON, ESQ. By P. O. HUTCHINSON. 8vo. 16s.

A NAVAL CAREER DURING THE OLD WAR. By Admiral MARKHAM. Demy 8vo. 14s.

SINNERS AND SAINTS. By PHIL ROBINSON. 10s. 6d.

PEN AND PENCIL SKETCHES IN BENGAL. By W. H. F. HUTCHISSON. Illustrations. 8vo. 18s.

ROMANTIC STORIES OF THE LEGAL PROFES- SION. 8vo. 7s. 6d.

"OUR SCEPTRED ISLE," AND ITS WORLD- WIDE EMPIRE. By ALEXANDER MACDONALD. 3s. 6d.

THE WESTERN PACIFIC. By WALTER COOTE. Illustrated. Small post 8vo, 2s. 6d.

VOICE, SONG, AND SPEECH. By LENNOX BROWNE and EMIL BEHNKE. Numerous Cuts and Photos. Medium 8vo. 15s.

GEORGE ELIOT: A CRITICAL STUDY. By G. W. COOKE. Crown 8vo. 10s. 6d.

WHITTIER (LIFE OF). By R. A. UNDERWOOD. 8vo. 10s. 6d.

THE CRUISE OF THE "FALCON." By E. J. KNIGHT. Illustrated. 2 vols. 8vo, 24s.

CEYLON IN 1884. By JOHN FERGUSON. Map and Illustrations. Crown 8vo. 7s. 6d.

'TWIXT FRANCE AND SPAIN. By E. ERNEST BILBROUGH. Illustrations and Maps. 8vo. 7s. 6d.

A SEA QUEEN. By W. C. RUSSELL. 3 vols. Crown 8vo, £1 11s. 6d. Also, small post 8vo. 6s.

SAILOR'S LANGUAGE. By W. C. RUSSELL. Crown 8vo. Illustrated. 3s. 6d.

(24)

Men
and
Women.

VICTOR HUGO AND HIS TIME. By Barbou. 123 Illustrations, royal 8vo, cloth, 24s.

THE MENDELSSOHN FAMILY LETTERS AND JOURNALS. Two vols., 8vo, cloth, 30s.

SANDRINGHAM; Past and Present. By Mrs. H. Jones, Second Edition. 8vo, 8 Illustrations, 8s. 6d.

ITALIAN RAMBLES. By J. J. Jarves. Square 16mo, cloth, 5s.

CID (BALLADS OF). By Rev. G. Lewis. Fcap. 8vo, 2s. 6d.

JOURNALISTIC LONDON. By J. Hatton. Fcap. 4to, 12s. 6d.

NARRATIVES OF STATE TRIALS in the NINE- TEENTH CENTURY. By G. L. Browne. New Edition. 2 vols., 8vo, 26s.

ANCIENT GREEK FEMALE COSTUME. Crown 8vo, 7s. 6d.

CONVERSATIONS AND JOURNALS IN EGYPT AND MALTA. By the late N. W. Senior. 2 vols., 8vo, £1 4s.

THE WAR BETWEEN PERU AND CHILE. 1879-1881. By R. Markham. 7s. 6d.

DAY'S COLLACON; an Encyclopædia of Prose Quotations. Imperial 8vo, pp. 1230, £1 11s. 6d.

THROUGH AMERICA. By W. G. Marshall, M.A. One Hundred Woodcuts. New and cheap Edition. Crown 8vo, 7s. 6d.

THROUGH SIBERIA By Henry Lansdell. New Edition. Numerous Illustrations. 8vo, 10s. 6d.

WHITTIER'S BAY OF SEVEN ISLANDS. 2s. 6d.

LIVES OF ILLUSTRIOUS SHOEMAKERS. By W. E. Winks. Crown 8vo. Eight Portraits. 7s. 6d.

EPISODES IN THE LIFE OF AN INDIAN CHAP- LAIN. By A Retired Chaplain. With many Illustrations. 8vo, 12s. 6d.

A HISTORY OF ENGLISH LITERATURE. By Prof J. Scherr. 8s. 6d.

STUDIES IN RUSSIAN LITERATURE. By C. E. Turner. 8vo., 8s. 6d.

ENGLISH DRAMATISTS OF TO-DAY. By W. Archer, M.A. Crown 8vo., 8s. 6d.

SIDNEY'S ARCADIA. New Edition. Small post 8vo, 6s.

(25)

BASE OF THE ALBERT MEMORIAL.

NEW VOLUMES OF "THE GREAT MUSICIANS" SERIES.

HADYN (JOSEPH). By PAULINE D. TOWNSEND.
Small post 8vo., cloth extra, 3s. *[Just ready.*

SCHUMANN. By J. A. FULLER MAITLAND. Small
post 8vo., cloth, 3s. *[Now ready.*

THE GREAT MUSICIANS,

EDITED BY F. HUEFFER.

Small post 8vo., cloth extra, price 3s. each.

1. **WAGNER.** By the EDITOR.
2. **WEBER.** By Sir JULIUS BENEDICT.
3. **MENDELSSOHN.** By E. ROCKSTRO.
4. **SCHUBERT.** By H. F. FROST.
5. **ROSSINI.** By H. EDWARDS.
6. **MARCELLO.** By ARRIGO BOITO.
7. **PURCELL.** By W. H. CUMMINGS.
8. **ENGLISH CHURCH COMPOSERS.** By WM.
A. BARRETT.
9. **JOHN SEBASTIAN BACH.** By R. L. POOLE.
10. **HANDEL. 11. MOZART. 12. BEETHOVEN.**

Handbooks of Elementary Art. By N. D'ANVERS.
Crown 8vo., cloth, very fully illustrated.

An ELEMENTARY HISTORY OF PAINTING—OLD MASTERS.
An ELEMENTARY HISTORY OF PAINTING—MODERN.
An ELEMENTARY HISTORY OF SCULPTURE OF ALL COUNTRIES.
An ELEMENTARY HISTORY OF ARCHITECTURE OF ALL COUNTRIES.

BLOSSOMS.

BOOKS FOR CHRISTMAS PRESENTS.

BLACKMORE'S LORNA DOONE. Édition de Luxe. Fully illustrated, cloth, 31s. 6d., parchment, 35s.

HARPER'S MAGAZINE, European Ed. Vols. 1–8, cloth, 8s. 6d. each.

THE RAVEN. 26 Illustrations by Gus. Doré. Imp. fol. 63s.

ROBIN HOOD, Merry Adventures. Illustrated, 15s.

FLORENCE, by Yriarte. 500 Illustrations, 63s.

FASHION, History of, by Challamel. 21 Coloured plates. 28s.

BUNYAN'S PILGRIM'S PROGRESS. 138 Illus., 3s. 6d.; gilt, 4s.

OUR VILLAGE. By Miss Mitford. Édition de Luxe. Fully illustrated, 10s. 6d.

BRETON FOLK. By H. Blackburn. 171 Illustrations by R. Caldecott. Small 4to. 10s. 6d.

ROCK ME TO SLEEP, MOTHER. By Elizabeth Allen. Fully illustrated. Fcap. 4to, 5s.

HEBER'S HYMNS. 100 Engravings, 3s. 6d.

IRVING'S LITTLE BRITAIN. 120 Engravings. Crown 8vo, 6s.

HISTORY OF ANCIENT ART. By Dr. von Reber. 310 Illustrations. 8vo, 18s.

ROBERT HERRICK'S POETRY. Illustrated by E. A. Abbey. 4to, cloth extra, £2 2s.

SIR ROGER DE COVERLEY. 125 Woodcuts. Small fcap. 4to, 6s.

HISTORY OF ANCIENT ART. By J. Winckelmann. Large number of full-page Plates. 2 vols., 8vo, £1 16s.

MEN OF MARK. Over 200 Photographs. 7 vols., 4to, £3 15s.

MODERN ETCHINGS OF CELEBRATED PAINTINGS. Medium 4to, £1 11s. 6d. Édition de Luxe, gilt top, £3 3s.

PATHWAYS OF PALESTINE, by Canon Tristram. 44 Photographs. 2 vols. folio, £1 11s. 6d. each.

THE RENAISSANCE OF ART IN ITALY, by Leader Scott. 150 Engravings. Medium 4to, £1 11s. 6d.

THE SOUTH AFRICAN CAMPAIGN, 1879. Royal 4to, cl. £2 10s.

THE AFGHAN CAMPAIGNS OF 1878-80, by S. H. Shadbolt. 2 vols., 4to. 140 Photographic Portraits of Officers, £3.

(27)

BOOKS FOR THE COUNTRY.

Heath (F. G.)—Autumnal Leaves. With Coloured Plates. 14s.

—— Fern Paradise. New Edition. With Plates and Photos Sm. 8vo. 12s. 6d.

—— Fern World. New Edition. With nature-printed Coloured Plates. Sm. 8vo. 12s. 6d.

—— Gilpin's Forest Scenery. 8vo. 12s. 6d.; New Edition. 7s. 6d.

—— Our Woodland Trees. With Coloured Plates and Engravings. Sm. 8vo. 12s. 6d.

—— Peasant Life in the West of England. Crown 8vo. 6s.

—— Sylvan Spring. Coloured, &c., Illustrations. Cr. 8vo. 12s. 6d.

—— The Fern Portfolio. A series of life-size facsimile pictures of Ferns. Imp. 4to. Published monthly. 1s. (No. 1, January 1884.)

—— Trees and Ferns. Crown 8vo. Illustrated. 3s. 6d.

—— Where to find Ferns. Crown 8vo. 2s.

BOOKS OF ANGLING, &c.

Fly Fishing—Salmon, Trout, and Grayling. By Dr. EDWARD HAMILTON. Small post 8vo., handsome paper, Illustrated, and with a Frontispiece Etching by Dr. SEYMOUR HADEN. Price 6s.
> Also large paper Edition, boards. 10s. 6d.

Fishing with the Fly. Sketches by Lovers of the Art, with Coloured Illustrations of Standard Flies, collected by CHARLES F. ORVIS and A. NELSON CHENEY. Square cloth, 12s. 6d.

An Amateur Angler's Days in Dovedale. Imperial 16mo., fancy boards. 1s.
> *₊* Also large paper Edition, printed on hand-made paper, 5s.

An Angler's Strange Experiences. By COTSWOLD ISYS, M.A. Profusely illustrated. 4to. 5s.

British Angling Flies. By MICHAEL THEAKSTON. Revised by F. M. WALBRAN. Illustrated. Crown 8vo. 5s.

Trout Fishing in Rapid Streams. By H. CUTLIFFE, 3s. 6d.

Notes on Fish and Fishing. By J. J. MANLEY, M.A. Illustrated. Crown 8vo. 6s.

Angling Literature in England. Sm. post 8vo. 3s. 6d.

Float Fishing and Spinning in the Nottingham Style. By J. W. MARTIN. Coloured. Crown 8vo. 2s.

An Evening's Fishing. In 18 Colours. Size, 14 inches by 10 inches. After Oil Painting by TARGETT. 5s.

The Book of the Roach. By GREVILLE FENNELL. New Edition Cloth, price 2s., post free.

LOW'S

STANDARD

NOVELS.

Small post 8vo, cloth extra, price 6s. each (except where otherwise stated).

[From Abbey's "Herrick."]

By R. D. BLACKMORE.
Lorna Doone.
Alice Lorraine.
Cradock Nowell.
Clara Vaughan.
Cripps the Carrier.
Erema.
Mary Anerley.
Christowell.

By WILLIAM BLACK.
Three Feathers.
A Daughter of Heth.
Kilmeny.
In Silk Attire.
Lady Silverdale's Sweet-heart.
Sunrise.

By THOMAS HARDY.
The Trumpet Major.
Far from the Madding Crowd.
Hand of Ethelberta.
A Laodicean.
A Pair of Blue Eyes.
The Return of the Native.
Two on a Tower.

By GEORGE MACDONALD.
Mary Marston.
Guild Court.
The Vicar's Daughter.
Adela Cathcart.
Stephen Archer.
Orts.
Weighed and Wanting.

By W. CLARK RUSSELL.
Wreck of the "Grosvenor."
John Holdsworth.
A Sailor's Sweetheart.
The "Lady Maud."
Little Loo.
A Sea Queen.

By JOSEPH HATTON.
Three Recruits.
(29)

By VICTOR HUGO.
Ninety-Three.
History of a Crime.

By CONSTANCE FENIMORE WOOLSON.
Anne: A Novel.
For the Major. 5s.

By HELEN MATHERS.
My Lady Greensleeves.

By Mrs. BEECHER STOWE.
My Wife and I.
Poganuc People.
Old Town Folk.

By Mrs. CASHEL HOEY.
A Golden Sorrow.
Out of Court.

By LEWIS WALLACE.
Ben Hur.

By Mrs. MACQUOID.
Elinor Dryden.
Diane.

By Miss COLERIDGE.
An English Squire.

By the Rev. E. GILLIAT. M.A.
A Story of the Dragonnades.

By LOUISA M. ALCOTT.
Work.

By the Author of "ONE ONLY," "CONSTANTIA," &c.
A French Heiress. Six Illustrations.

By Mrs. J. H. RIDDELL.
The Senior Partner.
Daisies and Buttercups.
Alaric Spenceley.
A Struggle for Fame.

AT THE KINDERGARTEN.

BOOKS FOR YOUNG PEOPLE.

Keraban the Inflexible. By JULES VERNE. Numerous Illustrations. Small post 8vo., cloth. 7s. 6d.

The Old-Fashioned Fairy Tales. By Mrs. BURTON HARRISON. With Numerous Illustrations by Miss ROSINA EMMETT, illustrator of "Pretty Peggy." Square 16mo., cloth extra. 6s.

The Story of Viteau. By FRANK R. STOCKTON, Author of "A Jolly Fellowship." With 16 full-page Illustrations. Crown 8vo., cloth. 5s.

Heidi's Early Experiences. A Story for Children and for those who love Children. By JOHANNA SPYRI. Illustrated. Small post 8vo., cloth extra. 4s. 6d.

Heidi's Further Experiences. A Story for Children and for those who love Children. By JOHANNA SPYRI. Illustrated. Small post 8vo., cloth extra. 4s. 6d.

Our Village Life. Words and Illustrations. By LORD H. SOMERSET. 30 Coloured Pictures. Royal 4to. cloth, fancy covers. 6s.

The Gold Seekers: a Sequel to "The Crusoes of Guiana." By LOUIS BOUSSENARD. Numerous Illustrations. Cloth extra, gilt edges, 6s. ; plain, 5s. [Ready.

Under the Meteor Flag; the Log of a Midshipman during the French Revolutionary War. By HARRY COLLINGWOOD. Fully Illustrated. Small post, cloth extra, gilt edges, 6s. ; plain, 5s.

Farm Ballads, Farm Festivals, and Farm Legends. By WILL CARLETON. Small post 8vo., cloth extra, 3s. 6d.

The Silver Cañon. A Tale of the Western Plains. By G. MANVILLE FENN. Numerous Illustrations. Small post 8vo., cloth, gilt edges, 6s. ; plain, 5s. [Now ready.

Charmouth Grange. A Tale of the Seventeenth Century. By J. PERCY GROVES. Fully Illustrated. Small post 8vo., cloth, gilt edges, 6s. ; plain, 5s.

(30)

Spinning-Wheel Stories. By LOUISA M. ALCOTT.

The King of the Tigers. A Story of Central India. By ROUSSELET. Numerous Illustrations. Small post 8vo., cloth extra, gilt edges, 6*s*.; plain edges, 5*s*.

Up Stream: from the Present to the Past. 4to. Fancy boards, 5*s*.

Perseus the Gorgon Slayer. 30 Coloured Plates. 4to. 5*s*.

The Boats of the World. 80 Coloured Illustrations. 4to. 3*s*. 6*d*.

The Green Ray. By JULES VERNE. Illustrated. 8vo., 5*s*.; gilt, 6*s*.; also boards, 1*s*.

The Crusoes of Guiana. By LOUIS BOUSSENARD. Illustrated. Crown 8vo. 7*s*. 6*d*.

Jack Archer. By A. G. HENTY. Crown 8vo., cloth gilt, 6*s*.; plain, 5*s*.

The Story of Roland. Illustrations. 6*s*.

The Story of Siegfried. Crown 8vo. 6*s*.

Red Cloud. By Lieut.-Col. BUTLER, C.B. Illustrated. 8vo. 7*s*. 6*d*.

The Mutiny of the "Leander." By B. HELDMANN. Illustrations. Sm. post 8vo. 7*s*. 6*d*.

An Old-fashioned Thanksgiving Day. 3*s*. 6*d*.—**Proverbs.** 3*s*. 6*d*.— By L. M. ALCOTT.

Dick Cheveley. 5*s*.—**Heir of Kilfinnan.** 5*s*.—**Snow Shoes.** 5*s*.— **Two Supercargoes.** 5*s*.—**With Axe and Rifle.** 5*s*.—By W. H. KINGSTON.

Young Naturalist.—**Round the Yule Log.** 7*s*. 6*d*.—By L. BIART.

Boy's Froissart.—**Boy's King Arthur.**—**Boy's Mabinogion.**—By S. LANIER. 7*s*. 6*d*. each.

Under the Sunset. By BRAM STOKER. Illustrated. 8vo. 6*s*.

Fairy Tales. By H. C. ANDERSEN. Illustrated. 4to. 5*s*.

The Flowers of Shakespeare. Coloured Plates. 4to. 5*s*.

The Cruise of the Walnut Shell. 5*s*.

Winning his Spurs. 74 Illustrations. Small post 8vo. 5*s*.—**The Cornet of Horse.** 5*s*.—By G. A. HENTY.

The Son of the Constable of France. Illustrated. 8vo. 5*s*.

The Drummer Boy. Illustrated. Small post. 5*s*.

No Longer a Child. By M. J. FRANC. Gilt edges. 4*s*.

Queer Stories. By EDWARD EGGLESTON, Author of "The Hoosier Schoolboy." Crown 8vo., cloth 4*s*. 6*d*.

BOOKS BY JULES VERNE.

CELEBRATED · TRAVELS · AND · TRAVELLERS.

Three Vols. Demy 8vo., 600 pp., upwards of 100 full-page Illustrations, 12s. 6d.; gilt edges, 14s. each.

I. The Exploration of the World.—II. The Great Navigators.—III. The Great Explorers.

The New Volume is **KERABAN THE INFLEXIBLE.** Full of Illustrations. Square crown 8vo., cloth extra, 7s. 6d.

☞ The letters appended to each book refer to the various Editions and Prices given at the foot of the page.

ae Twenty Thousand Leagues.	*bcd* Martin Paz.
ae Hector Servadac.	*bcd* The Child of the Cavern.
ae The Fur Country.	The Mysterious Island, 3 Vols.:
af Earth to the Moon.	*bcd* I. Dropped from the Clouds.
ae Michael Strogoff.	*bcd* II. Abandoned.
ae Dick Sands.	*bcd* III. Secret of the Island.
bcd Five Weeks in a Balloon.	*bcd* The Begum's Fortune.'
bcd Three Englishmen and Three Russians.	*bcd* The Tribulations of a Chinaman.
bcd Around the World in Eighty Days.	The Steam House, 2 Vols.:
bcd A Floating City.	*bc* I. Demon of Cawnpore.
bcd The Blockade Runners.	*bc* II. Tigers and Traitors.
bcd Dr. Ox's Experiment.	The Giant Raft, 2 Vols.:
bcd Master Zacharius.	*b* I. Eight Hundred Leagues on the Amazon.
bcd A Drama in the Air.	*b* II. The Cryptogram.
bcd A Winter amid the Ice.	*b* Godfrey Morgan.
bcd The Survivors of the "Chancellor."	*d* The Green Ray. 5s. plain; 6s. gilt edges.

a Small 8vo, numerous illus. cloth, gilt edges, 10s. 6d.; ditto plainer, 5s. *b* Large imperial 16mo., numerous illus., cloth, gilt edges, 7s. 6d. *c* Ditto, plainer binding, 3s. 6d. *d* Cheaper Edition. 1s.; cloth gilt, 2s. *e* Cheaper Edition as (*d*), in 2 Vols. 1s. each; bound in cloth, gilt edges, 1 Vol., 3s. 6d. *f* Same as (*e*), except in cloth 2 Vols. gilt edges, 2s. each.

www.ingramcontent.com/pod-product-compliance
Lightning Source LLC
Chambersburg PA
CBHW030103030726
47498CB00007B/2238